On the run from trumped-up murder charges, Alex Dawson and his boyfriend Sev settle in a small town in Vermont on the recommendation of Sev's mob-boss cousin Bella. Chickadee is so tiny that it has only one major employer in the depths of the Great Depression: Trask & Co. Maple Sugar Mill. It's a quiet place. That is, until Walter Trask is found in his own maple grove with his head smashed in.

Alex doesn't want to have anything to do with the death, but things get much more personal when Bella is falsely arrested. Determined to free her and even the scales, Alex scours the town for clues as to what really happened. He quickly learns that small towns have big secrets that people may be willing to kill for. And if that weren't bad enough, Alex and Sev's once-sweet relationship is turning bitter under the combined pressures of isolation, anxiety, and jealousy. Alex needs to find the true murderer quickly before Bella is turned over to the feds, or worse, Sev walks out of his life forever.

BOILING OVER

The Caro Mysteries, Book Two

Thea McAlistair

A NineStar Press Publication

Published by NineStar Press
P.O. Box 91792,
Albuquerque, New Mexico, 87199 USA.
www.ninestarpress.com

Boiling Over

Printed in the USA
First Edition
January, 2020

Print ISBN: 978-1-951880-20-0

Also available in eBook, ISBN: 978-1-951880-05-7

Dedicated to my mother, uncle, and grandmother.

Their love for mysteries is enormous, but not nearly as enormous as their love for me.

Chapter One

WHEN SEV FIRST asked me to run away with him, he'd mentioned exotic places like India and Australia, warm countries far away from the seedy city we were living in. It had sounded romantic and wonderful, and when we finally left—well, fled—I had hopes of going somewhere like that. Instead, we ended up in Chickadee, Vermont.

Chickadee was a small town, about a half-hour drive from the Canadian border and about a six-hour drive from our old home in Connecticut. In all my twenty-three years, I'd never set foot in the countryside, and now there was all this empty space. Blue sky. Trees. *Cows*.

"Bella wants us to stay here?" I asked as I gaped at the maple forest flashing by the car window. "It's so...rustic."

"Well, just think, Alex," grumbled Sev, his faint Italian accent tinged with unease as he guided the rickety borrowed Oldsmobile over bumps on the dirt road, "it's better than the alternatives, yes?"

Considering the alternatives were *dead* and *arrested for murder*, he was right. Less than a month ago, I'd been living my dull life, writing during the day and serving as a bodyguard for the mayor in the evenings, and then all hell broke loose. Now nine people were dead, including my friends Martin and Donnie, and the corrupt cops wouldn't even think of hearing my side of the story. Targeting the big guy with a chip on his shoulder the size of New England was almost too easy for them.

"It's pretty here!" chimed Pearl from the back.

I twisted to look at her. She perched on the edge of the seat, her already-large eyes expanded in wonder. Her cat, Daisy, sulked in a metal cage next to her. I still wasn't sure it'd been the brightest idea to take a six-year-old on the lam with us, but it was too late now. At least she seemed to be enjoying the trip. And why wouldn't she? *She* wasn't the one running from murder charges.

"Bit different from the city, huh?" I asked, careful to keep my voice cheerful for her.

She nodded and returned to staring at the trees.

I slumped back into my seat, grateful she didn't seem to share my nervousness.

Sev nudged my arm. "Which road do I take?"

I straightened and peered out the windshield. We were coming up on an intersection, if a split of one dirt track into two could be called that. I scrambled to unfold the map I'd crumpled in my distraction. Sev's cousin Bella—the most notorious gangster in Westwick—had given us these directions and all our fake identification papers first thing that morning.

Why Bella had chosen Chickadee to hide us from the cops was a mystery. She hadn't given me a straight answer when I asked, only that she had friends there and Sev would be working with one of them. Most likely the location had something to do with the rum-running routes she'd controlled until about six months ago. While the end of Prohibition had cut the bottom out from under her main moneymaker, there were many other ways to make an illegal living, and why leave when she already had a foot in the door?

"Left," I said, tracing the hand-drawn line with my finger. "Looks like another mile and we reach town."

Sev obeyed, taking the left fork. The car turned in a wide arc around yet more trees. Both sides of the road were obscured by underbrush and shadow. Sev swore under his breath in Italian and slowed even more.

"They should clear this," he muttered. "Someone's going to get hit one day."

"Who's going to get hit?" I answered. "There's no one out he—"

Sev slammed the brakes as a figure darted from between the trunks. I jolted forward and got the wind knocked out of me as I smacked into the dashboard. Pearl screamed, tumbling into the back of my seat. The rattle of the cat cage almost drowned out Daisy's yowls.

Blinded by pain, I groped for Sev. "Everyone okay?" I gasped.

He grabbed my hand and squeezed. "Fine," he said.

Pearl wailed. I turned, ignoring the objections of my bruised ribs. She huddled in the space between the back bench and the front seat, clutching her wrist. My already-pitching stomach dropped. I'd brought her with us to get her away from all the pain in her past, and now here was more. I scrambled out the door and around the back to get her.

"You're all right; you're all right," I mumbled in an effort to convince myself my assurance was true. "Can I see?"

Pearl snuffled and presented her arm. Already her wrist was red and swelling. I held back the curses bubbling in my mind. In a flash of anger, I whipped around to see what jackass had done this.

To my surprise, I only saw a girl straddling a sturdy bike. She was maybe sixteen or seventeen, wearing men's dungarees and a gingham shirt. Freckles were splattered across her face, and ash-blonde braids draped down her back. She gnawed on her lip, her eyes huge with fear.

"I'm so sorry," she squeaked. "There's almost never anyone out here—"

"Alex?" Sev called. He sounded muffled. I looked at the driver's side door. He had gotten out and had one hand curled around the lower half of his face while the other scrambled in a pocket. "I think I might have been mistaken when I said I was fine." He pulled out a handkerchief, and I saw both his nose and his upper lip were bleeding.

Fear, anger, and unbidden memories tangled up in my mind, freezing my mouth in one slack-jawed position, keeping me mute.

"Alex? Alex Carrow?" said the girl on the bike.

It took me a second to recognize my own fake last name. "Uh, yeah? How do you know?"

"Sorry, anyone new in town is big news. You're renting the Reed place. I'm Fran, Fran Gaines. My family lives next door."

It would be my luck for us to almost get killed by someone we were going to have to see every day. "Charmed. Tell me, kid, you have a doctor around here? Or someone who can at least have a look at Pearl's wrist?" I glanced at Sev, blood leaking from between his fingers and giving me heart palpitations. "And ice?"

"There's no doctor in Chickadee, but Mrs. Manco could set her in a splint until you can get to one. And she has an icebox. Follow me." She took off down the road.

Follow her? How? I had no idea how to drive.

"*Andiamo*," Sev waved for me to get back into the car.

"You need two hands," I protested.

He shrugged and pulled the handkerchief away from his face. He had a split lip, but at least his lovely proud nose didn't seem crooked. "It is mostly stopped now."

With no choice, I jumped into the back seat of the car with Pearl. She curled, whimpering, against my side. I held her as the car jolted and skidded at odd turns. I wished, not for the first time, that Martin and Donnie were still alive. They would have known what to do.

I glanced at Sev more than a few times. I could tell he'd lied to get me into the car—fresh blood was smeared across his chin. And yet he showed no sign of pain or distress. No cringing or tears or labored breath. His calm personality kicking in, or was this sort of emergency driving usual for him? I hadn't asked if he'd done anything for Bella besides laundering her ill-gotten gains, but life in a mob family often took peculiar turns. Learning he'd driven getaway cars or moved injured friends while injured himself would not have surprised me.

The trees thinned, and I caught a glimpse of town through the windshield. Rustic didn't even begin to describe the place. Of the twenty or so buildings I saw, most were built with clapboard, a few with simple brick. The tallest one was a church, and even its white-painted steeple looked shorter than my boarding house back home.

Not home anymore, I told myself. As much as I had wanted and needed to leave Westwick, I still had trouble wrapping my mind around the fact that I couldn't go back. Emma had called the cops on me moments before I confronted her about her killing spree, and considering she was now very dead, there would be no calling them off. According to Bella, the cops were still sniffing even ten days after Sev and I fled to Boston.

Fran veered a hard right on the outskirts of town where only a few houses were scattered. We followed carefully. The few people out stopped and stared. And who wouldn't? An unfamiliar car going about ten miles an hour had to look pretty suspicious. Maybe Bella had done this on purpose: sent us somewhere where a gang of yokels would tar and feather us for daring to intrude. I kept my anxieties to myself though. Pearl sniveled next to me, and Sev's knuckles had gone white from gripping the steering wheel.

Fran skidded to a stop in front of a small house—more of a shack if I was being honest—with green shutters. With all the care of a mother laying her baby to sleep, she propped the bike against the nearest tree before scampering to the door.

While Sev killed the engine, I checked on Pearl's arm again—still red, swelling more. My anger flared, but I remembered how Donnie always told me to breathe before letting my temper get the better of me. So, I heaved in a lungful of air to tamp everything down before I opened the car door.

By the time I got myself and Pearl out, Mrs. Manco had already stepped outside. She had a darker complexion than I expected, closer to Sev's Mediterranean olive than my English ruddiness. In fact, she looked almost like a younger Bella with her dark hair and eyes. Unlike Bella, however, everything about this woman was small and simple, from her delicate bun to her tiny booted feet. She wiped her hands on a faded floral apron as she stared at the strange car haphazardly parked in front of her house.

Fran started in right away. "Sorry to bother you, Mrs. Manco, but they had an accident on the way here."

Shrewd kid, leaving out the part about how she'd been the one to *cause* the accident. I interrupted her as I stuffed my own clean handkerchief into Sev's hand. "My name is Alexander Carrow, and this is Se—" I almost tripped on Sev's fake name. "Seb Arrighi. And this is Pearl." I nudged her forward. "We heard you might be able to set a splint."

Mrs. Manco's eyes widened as they tracked between the three of us. "Bella's friends?" Her words came out in an Italian accent much thicker than Sev's. She hurried forward. "I was not expecting you to come today."

Well, we'd found one of Bella's contacts. Somehow I hadn't expected a housewife. "I'm sorry; how do you know Bella?" I asked.

"Oh, how rude of me. I am Cristina Manco," she answered. She knelt in front of Pearl. "Please call me Crista. I knew Bella from childhood, and my husband worked with her."

Recognition lit in Sev's eyes. "Is his name Leo, by any chance?"

Crista paused as she reached for Pearl's wrist. "Yes, his name was Leo." She glanced at Sev. "I'm afraid he passed away about two years ago."

"My condolences. I met him several times, and he was always a pleasure to speak with."

"Thank you." Crista went back to examining Pearl. "Some good news for you: it's just a sprain. No doctor needed. I will wrap it up for you." She straightened and stepped up to Sev. "Now you."

Her fingers touched his face, and heat bloomed up my neck and all the way into my ears, making them itch. *Are you really going to be jealous about this? She just wants to help.* But I couldn't squelch the jealousy. I hadn't been in love in a very long time, and even the hint anyone could get between us was overwhelming.

"Well, your nose isn't broken," said Crista as her hand moved away. "We should get you something to clean up with though. Please." She gestured at her house. "*Bienvenue.*"

I didn't particularly want to walk into the home of a stranger, but she was willing to help Pearl and Sev, and that was good enough for me. Besides, she wasn't a complete stranger. Sev apparently knew her through her husband. Leo must have been up to something illegal if he worked for Bella. Bootlegging perhaps? Sev hustled Pearl through the front door as I salvaged Daisy's cage from the car.

Fran made to follow us in, but Crista held up a hand. "Thank you for bringing them. You may go."

The girl froze midstep. "I hoped I might show Mr. Carrow around town?"

Underneath her wide-eyed pleading look was an expression I'd grown to recognize and fear in young women: infatuation. Oh Lord, just what I didn't need, some kid thinking she fell in love because I had a strong jawline.

"I'm sure Mrs. Manco knows best," I said. "But if we need a guide, we'll come straight to you, okay?"

Fran's eyes darted between the two of us before she moved toward her bike. "Sounds fair enough. I'll be heading home now, ma'am."

Crista nodded her acknowledgment and raised her face to me and gestured at the door. "After you, Mr. Carrow."

The living room reminded me of nowhere so much as Martin's home in its tidy shabbiness, and another pang of sadness echoed through me. At the far end was a fieldstone fireplace, unlit in the over-warm June weather. Next to the fireplace was a scuffed rocker. Pearl had taken a seat in a patched-over armchair across from an equally threadbare couch. Sev hovered in the middle of the room. I placed Daisy's cage on the floor, hoping the faded rug and pitted wood might muffle some of her howls.

Crista followed me inside and slipped through an interior door to the immediate right—a kitchen, by the smell of bread emanating from it. As I stood there, I was struck by how the only sounds I could hear were the cat's complaints and Pearl's soft, pained sniffles. Such deep quiet sent a chill through me. In Westwick, and in Boston, there'd always been some kind of background noise—cars, children, factories. Here, there was nothing, and it felt like there was emptiness beyond the four white-painted walls.

Crista reappeared within a moment, holding a bundle of rag strips and a soaked dishtowel. I edged out of the way to stand next to Sev. She handed him the dishtowel, and he started wiping the blood off his face.

He saw me anxiously watching him and smiled. "See? Not so bad. A little cut."

Cleaned, the laceration on his lip was barely anything, and his nose had stopped bleeding. I relaxed a little but couldn't shake the panicky feeling coiled like a spring in my chest.

"I apologize for Frances," said Crista as she crouched in front of Pearl. "She can be difficult." She glanced at us. "Her parents fight a lot."

"I'm sorry to hear that," I said.

My own condolences rang oddly in my ears. Already everything I said in this place sounded like stilted dialogue in a play. And I *was* acting, wasn't I? I wasn't Alex Dawson anymore—queer writer and terrible bodyguard—but Alex Carrow, and I wasn't quite sure who he was supposed to be. The papers Bella had given me were a driver's license and a birth certificate with false names and dates. Nothing that made a person a person. While Sev and I had agreed on some points to cover our mutual existence, I hadn't bothered making myself a background. I'd have to make something up on the fly. Hopefully, Sev had put a little more effort into these false identities than I had.

Crista took Pearl's wrist again and began wrapping the bandages. "You will leave this on the rest of the day and tonight, yes?"

"Yes, ma'am." She nodded. "Miss Bella told you we were coming?"

My heart skipped a beat. This kid was going to be my death. Casually chatting about Bella Bellissima, the mobster queen? It was like asking for more trouble. Not that Bella was anything more than an overbearing aunt-like figure to her. Bella must have done quite the complicated dance in the last few days to keep Pearl from seeing anything too unseemly. Then again, maybe her criminal empire had been quiet. There *had* been her husband's funeral to attend to, after all.

"She sent a telegram earlier this week to say you might be coming and again this morning saying you were on your way," said Crista. "You are welcome at any time." She tightened the gauze and kissed the back of Pearl's hand. "And a kiss to make it better."

Pearl giggled through her tears as she took her arm back.

Sev cleared his throat. "*Gattina*, why don't you play outside for a little while? Alex and I would like to talk to Mrs. Manco, and it would be very boring." He gave me a look. "Isn't that right?"

"Uh, yes. Like chores and...taxes." Shit, I was even worse at this than I thought. "Stay in the yard. Don't go wandering into those trees."

Unperturbed by my bad acting, Pearl shrugged. "Okay. Can I take Daisy?"

"Sure. But don't let her out. If she gets lost, we'll never get her back. And be careful with your wrist!"

Apparently, that was good enough for her because she sprang up and grabbed the cage. Daisy yowled her displeasure but, thankfully, didn't try clawing through the bars. Once they were gone, I allowed myself a small sigh of relief.

"Our apologies," Sev said. "We did not mean to surprise you by arriving so quickly. We only knew we were coming ourselves around eight o'clock."

Crista shrugged. "I think we are all rather used to, ah, emergencies when we work with Bella." She nodded at us. "I imagine something must have gone very wrong if she sent you here."

Sev snorted. "Wrong is an understatement."

Her eyes scanned Sev's face, lingering on the scar running down his left cheek from eye to chin. A souvenir of prison, though she had no way of knowing. Still, if she knew Bella, she had to know men with scars like that were not to be trifled with.

"Well, I am happy to help," Crista said. "I consider it returning the favor. Bella has been very good to me since Leo died."

Bella, good to people? What a riot. Then again, she had poured what had to be hundreds if not thousands of dollars into setting up this new life for us. And she had a soft spot for her now-deceased daughter and husband. She might want to help a childhood friend, particularly if said friend was now the widow of a man in her service.

"In any case," Crista continued, "you may tell me your story or not. Either way, I will still help you. I will make you answer one thing though: Is the little girl safe?"

"She is," Sev replied. "She is not running from anything. It is us who need to hide."

Crista's eyes narrowed. "Then why bring her?"

I took a breath. Time to test our story. "Why wouldn't we? We're her family."

"My stepdaughter," Sev added. He gestured at me. "Alex is my late wife's brother."

Crista's gaze tracked between us, looking for the lie, maybe. After a second, she nodded. "I can imagine how hard raising her by yourself must be."

"I am not by myself." He smiled at me. "But yes, it is a new experience."

Christ, he was a much better liar than me. *I* almost believed Pearl was his daughter, and I knew he'd met her less than a month ago. Crista was buying it. Her expression switched from squinting suspicion to pouting pity.

"If you'll forgive me, what was your wife's name?" she asked.

"Marianne," I said quickly. Maybe too quickly. "And we had a brother named Martin who died a few days ago."

Sev's brow furrowed for a moment before smoothing back to placid earnestness. We had agreed on the fictional woman's name, not that Martin was supposed to be family as well. But Pearl would start talking about him at some point and having him be her other uncle would make everything sound a little less peculiar. While Martin would have never hurt a fly, grown men taking care of children who weren't their own always raised a few eyebrows.

"I'm very sorry for your loss," said Crista. "Both of you."

"Thank you, we miss them both very much," Sev murmured. "Now, *signora*, if you will excuse us. We thank you for your help and your hospitality, but I believe Alex and I must go find this house we are to be living in."

"Yes, of course!" She took the now-bloodied dishtowel from Sev. "It's on the other side of town. Not far though. I can point your place out from the porch." She smiled. Even her teeth were petite. "I will meet you outside in one moment. I must put this away." She disappeared through a door on the far side of the room.

As soon as she left, Sev smiled at me. "How friendly she is."

I tried to smile with him. "Yeah, friendly is one way of looking at it. You did a good job there, selling the dead wife thing."

He shrugged. "Loss feels the same, I think, no matter how it happens."

I winced. How stupid of me. He'd given up everything for me—nice home, easy job, his mother's love, all in the last few weeks—and here I was asking how he managed to sound so pained. "I didn't mean—"

"I know what you meant." His smile turned sad. "That's one of the things I like about you. Your face shows everything, even when your words are not the best words."

I laughed uneasily. "Right, tell the writer his words aren't good. Good revenge."

He stared at me a moment before heading for the front door. If my face was an open book, his was a lockbox of state secrets. The easy grins, I'd already learned, were a front for so many other emotions. Had he actually forgiven me, or was he still hurt? My stomach knotted up thinking about the latter.

"Sev."

He turned his head. "*Caro*." He walked outside without another word.

Chapter Two

RENDERED SPEECHLESS WITH anxiety, I followed Sev outside. Pearl sat near the car, singing to herself while chucking handfuls of grass at Daisy through the bars of the cage. The cat looked displeased at this particular turn of events. At our approach, Pearl scrambled to her feet.

"Daisy doesn't want to eat it," she declared.

"She doesn't eat grass," I said. "She's a carnivore."

"What's carnivore mean?"

"It means she eats only meat. Come on, time to get back in the car."

She froze. "I don't want to."

What? "It's too hot for games—"

"I don't want to!"

My eyes fell on her bandaged wrist. She probably had a point. If I'd been knocked around, I wouldn't want to go back inside either.

"Hey, Sev?" He paused opening the driver's side door of the Oldsmobile to look at me. "How do you feel about walking up and coming back for the car? Pearl's not keen on being a passenger right now."

"Ah. Well, I don't mind. One moment."

I caught a glimpse of something slipping into his trouser pocket. His cigarette case? No, he tended to carry that in his jacket. His knife then. He'd gotten a new one almost as soon as we got to Boston. His old one had sunk to the bottom of the Westwick River as bloody evidence.

He'd only killed Emma to protect me, but I knew she wasn't his first kill. Sev was so gentle and affable with me, but a mob man was a mob man until he died, and there would always be an element of danger to him.

Crista's voice snapped me out of the hole I was digging for myself. "Are you all right, Mr. Carrow? You're looking lost."

In her accent, Carrow sounded like *caro*. Sev winked at me. He knew my false name was Bella's little joke. *Caro mio*, my beloved. At least the pseudonym covered any slip-ups he might make. Sev's name had proved harder to disguise. Severo wasn't exactly the most common name on the census, so his new papers said Sebastiano. We'd blame any hitch in my abbreviation on an early mishearing and refusal to adjust.

It took me a second to gather my thoughts. "Pearl's a little afraid of the car right now, so we were hoping you'd give us walking directions?"

"Oh certainly." She stepped off the porch. "I'd be happy to take you, even, if you are ready."

"Ready when you are," I said, hoping the smile I'd plastered on my face disguised my nervousness. "Come on, Pearl. We're going to take a little walk across town."

"Okay." She hauled Daisy's cage up with a grunt and shoved it into my arms. "You'll have to hold her. She's too heavy for me to carry all the way."

In ordinary circumstances, I would have laughed myself hoarse at the proposition of lugging a cat for over a mile, but since nothing about the circumstances were ordinary, I resigned myself to being Daisy's lackey. Besides, Pearl had had too many things go wrong in her short life. If I could lift the burden of just one thing, even if that thing was a cat, I would do it.

It was about a five-minute walk into town, and the trip might have been less if Pearl hadn't stopped to exclaim about every plant and insect. I knew very little about nature, and so had nothing useful to say. Crista, however, seemed to know everything's name, range, and food source from memory. Before we even reached the first storefront, I'd been educated on at least six types of shrub, three species of beetle, two breeds of butterflies, and the life cycle of cicadas.

"Mrs. Manco knows a lot," Pearl exclaimed. "Maybe more than you!"

Had I just been insulted by a first grader? "She sure does know about bugs. Oh, hey, look, we've made it into town."

As I suspected from my glimpses on the drive up, Chickadee wasn't so much a town as one long street with a handful of intersections. The first place we passed was a grocer, followed by a hardware store. Across the street from those was a garage with several truck hulls rusting by a gas pump out front. A barber, a diner, a clothing shop. Baker, butcher, drugstore. Townhall was little more than a brick square. The library next to it wasn't much either, only differentiating itself from the other municipal buildings by having tall rounded windows to let in light. Bank. Post office. The white church I'd seen from the road, as I suspected, was only about forty feet high. Methodist said the billboard in its yard.

Sev asked Crista something in Italian, and she answered in the same language.

I shifted Daisy's cage to my other hand. The barely healed injuries down my arm from the knifing Pearl's father had given me ached. "Huh?"

"Sorry." Sev smiled. "I asked her if this was the only church in town."

"And it is," she said. She pointed somewhere to our right. "I have to go to the Franciscan mission about five miles away."

"And you walk there?" Sev asked. She nodded. He tsked. "That's no good. Sunday, I will pick you up, and we will go together."

She showed her petite teeth again. "Thank you. You're very kind."

I clenched my jaw against the jealousy. *Stop being ridiculous*. Sev was always polite. He would never allow a lady to walk miles to go to church. Besides, he didn't go for women. Right? I had never bothered to ask even though I knew some people went either way. Was it even my business to ask? He had picked me and gone above and beyond to prove it. And she had to be, what, forty years old? That was a big jump. Then again, *we* had a big age difference—

"Alex?" His hand on my arm made me flinch. "Are you all right? You're very red."

"Just hot," I mumbled. Not a lie, exactly. I did feel too warm, and in our rush to flee Boston, I'd put on a wool jacket without thinking. I'd been pouring sweat all day.

"Well, here." Sev took Daisy's cage. She growled and took a swipe at me as she passed between our hands. "We will stop for a minute." He waved at a window ledge a few feet away. "Sit, *Gattina*, wait a moment."

I considered protesting, but I was glad for the chance to suss out all the negative emotions pouring through me. To *breathe*, as Donnie would have said. His voice still bounced around in my head sometimes, echoes of his fatherly wisdom. What was I going to do without him and Martin making sure I kept my nose clean?

Pushing their memories away, I scrambled for something else for my mind to latch on to. I settled on watching the other pedestrians. There were quite a few, considering it was a Wednesday afternoon, people running errands among the few stores. Normal, if less populated than home. Except something about it seemed odd. It took me a minute to place my finger on it: I was only hearing English. No Yiddish or Chinese or Italian. Not even an Irish accent. And Sev and Crista were by far the darkest-complexioned people on the street. Even as I watched, a man passed a few inches from them and gave them a hateful glare.

Breathe.

A blonde woman in a sculpted brown hat had emerged from the door of the post office a few feet to my right. "Crista, how nice to see you," she exclaimed. "Are these our new guests?"

Great, more people. I looked to Pearl in the hopes she would be so fidgety I could justify continuing along, but she seemed content enough poking at some kind of beetle crawling on the nearby wall. *Damn.*

"Hello, Judy, yes! Everyone, this is Judith Howe." Crista made introductions for us, and hands were shaken all around. Judith was young, perhaps twenty-five, and had a pink Cupid's-bow mouth and round cheeks—very pretty by Hollywood standards.

"Pleased to meet you," said Judith. She glanced up at me through long lashes. If I had ever been in for the ladies, that look would've wound me up fast. "I'm sorry, Crista, dear, I don't mean to badger: Have you seen Walter at all today? I was supposed to meet him in his office at two, but everyone at the factory says he never came in this morning. I checked with Joe, and he says he didn't even see him while delivering the mail. I would ask Mr. Gaines, but he's in Burlington and won't be back until later."

At Walter's name, Crista's eye twitched. Judith didn't seem to notice. "I'm afraid I haven't. But, well, Walter is often gone, isn't he?"

"He hasn't gone on a business trip in the last six or seven months. And he's never broken a luncheon date with me."

"I'm sure he's somewhere." Crista glanced around as if she expected to see him lurking nearby. "Oh, maybe Mr. Parrish has seen him." She waved at a man coming out of the library with a stack of books under his arm. "Mr. Parrish!"

The man noticed and waved back before jogging across the road. Now Judith looked uncomfortable—she blanched like Crista had called over a Bengal tiger. I couldn't fathom why. Parrish was a beanpole, very slim and as tall as me, and his thick glasses made his blue eyes seem far too big for his face. One punch from someone my size and he'd be flat on his back, if not knocked out. Even a delicate woman like Crista might have been able to toss him over. Hell, maybe even Pearl could if she aimed right.

"Hello, Mrs. Manco, Miss Howe." His nasal voice warbled as he pushed his glasses up with one finger. "What can I do for you?"

"Have you seen Walter today?" Crista asked.

Mr. Parrish shook his head. "Not since yesterday." He turned to me and Sev and extended a hand. "You must be Mr. Carrow and Mr. Arrighi. Arthur Parrish. I'm the local librarian." He smiled at Pearl. "I hear you're staying for the summer, and I do hope you'll stop by sometime."

Christ, did *everyone* in town know who we were already? Crista must have gone around and blabbed as soon as she got the note from Bella. "Fine by me," I grumbled.

Sev gave me a brief warning look. "We're very pleased to meet all of you." He beamed at the small crowd now surrounding us. "I apologize for Alex, he's a little overheated. So, if you'll pardon us, I think we should go so he can get some rest."

There was a flurry of farewells as Judith and Arthur excused themselves from the conversation and went their own ways. Arthur walked toward the north, Judith to the south, but after a few yards, she turned her head and paused as if checking up on him. I shook my head. The last thing I needed was to get involved in some small town's petty business.

I unfolded myself from my awkward seat, and after convincing Pearl to put down the bug she had collected, the rest of us continued down Main. As we passed the schoolhouse, I noted a sweet smell hung in the air. Maple. The source was an enormous brick building farther up the street. The sign running between the first and second floors read Trask and Co. Maple Sugar Mill in bold, red letters with gold outlining. I glanced at Sev. This was where Bella had said she'd gotten him a job.

"Big business?" I asked.

"The only business, besides the few shops," Crista answered. "Walter Trask owns it."

"Is this the Walter they were looking for?" Sev asked.

There it was, the twitch again. "Judith has a nervous disposition. Sometimes he goes up to his groves to check for blights and forgets to tell people. He's always back by sunset."

Odd. But if everyone in town was as irritating as the people I'd already met, I might also conveniently "forget" to tell them where I was going so I could hide in the woods in peace for a while. Or Bella might have sent him on some kind of illegal jaunt that took longer than anticipated.

There was nothing on Main Street after the maple syrup factory, and we continued walking for another few minutes. A row of houses was perched across a ridge running perpendicular to the road. Not a street, exactly, but it had the ambition to become one. The house second from the left had a bike parked in front. Crista pointed to the building on the end.

"That is the Reeds' house where you'll be staying," she said. "This is their summer home, but they're not there often."

The house did look quite summery with sunflower-yellow shutters against the white walls. It had all its shingles and no haphazard patching jobs. The bricks in the walk were even, and someone had gone through and ripped up all the little plants that had undoubtedly grown in the cracks at some point. Perhaps the most luxurious thing about the building was the open porch with a suspended wicker swing. I almost opened my mouth to protest such opulent surroundings, but luckily Sev got the first word in.

"It's very beautiful, and the Reeds have been very generous about letting us stay." Sev passed Daisy's cage back to me and produced a key from his jacket pocket and handed it to me as well. "Why don't you go inside and lie down. I will go back with Crista and get the car."

"Oh, yeah, sure. See you in a few."

While they turned and headed back the way we'd come, I led Pearl into the house. Like the outside, the walls were painted a vivid white. I stood in the foyer with a staircase and stared straight into a kitchen at the back. To my left was a closed door. The right opened to a tasteful parlor with maple-wood furniture. I shut the front door and set Daisy's cage down as Pearl bolted up the stairs.

"I want to see my room," she exclaimed as she ran, leaving dusty footprints on the polished floor.

I sighed as I pried open the latches on the cage. Daisy shot out and up the stairs, no doubt very grateful to no longer be cooped up. I set the cage outside so the smell of ammonia didn't permeate the interior of the house.

When I came back in, I opened the closed door in the foyer. The room beyond was an airy and bright bedroom with two windows, one in front and one on the side. A double bed with a brass headboard took up most of the space, and the heavy wooden dresser sitting beside it was almost as large. A vanity mirror across reflected the door and myself.

I blanched at my own image. Even from several feet away, the bags under my eyes and the spot I'd missed while shaving in a rush that morning were obvious. My hair, too, was a disaster of dust and sweat, making it at least two shades darker blond than usual. No wonder Sev had thought I needed a rest.

Ignoring my own dishevelment, I wandered through the rest of the downstairs. There was nothing exciting about the living room. No china displays or knickknacks littered the mantle or shelves. No books, not even throw pillows. Either the Reeds had never bothered decorating a place they only lived in for three months out of the year or they had removed anything tempting enough to steal.

The kitchen was far more impressive to me. Among the appliances was a refrigerator, not an icebox, in pale green. The oven and range were the same color, a matching set to the refrigerator. A phone was mounted on the wall, not green. The table in the center looked solid and had no cut marks. The counters were also unscarred. On the far wall was a back door, and when I pushed the curtain away from its window, I got a spectacular view of forested mountains.

Another door was awkwardly placed on the wall opposite the sink. I opened it, expecting a closet, and instead found a bathroom. A peculiar place for one, but it was clearly a recent addition to the building, and one in a strange location was better than having none at all. I'd spent the majority of my childhood living in a slum with no running water, and functional plumbing was something I never took for granted.

As I headed back toward the front, I heard the car pull up. A few moments later, Sev stepped in the door with two suitcases, and he brought the smell of rosewater and tobacco with him. Unlike me, he'd gotten a chance to groom before Bella swooped in, and he didn't look as sweaty or scruffy as I did. Or maybe that was because his clothes were his own, tailored to fit his trim frame, unlike mine, which were secondhand and far too small. On seeing me, he smiled, his golden eyes acquiring crow's feet at the corners.

"Will you help me get the last of the bags?"

I let him lead me back out to the car. There were two more: Pearl's suitcase and some kind of wooden case Bella had brought for us. The case was heavier than I thought, and I almost dropped it. Cursing, I opened it to see what on earth she had decided to burden us with. It was a small typewriter. A scrap of paper had been left on it.

I heard the police impounded yours—Bella.

Sev read the note and smiled. "How sweet of her."

I snorted. He knew as well as I did nothing Bella did came purely from the goodness of her heart. Hell, he knew her temperament even better, having spent the better part of his adult life cowering under her iron fist. Still, he had a soft spot for her I couldn't figure out. Every horrible thing she did, he forgave her, through and including getting him disowned. We had argued about how lightly he took her abuses before but tucked the issue away for some other time, and this wasn't the moment to dig it up. I grabbed Pearl's suitcase and got out of the way before my mouth ran away with me.

The bag was so light, it was no problem to hustle up the stairs. Before I even got to the top, I heard Pearl chattering to Daisy. On reaching the landing, I realized the second floor was much smaller than the first and didn't extend completely over the kitchen. The hall ended and had a door on either side. Pearl's voice drifted through the open one on the left.

She'd already made herself at home in the small, slant-ceilinged room by taking off her shoes and sitting cross-legged on the bed with a pillow in her lap. She'd also thrown open the window to catch a breeze. Daisy prowled along the top of a dresser, her nose twitching with every step.

"This room is mine," Pearl declared.

"It's all yours," I answered as I swung the suitcase onto the foot of the bed. The new scar on my arm twinged.

"Which room is going to be yours?" she asked. "The one downstairs is bigger, but the other one up here is closer to me, so I think you should have that one."

I had been too preoccupied with everything else to think about sleeping arrangements. I'd taken for granted that once we got out from under the stern eye of Sev's great aunt, we could sleep wherever we wanted, but that couldn't be the case. While Pearl, on her own, likely wouldn't care or even think to ask why Sev and I shared a bed, she had a big mouth, and it was only a matter of time before someone else found out.

"Yeah, sounds great," I said. "Let's have a look at it, shall we?"

I edged into the hall and pushed open the other door. The room was the mirror image of Pearl's with a bed with a wooden headboard tucked against one of the vertical walls and a wooden dresser against the other. Unfortunately for me, I was a good six feet tall, and the peaked ceiling made half the room inaccessible unless I wanted to start crawling. The things I did for this kid.

"Perfect," I said. "So, tell you what, why don't you start putting your clothes away, and when you're done, we'll see about finding supper, all right?"

Pearl nodded and snapped her luggage open before I even turned around. I headed back downstairs, taking small solace in the fact that at least she was still having a good time.

"Sev?" I called once I hit the ground floor.

"*Ecco!*" he answered from the bedroom.

I followed his voice to find him poking around the vanity. He looked up and smiled at me through the mirror's reflection. His eyes glinted gold in the sunlight. God, I could look at him forever.

"Such a beautiful place, don't you think?" he asked.

I tried to reflect his smile. "Yeah, it's great."

He sighed and shook his head. "You're not a very good liar, *caro*. I wish you wouldn't try. What don't you like about it?"

"I don't not like it," I said. I hoped the heat rising around my neck again wasn't showing red on my skin. "It's just... It's a lot in one day. A month ago, we were living our lives, and at nine this morning, we were in Boston, and now we're here. It's too much, Sev. It's just too much."

"I know it's not what we wanted, but we are safe, and that's what matters." He crossed the room. He pulled me toward him and slid a hand behind my back. "Come, lay down with me."

I hesitated. "Pearl's right above us."

He laughed softly. "I said lay down, not let me ravish you." His hand drifted down and squeezed as his grin turned wicked. "Not that I don't want to."

My skin immediately set on fire. Despite my grumpiness, I was absolutely starved for affection after a week in forced isolation. My lips met his, desperate and longing, and above all, anxious. Everything was terrible, terrifying, and he was the only brightness, the only thing I could see in the world. I needed him, body and soul.

Too soon, he turned his face away. "I thought you wanted to be careful?"

"I do." I sighed. "Sorry."

He shook his head. "Nothing to be sorry for." He ran his hand up and down my back. "Let's lay down, just for a minute. I can see you're tired."

Tired didn't even cover half of it. He led me to the bed, and I slumped onto it. Sev crawled in after me, curling along my side with a hand on my chest. I clutched it with my own, hoping some of his calmness might transfer through our touch. It almost worked. Finally sensing a bit of safety, the ache in my ribs and shoulders started to ebb away. I kissed his head and relished in the rosy scent of his curls. He chuckled and turned his face up to mine. I kissed his lips briefly, just long enough to feel their softness. He smiled against the kiss.

"Did I tell you that you have beautiful eyes?" I asked once I gathered enough willpower to break away.

A light blush spread up his cheeks along with a smile. "Only every day."

"Then did I tell you thank you for saving me?"

The smile cooled slightly. "Also every day." He kissed my shoulder. "Did I thank you for saving me?"

"A crap job is a little different than a gun to your head."

"It wasn't the job. Just because you didn't see the gun didn't mean it wasn't there." His fingers curled into my shirt as if that could make us closer. "A life of lies is a life in prison, just without the bars. And I would know, I have done both. With you, I am free."

My turn to blush and to try to pull him closer. "Then you're welcome."

We lay in silence for a few minutes, dredging what comfort we could from each other, the breeze from the window cutting through the heat. It was almost like peace, but not quite, because even there, my brain flickered through possibilities and excuses. If Pearl appeared in the doorway, how would I explain this? What would we tell anyone? We had to look suspicious, or at the very least incongruous. We couldn't hide and ride it out either. Too many people had already somehow heard of our coming. "Talk to me, *caro*," Sev murmured. "I can tell you're thinking of something. You're making faces."

I knew he wouldn't buy a lie, so I didn't try one. I opened my eyes and twisted to look at him, careful to keep his hand in mine. "Don't you think it's weird half the town knew we were coming? Crista had to have told them."

He raised a shoulder. "Or maybe the Reeds told people. So, they know we're here? They'd have to find out sometime. They'd certainly find out when I showed up at the factory tomorrow. Anyway, they don't know why, and they don't suspect anything." He smirked and edged forward to kiss me. "Nothing at all."

The phone rang.

I broke away from Sev with a curse.

He huffed a laugh. "Someone should get that."

"It's probably someone looking for the Reeds," I said. "Ignore it."

The ringing persisted, jangling my already scattered brain out of sorts. I closed my eyes again and willed the ringing to stop.

"Alex?" Pearl shouted from upstairs. "There's a phone ringing."

A step creaked, and I clambered out of bed in case she had decided to take it upon herself to come down and answer the phone herself. I dove for the door. Yes, there stood Pearl about to descend the staircase. My heartbeat, only recently slowed, picked up again at the close call.

"Yeah, I know," I said. "It's not for us though. We don't—"

"I will get it." Sev brushed past me, dragging the ghost of the lost moment behind him. Annoyed, I followed him into the kitchen. He picked up the receiver with more grace in the movement than I had accumulated over my whole lifetime.

"Hello?"

"Tell them we're not home."

He waved a hand to silence me. "Bella," he mouthed.

Bella? I checked my watch. We'd left her in Boston all of six hours ago. What could she want? Sev ignored my questioning looks, turning away and carrying on an overloud conversation in Italian. I huffed and sat in one of the chairs. It wobbled. Of course, I'd picked the broken one.

He switched to English. "Fine, fine! Hold on." He held the receiver out to me. "She wants to talk to you."

"What for?" I asked as I stood. "I'm not the one related to her. Hello?"

"Alex." Bella's husky voice dripped syrup thick with a false sweetness that sent chills down my spine. "How are you?"

"Why are you calling?"

"I will assume not well."

I rolled my eyes and was grateful she couldn't see me. "You expect me to believe you just wanted to check up on us?"

"You know, if I didn't want you alive, you wouldn't be."

Touché. I sighed. "Thank you for getting us this place, *signora*." I leaned heavily on her honorific but not enough she could be sure I did it sarcastically. "It's very pretty. And rural."

"It's close to the border, which is why you're there and not still in Boston. Walter Trask will take care of you, and if the cops pick up the scent again, I will have him take you to Canada. He will be coming by your house in the evening to talk."

"You sure?"

"Yes, why?"

"I heard he never showed up for work this morning."

Another awkward pause. Apparently, he wasn't on a job for her. "Put Severo back on."

Under any other circumstances, I would have been happy to get away from Bella, but her tone had a perplexed edge to it, and that worried me. Walter Trask disappearing was not part of her plan.

Sev picked up the conversation again, but it didn't last very long. Most of what I understood consisted of him protesting something. I was surprised. Bella didn't like to be crossed. He put an end to the conversation and hung up with a grunt.

"Do you believe her?" he exclaimed. "She wanted us to go looking for him. Ridiculous!"

"You told Bella Bellissima her idea was ridiculous and you weren't going to do it?"

He opened his mouth then closed it. "Yes, I did." He chuckled. "All it takes is three hundred miles between us."

"Still. I'm impressed. That was pretty brave."

He smirked and caught me around the waist. "I learned it from you."

I giggled against his lips like a lovesick teenager, all thoughts of jealousy banished. How could I have even let the thought into my mind? I was just jittery. He was right; we were finally safe.

"Alex!" Pearl's shrill shout echoed down the stairs. "Can you help me? The shelf is too high."

I groaned and let my face linger next to Sev's for a moment before moving away. "I'll be right there."

Sev laughed. "Children always know when you're busy, don't they?" He smacked my rear. "Go on before she comes looking."

Chapter Three

FACED WITH AN empty pantry, the three of us took a walk down the hill to eat supper at the diner and pick up a few groceries. I felt the eyes of the locals on us, scrutinizing everything we did. Sev didn't seem to notice, though, nor did Pearl. So, I squirmed alone, sure someone sensed that not only were Sev and I a couple, but also that we were running from the cops.

By the time we got back home, I was exhausted and wanted nothing so much as to fall into bed. Sev rolled his eyes when I explained to him how I'd need to stay upstairs, at least for the time being. I'd promised Pearl I'd be close to her, and that was what I would do.

I came to regret making that promise within the hour. The room was boiling hot, so I cracked open the window. While the gap caught a slight breeze, it also let in several mosquitos, only a handful of which I managed to kill before they left little red welts across my arms and neck. And they weren't the least of my bug problems. A million cicadas screamed unseen. Their chorus was worse than the traffic noise in Boston. So much for the quiet that had unnerved me on arrival.

Eventually, I fell asleep or at least dozed. I'd had bad dreams almost every night since Donnie was murdered, and that night was no different. *A basket of laundry strewn down the stairs. The white tablecloths of the Ostia spattered with blood. Broken glass crackling beneath my feet. Logan's skull exploding into a million pieces as his daughter laughed behind me.*

I jolted awake and promptly smacked my head on the low, slanted ceiling. "Shit!"

"Alex said a bad word!" Pearl's voice echoed in the hallway.

I blinked. Right, Vermont. And morning, judging by the sunlight filtering through the sagging curtains. The air had somehow gotten more stagnant and warmer overnight. The bugs, however, had thankfully flown off. I groaned as I unpeeled myself from my sweat-soaked sheets.

Pearl appeared in the doorway, already dressed and with her brown hair done up in pigtails with red ribbons tied in bows. "Mr. Sev says breakfast is ready."

I contemplated trying to start coaching her on calling him Sev since he was supposed to be her stepfather, but I decided I was far too tired. Plus, the spikes of pain from the new goose egg on the top of my head rattled my thoughts.

"Tell him I'll be down in a minute," I mumbled.

Pearl nodded and slipped out, the tails of the ribbons fluttering. I groped for my alarm clock, realized I didn't have one anymore, cursed again, and reached for my watch. Ten to seven. I sighed. Between the night job and the haphazard nature of writers, I couldn't remember the last time I'd voluntarily woken up before nine. But this was a different life, and maybe Alex Carrow was a morning person. Likely not, but I'd at least give it a try. Positive side, at least this was definitely early enough to see Sev off to his new job. Job at what, I didn't know. It certainly wasn't managing a nightclub, which would be quite the change.

Somehow, I managed to get dressed without smacking my head again or tripping into the unfamiliar furniture and stumbled down the stairs. Pearl sat on the parlor floor doing a puzzle, Daisy curled next to her on one side. Silently, I thanked Bella for showering the kid in toys and gifts. I knew the spoiling came from some weird transference, as Freud would say—Bella's own daughter had died very young almost two decades ago—but the gifts kept Pearl quiet and amused, and I needed all the peace I could get.

As I approached the kitchen, the smell of burned coffee reached me. The source became obvious when I discovered Sev scrubbing a percolator in the sink. Wet grounds were smeared across the counter. He had already dressed and styled in his gray suit—the one he'd been wearing when we met, the night Donnie died. I shook my head to try to uncouple the terrible memory from how handsome he looked.

"Sorry, there is no coffee," he said. "The pot broke."

"Oh. Well, that's okay." I extended a hand. "Do you want me to have a look at it?"

"No, I have it. *Mangia.*"

He waved at the table where he'd dumped the typewriter box. A plate with a piece of bread and a single egg rested on top of it. This was what I had rushed down to eat? Still, he had tried. He'd worked nights back in Westwick, same as me. By all rights, he ought to have been groggy and stumbling around, not cooking breakfast. And aside from the coffee, he hadn't made too much of a mess. Boiling eggs wasn't all that difficult.

I slid into a chair. *Damn, wobbly one again.* "I should be the one making breakfast. You've got a big day in front of you."

He shrugged and ran a hand over his slicked-back curly hair. "I figured I might as well. I was already up. I was too hot to sleep."

"Same. But just think, India would have been worse."

He gave me a perplexed look, but then he laughed. "I imagine we could ask the locals how they stand it. I'm sure they know lots of things we don't."

"If I'd known you were awake, I would have come down." Thoughts of cuddling next to him floated by, but in this weather, that would have been akin to lighting ourselves on fire. "Could have talked then, at least."

"Perhaps tonight," he answered with a smirk. "Though I think you need sleep more than you need my company. You have such dark circles." I shrugged. Yes, I definitely needed some sleep, but I'd stay up a hundred nights if I could talk with him through them all. Then again, he probably didn't want me sacrificing something necessary for him. To stop my already twisting thoughts, I changed the subject.

"What's Bella having you do, anyway?" I asked.

"Ah." He smiled sheepishly. "The business is growing and they're thinking of making some new investments—"

"She wants you to cover up smuggling, doesn't she?"

"Don't say it like that, *caro*. It's not like anyone is getting hurt."

I didn't want to get into an argument about the accuracy of that statement, so I let it go. "Did you do Pearl's hair?"

"She asked if I could tie bows, so I did. Should I not have?"

"You're fine. She trusts you, at least."

I glanced at the hall to make sure she wasn't on her way in and lowered my voice. "I don't know how we're going to do this. I don't know the first thing about raising kids, let alone girls."

"Well it was us or Bella or the state, and I think even at our worst, we will do better than either of those. And we will not be the worst. You may not have grown up with other children, but in my family, they were inescapable." He finished cleaning up and turned around. "And believe me when I tell you, she is as good as they come. We will not have a hard time."

"Yeah, I guess. What ab—"

A banging, rattling sound made me jump in my seat. My head filled with the nightmares I'd just escaped—memories of gunshots, of Donnie and Martin bleeding out in my arms—and my chest ached as I struggled to breathe. Then, as quickly as the panic came up, it dissipated, leaving me gasping, staring wildly at nothing. Sev watched me with confusion and concern, hand reached out like he meant to stop whatever was happening.

The banging continued, but now I knew it for what it was—someone knocking on the back door. I turned, heart still pounding, to see Fran's face at the window. She waved and smiled. I groaned.

Sev patted me on the shoulder as he slid past me to get the door. He tried to block her path, and she darted under his arm. She had swapped out the dungarees for a flower-patterned dress, and her hair was now in one long braid down her back. I got the impression this was her Sunday best. Or courting clothes, in her mind.

"Hello, Mr. Carrow," she said. "I didn't mean to scare you."

"Hello. Are you going to say hello to Mr. Arrighi, or is he chopped liver?"

She froze and embarrassment passed across her face. She twisted to give him a quick smile and awkward wave before turning back to me. Behind her, Sev rolled his eyes as he closed the door.

"They're gathering a search party to look for Mr. Trask," she said.

He was still missing? Not good. I looked at Sev. "Well, I guess you're not starting work today."

"No, no one's at the factory," said Fran. "They're all out looking."

Was she trying to talk us into joining them? "I mean, we'd love to help, but we don't know what he looks like. So, go on without us and—"

"Oh, I'm not going either. That's why I came here. I figured you and Mr. Arrighi wouldn't even know him if you saw him, so it would be silly for you to go. Can I sit?"

She slipped into the chair next to me as quickly as an eel. I had to admire she had the guts to go straight for what she wanted. Sev, practically shaking with suppressed laughter, started rooting through the cabinets.

"Can I get you something to drink, Miss Gaines? Tea? A glass of milk?" he asked.

I shot him a warning look. He smirked.

"No, thank you," Fran replied, still not taking her eyes off me. "I can't stay too long. I told Mrs. Davidson I'd watch her twins while they were out looking for Mr. Trask. I'd rather sit with a bunch of babies than go out looking for that old le—" Her eyes widened as she caught herself. "For Miss Howe's beaux."

My brain had a hard time piecing together all the things she'd said so rapidly. Trask was old, or at least old enough a sixteen-year-old might think so. Forties, maybe fifties? Not shocking, considering he owned and operated a whole factory. But Judith Howe wasn't much older than me. I'd heard of sugar daddies, but going out with a maple syrup magnate would be taking it somewhat literally. And what else had Fran been about to say? Lech?

"Anyway," she continued, "I'm sure Mrs. Davidson wouldn't mind if you stopped by while I was there. They are babies, after all. They just sit there in the crib." She smiled again. I imagined she thought she looked cute or maybe seductive. Mostly she was making me uncomfortable.

I caught Sev's eye over her shoulder and willed him to understand that we needed Fran out of our kitchen. *Now.* In a testament to our love, he managed to stop snickering behind his hands and approached the table.

"Miss Gaines." He said her name so sweetly that if I had been her, I'd have swapped my affections in an instant. "I'm sorry to interrupt. You have found us in the middle of breakfast," he gestured at the plate still perched on the typewriter case, "and since you promised Mrs. Davidson you would babysit, I think you should go over there. What if they are stalling the search party for them? Mr. Trask might be hurt somewhere, and you wouldn't want to delay his help, would you?"

Her cheeks went scarlet, and her brow furrowed. "You're right, how silly of me." She stood. "Excuse me." With three steps, she was back across the kitchen. The door banged again as she shut it hard.

Free of her at last, Sev burst out laughing.

"It's not funny, you know," I snapped.

"Well it wouldn't be, except you made such horrified faces."

I did have to admit it was probably amusing to watch me flounder my way through someone else's farce but still. Fran was going to be trouble, and we didn't need more. "Do you think we should tell her parents what she's up to?"

"Now, now." Sev draped his arms over my shoulders and pressed his face into my hair. "She's infatuated with you is all. Not her fault. It's hard not to be."

"She's what, sixteen? Seventeen? That's a seven-year difference."

Sev cleared his throat. "*Caro*, I hope you remember *we* have a seven-year difference."

"You know what I mean. She can't even be done with school yet."

"Well then, we should be pleased she's in love with you and not someone who would take advantage of her. Because you know some other people would."

"Yeah." Another thought slid into place. "Do you think it's weird she doesn't like Walter Trask?"

"Well, she can't like everyone. Perhaps she is angry he shooed her out to defend his own boyfriend as well?"

I chuckled. "Yeah, maybe."

My body still thrummed with anxiety from the banging door. I sat there for a moment, searching for comfort in Sev's arms, but instead of comfort, his touch made me feel like I was going to shatter. I needed to smoke. Bad. I wiggled out of his grip. "Can I steal a cigarette from you? I left mine upstairs."

He sighed and produced both his silver cigarette case and lighter out of a pocket. "I should start charging you for these."

I shrugged as I lit it. There weren't too many things we weren't sharing already. Anyway, bumming cigarettes was better than sniping at him. I just needed a minute to breathe.

Pearl wandered into the room, Daisy not more than five feet behind her. The cat padded her way across the room to sit and stare at nothing. Pearl crept up to the table, eyeing my toast. When she got next to me, she stopped cold and squinted.

"I don't like that," she said.

Were kids always this cryptic? "What don't you like?"

"The smoke." She wrinkled her nose. "It makes my eyes and throat hurt, and I cough."

That was about par, considering how the rest of my morning had gone. How had I not known she was allergic before? When I thought about it, I had never seen her father smoke, and Martin hadn't gone in for it either. And I hadn't been around Pearl for more than an hour at a time until yesterday. I sighed. Well, smoking outside wouldn't kill me.

I slid out of my seat and went to the back porch. I leaned on the rail running about waist-high and stared into the trees. I had to admit the view was pretty. I just didn't know what to do with it. No people, no cars, no other buildings in view. The only things I could hear were birds and Sev and Pearl's voices drifting through the screen door, and they weren't enough to drive away the silence choking me here. It itched across my back and burrowed into all the hollow places inside me, where it grew into something vicious. My grief multiplied in the quiet calmness, and even the smoke couldn't drive it out.

Something rustled by my leg, and I glanced down in time to see Daisy streak past me and down the stairs into the open yard. Her calico form continued at a dead sprint toward the forest on the edge of the property and disappeared into the brush. My breath caught and the smoke went down the wrong way. As I choked, Pearl screamed and pushed out the screen door I apparently hadn't properly closed.

"Daisy come back!" she cried. I managed to catch a fistful of her dress as she rushed by.

"You can't go running off," I wheezed. "Especially not into the woods." Woods where a grown man was lost, at that.

Her green eyes filled with tears, and she began to wail.

I had no problem letting the cat go. Those things came back, right? They knew who fed them. Daisy, in particular, was very good about knowing where she had the best chance of getting food. But that had been back in Westwick. In the country... Would a city cat even understand where it was?

"All right, all right," I said. "Me and Sev'll get her. You stay here, okay? Sev!"

"Already coming." He appeared in the doorway behind me with the cage and without his jacket or tie. Smart man. I knew I liked him for more than his smile.

I crushed my barely smoked cigarette under my heel. "Lock the doors and don't open them for anyone but us, got it?"

Pearl sniffled and nodded. I snatched the cage out of Sev's hands and tramped down the stairs, determined Pearl not see how guilty I looked.

IF I HAD been hot before, it was nothing compared to how I felt after several hours traipsing through the woods. Sweat dripped into my eyes, making them sting. At some point, something snagged the cuff of my pants and ripped a jagged hole. Again, the mosquitos attacked, and I had to wave my arms to keep the other bugs away. Cicadas rattled, the remains of their carapaces littering the ground. I was *fairly* sure we weren't lost, but only because I refused to consider the possibility.

"When I get my hands on that fucking cat, I'm going to strangle it," I muttered as I crunched through the underbrush.

"Hush. What if Pearl heard you say such things?" Sev panted. His curls were fraying in the humidity, and he'd undone the top buttons of his shirt. He paused to wipe his face with his handkerchief, and I took the opportunity to stop too. I dropped the cage and massaged my scarred arm.

"Well she's not here to hear me. And anyway, I don't care. Should've left the stupid thing in Connecticut."

"You know Pearl wouldn't have come if she couldn't have Daisy," he answered. "Besides, Bella put a lot of work into capturing that cat again. She wouldn't want the effort to go to waste."

"It's about to. What if it, I don't know, fell in a river or got eaten by a wolf?"

"I do not think there are wolves anymore."

"Good, because if I found one, I would feed the cat to it."

He rolled his eyes and flapped a hand near his face. "If you're going to be angry about it, you should go back. I'll stay and look."

"No," I groaned. "I let the thing out, the least I can do is bring it back."

I scanned the area. A cat might be anywhere. Trees rose up on all sides, maples mostly. Others I couldn't identify, having lived my entire life in a mess of concrete and steel. Hundreds of shrubs and little plants sprouted underneath the trees, which made walking difficult and even a hazard. They hid quite a few popping roots, fallen logs, and all kinds of little burrows. The one indicator we were anywhere near civilization was the single-file dirt track meandering alongside a creek.

Something rustled in the undergrowth somewhere to the right. A flash of orange. A fox or our quarry?

Sev saw it, too, and a smile spread across his face. "Aha, now we have you." He crept forward, and I quietly propped the cage, so its door faced the sky.

The plants shook again, and the flash of orange sped to the right near the dirt path. I cursed our bad luck. Now it was going to be at least another half hour of chasing. I was exhausted, parched, and starving, not to mention craving the cigarette I hadn't gotten to finish.

Sev sighed. "Well, she can't go too far," he said. "Stay here. I am going to follow the road." He indicated the track. "I will come back with Daisy or in five minutes. Whichever is first. Then we go home, cat or no, I promise."

I threw up my hands in resignation. I was too tired and hot to argue. He followed the path as it curved out of sight, and I leaned against the tree and stared at my watch. Five minutes? I'd go after him in four.

At three minutes and twenty-two seconds, I heard him cry out. All my nervous energy came crackling back, and I ran up the path yelling for him, leaving the cage behind. Thankfully he hadn't been too far, and he appeared, stumbling back along the road. He was doubled over, handkerchief across his face. He saw me and stopped, only to turn and vomit into the underbrush a moment later.

I skidded to a stop in front of him and grabbed his shoulders, scanning him for any sign of injury or illness.

My heart beat a hundred times a second. "Are you all right? What happened?"

He nodded but continued to gag into his handkerchief. He raised his head and gulped for air. His face had gone ashen. "I think I found Walter Trask."

Chapter Four

THE BODY WAS barely recognizable. Not that I would have been able to tell it had belonged to Walter Trask, but the other people who had come running when they heard Sev yelp assured me that it was. Something about a birthmark covering the entire back of his hand. They couldn't have been able to tell from his face. Besides the fact that a chunk of his head had been smashed in, some predator—hell, potentially even Daisy—had gnawed on his nose and gotten at his eyeballs. The remaining skin had turned a bizarre mixture of maroon and yellow. Not surprising Sev had thrown up. I was on the verge myself.

Somehow in the search for the cat, we had stumbled onto Trask's property, more specifically, the grove his factory tapped into for maple sap. The search party out looking for him had been only a hundred or so yards away. I glanced over them while we waited for the cops to show: a good fifty people had turned out, including Arthur Parrish and Judith Howe. Crista was absent.

Aside from the body, the scene of Trask's death wasn't much to look at. This patch of forest looked like the rest as far as I was concerned, except for the wider path and the little plug holes in the nearest trunks. Oh, and the bloody branch as thick as my upper arm laying in the dirt beside him.

Deputy Sheriff Robert Kelly let the sheet drop back over Trask's head, and the stretcher-bearers hauled the body back toward the main road. He turned to Sev and me. "So, did you know him?"

Sev shook his head. He was still pale and kept his now vomit-stained handkerchief close to his nose. I suspected it smelled like bile, but maybe it was easier than smelling the rot. Trask may only have been dead for about a day, but the heat had done his corpse no favors.

The sheriff looked at me. "How about you?"

"No? Look, we just got into town yesterday and—"

"According to some of the other people I talked to, he went missing before you arrived."

"And?"

Kelly looked me up and down. "And maybe you took a detour before showing up."

Another corrupt cop in my life? And this one was Sev's age, maybe even younger. "We don't even know who he is, why would we kill him? And anyway, it might have been an accident." I pointed at the bloody branch. "Could have fell on him, couldn't it? Going to start questioning the tree?"

"Alex, don't," Sev hissed.

Judith Howe, with her doll-like face, appeared at my side. Her eyes were red-rimmed, but she held herself proudly. "Bobby Kelly, you leave them alone. Just because they're strangers doesn't mean they're murderers," she said. "You should know better, not having been born here yourself."

Kelly turned nearly as red as his hair as he sputtered something about how he was doing his job, but now had other things to do and "Thankyouverymuchforyourtime." As he scrambled away, a smug smile spread across Judith's face.

"Sorry about that," she said. "He's gotten a big head since he joined the force." She nodded at Sev. "And I'm afraid he doesn't like foreigners much."

"I've lived here since I was nine," Sev snapped. "I have citizenship and everything."

"That won't matter much to Bobby. You only have to look the part." She peeked at his back and lowered her voice. "I would avoid him as best you can."

Amazing how I'd found a cop even shadier than Harlow. Maybe I needed to carry rabbit's feet and clovers to counteract this string of bad luck. "Thanks for the warning," I said. "It's decent of you."

"Mmm. It might be the only decent thing you'll get out of anyone around here. I hear you're from the city, so I'll remind you small towns are different. Everyone knows everyone else's business, and they aren't particularly forgiving."

She stepped away without a goodbye and averted her eyes like somehow even looking at us was social poison. Maybe it was. Another glance at the search party showed a good number of them were whispering to one another and casting suspicious looks at us. Well, if they didn't want anything to do with us, so much the better. I didn't need annoying neighbors poking around.

"So, can we go, officer?" I called.

Kelly spun and glared. "Yes, but don't go leaving town."

Sev and I started back toward the house, following the road. Once I was sure no one else could hear me, I let my rage loose. "I swear to God," I roared, "if I have to deal with one more cop who has it out for me, I'll—"

Sev laid a hand on my arm. "You will talk to him calmly and honestly. There is nothing to implicate either of us, and getting angry is only going to get us into trouble. And we cannot afford more trouble."

"We can't just sit and take it either."

He sighed but didn't say anything else. His silence grated on me. Clearly, he wanted to make an argument, but what could he say? That it was better to allow ourselves to be bullied by some small-town sheriff with a crooked moral compass?

Breathe. Donnie had always told me to breathe before I made any rash choices. Frustration had me spoiling for a fight and didn't care if my anger aimed at the right person or not, and Sev was definitely not the right target. He was one of the few nice things I had. In fact, he was the best thing by far, and the last thing I wanted to do was hurt him. So, I clamped my mouth shut and followed him home in silence.

To my fury and astonishment, when we got there, Daisy was sitting on the porch licking a paw. She didn't even look dirty. Most likely she had run, seen how terrible it was out there, and doubled back immediately. A stream of curses bold enough to make a sailor proud escaped my lips. Daisy stopped grooming and stared.

"Don't move," Sev whispered. He inched up the stairs making kissing noises and coaxing her in Italian. Daisy watched him, tail flipping. Then she stood and arched into a stretch. I braced, ready for her to fly down the stairs again. Instead, she rubbed her head against Sev's outstretched hand.

"Seriously?" I growled.

"Hush." Sev scratched her behind an ear. "*Che bella gattina, che dolce. Vorrei entrare? Si? Bene.*" In one motion, he scooped her up. She meowed in surprise but didn't struggle as he carried her to the door.

I'd never unlocked a door so fast in my life. We tumbled in, cat still clutched in Sev's arms. I slammed the door shut and bolted it, only to remember a second later that cats couldn't pull doorknobs. Sev released Daisy, and she skittered across the tile floor. Pearl, most likely having heard the commotion from the kitchen, ran in.

"Daisy!" she exclaimed as the cat streaked past her. "Thank you," she called over her shoulder as she turned to give chase.

I sighed and slumped against the counter, dropping the cage onto the floor with a clatter. "Well at least *that's* over with."

Sev didn't answer. Instead, he stood frozen, staring at the hall. Confused, I followed his gaze. Bella stood in the doorway to the foyer, a look of amusement on her face. Oh Christ, no. Anyone but her.

"How nice to see you boys," she said. "And so soon."

"I told Pearl not to open the door to anyone," I mumbled, mostly to assure myself I had actually said it.

"I'm not just anyone, am I?"

She stepped into the kitchen, her shoes clacking. She was still in black, of course—her husband had been murdered about ten days ago—but somehow, she made even the sack of a mourning dress she wore look regal. The rosary made of simple ceramic beads wrapped across her hand glinted and glimmered like a bracelet made of pale sapphires. The Queen of Sin indeed.

"Aren't you going to offer me anything to drink?" she continued. "Really, Severo, I know you know better than to mistreat company. *Vorrei un cafe.*"

Her words seemed to snap him out of his shock. "*Abbiamo solamente te.*"

She rolled her eyes. "Fine, tea."

He dove for the kettle, muttering what sounded like apologies in Italian. I, on the other hand, wasn't about to be intimidated.

"What are you doing here?" I demanded.

She raised her face to me, and her eyes met mine. They were coal black, unreadable. After a few seconds of silence, she turned away and took a seat at the table. Her silence made me twitchy. I assumed that was the point. I peeked back into the hall, expecting to see at least one bodyguard. No one.

"Kind of rude to make your guard wait outside, don't you think?" I said.

She hesitated before she said, "I came alone."

Sev stopped fumbling with a rose-patterned tea set he'd apparently found somewhere in the cabinets. "What?"

I might not have found her solitude odd except for his surprise. I had seen Bella without guards before, at the Ostia and at the warehouse gambling den. But those had been places she owned where she was surrounded by dozens of people. Just because I hadn't noticed any guards didn't mean she hadn't had any nearby.

"Then how'd you get here?" I asked.

She gave me a perplexed look. "I drove here, same as you."

Oh. I had always made the assumption she had a chauffeur. She had enough money for one. Learning that she could be mobile on her own was like learning that cockroaches could technically fly: horrifying and yet not terribly unexpected.

"Bella." Sev took a step forward. "*Ch'é il problema*?"

She twisted her wedding ring, the only piece of jewelry left of the treasure chest she had worn when I first met her. "Romero divulged our hiding place, and then I had to take you from Boston." I nodded, understanding her fear and frustration. One of her personal bodyguards had told Logan where to find her, resulting in her husband's death, and only a week later, she had been betrayed again. She continued, "And now you say Walter Trask is missing—"

"He's dead," I said. "They found his body. Or actually, Sev found his body maybe an hour ago."

Bella's eyes widened. Otherwise, she managed to maintain her composure. "Then I am glad I decided to come here and not go back to Westwick this morning."

"You're *glad* to be somewhere where they murdered one of your men?"

She shrugged. "It's quieter here. And for all his faults, Severo has always been very good to me. He would not betray me. And I know I have nothing to fear from you."

The shriek of the kettle made me flinch, and I ducked away to shut it off, hoping she didn't see the flush in my cheeks. She wasn't wrong about me being useless and cowardly. I hadn't even been able to defend myself from Emma when I had a loaded gun in my hand. I glanced at Sev. He had gone pale again, maybe even paler than when he found Trask. I looked away. If both he and Bella were frightened, things were very bad.

"So, your plan is to hide?" I said as I poured water into the teapot.

"I am not hiding," Bella snapped.

"Well, you ran away, at least. Great way to show how powerful you are."

Bella's eyes narrowed, and she turned to Sev and asked him something in Italian. I glared at him.

"She asked if you are always this sarcastic," he said.

"I'm just saying, I don't know how you coming here helps anything besides putting me and Sev in the line of fire again. Pearl too."

At Pearl's name, Bella recoiled like I'd smacked her across the face. "I wouldn't dare put her in danger!"

"What do you think you're doing by coming here when you're afraid for your life?"

"Not my life," she replied. "Not yet, at least."

"Fine, business. Or whatever you call your little setup."

She shrugged, her eyes cast into her lap, fingers worrying the rosary beads.

Sev regarded her for a moment before glancing at me. He had an expression a kid might have when asking a parent if he could keep a stray cat he found. Before I could protest, he turned back to Bella with a gentle smile. "Of course, we would love to host you while you have a small break. We have the house for the summer, after all."

"*Grazie.*" She lowered her head by way of acknowledgment. "Now," she gestured at the teapot in my hands. "Offer your guest a drink."

Chapter Five

SOMEHOW, I SURVIVED about ten minutes of that bizarre tea party in my dazed state before I *had* to go out to smoke. I went to the front porch, intent on putting as much distance between Bella and myself as possible. I was still reminded of her though. Beside our borrowed ten-year-old Oldsmobile was a shiny new Model B Ford. Huh. I'd almost expected a gilded carriage from her.

"Alex?"

I turned to see Sev slipping out the door, his own cigarettes in hand. I exhaled, and the smoke hung as a cloud in the humid air. "Are you *insane*?" I hissed. "Inviting Bella Bellissima to stay with us?"

"She's alone and scared—"

"All the more reason she shouldn't be here! I don't want to be part of anything she's afraid of."

He sighed and leaned on the railing. "We owe her."

"No, we don't. She can't even keep us safe for more than a week. And don't start telling me about family honor or something because she's the reason you were stuck in that life. Like prison, you said yesterday."

"I know what I said." He huffed smoke out through his nose. "It's more complicated than that."

I opened my mouth to retort and found nothing. For half a second, he looked angry, but the expression melted away as he reached over and ran his hand down my arm. "I'm sorry, *caro*. It's too hard to explain now. Maybe later."

I nodded, even though I wanted to know right then. "Okay, later." I leaned in to kiss him and got a mouthful of smoke with the sour aftertaste of stale vomit. I struggled not to grimace.

A car coming up the hill caught my eye—and not just any car—a police car. It was a boxy, black-and-white thing with a yellow star painted on the side. I watched it carefully, and soon my suspicions were confirmed when it pulled up in front of the house. Kelly popped out of the driver's door, and a second cop slipped out of the other. The new officer didn't look like much, wider than average with dueling bald spots, one in the front and one in the back. I grunted and tossed my cigarette onto the ground as they approached.

"You said we could go," I said.

"And I said I might have questions for you," Kelly answered as he mounted the stairs.

"No, you said not to leave town." I spread my arms. "And here we remain."

Sev kicked the back of my heel as a warning. "How can we help, officer?"

Kelly moved toward the door. "Maybe we should take this inside, so we don't give the neighbors something to gossip about."

Sev's shoulders tensed up, and he glanced at me. I tilted my head slightly and hoped he understood that as a definite no. Refusing might look suspicious, but once we were out of the public eye, they could do anything they wanted, from planting evidence to outright killing us. The second officer, in particular, seemed to be a bit trigger-happy; his hand hadn't left his sidearm since getting out of the car.

"I'm afraid my daughter is resting inside," Sev said. "The heat has been too much, and I'd rather we not disturb her. We're happy to answer any of your questions out here. We have nothing to hide."

Sweat pooled in the space behind my shoulders as Kelly cracked his jaw. He scanned over both of us before turning his attention to the cars in the drive. "Funny, two cars for a family of three and nowhere in particular to go. At least, that's what I hear."

"My cousin has stopped by for a visit."

"Well, I want to talk to him too. Get him out here."

Sev smiled, but nervousness pulled on the edges of it. He turned toward the door. "Of course, one moment—"

"And *don't* leave my sight."

Sev's hand froze on the knob, and he nodded once before easing the door open. I kept a close eye on the officer's fingers drumming on his holster. "Bella," Sev called, careful to keep his face and hands in sight, "we have some unexpected guests."

For a terrifying moment, there was no response. Then came the slow *click-click-click* of heels on hardwood until Bella appeared, head held high. She took a deliberate step over the threshold and closed the door behind her. Her face showed no sign of fear.

"Sheriff Kelly," she said with a smoothness I envied, "how lovely to see you again."

Kelly, on the other hand, gaped. Then the shock gave way to smugness. "Mrs. Ferri. Didn't think I'd see you back here."

"You, uh, know each other?" I asked.

"She was here when Leo Manco went missing, weren't you?" Kelly answered.

Bella had no reaction.

"I thought Leo Manco was dead?" I said.

Bella snorted. "He is. Sheriff Kelly seems to think he can pass off his incompetence as trickery on my part." She bristled. "Did you ever apologize to Mrs. Manco for taking nearly a week to even go looking for her husband's body?"

Sev placed a restraining hand on her arm and muttered something in Italian.

Kelly glowered and took a step forward, so he was right against them. "Speak English."

Bella turned to him, still impossibly cool. "I did not realize there was a law here that said I must. Did you start fiddling with them since I have been here last?"

He prodded her in the chest. "Listen here, bitch—"

Her hand flew out so fast I almost didn't see it, but there was no missing the crack of it against Kelly's cheek. He flinched and fell back a step with a yelp.

The other officer, already poised, drew his gun. My heart jumped into my throat and tried to choke me as all my strength fled. I was unable to move, barely able to breathe, as the memory of Emma's gun in my face flickered into my mind. Somewhere past the ringing in my ears, I heard a woman scream. It wasn't Bella though. She stared straight at the cop, as if daring him to find the courage to shoot her. The officer, still with his gun drawn, turned his head. He hastily lowered his weapon. Kelly grabbed Bella and twisted her around, a set of handcuffs sliding off his belt.

"Bella Ferri, I'm arresting you for assaulting an officer," he announced. "Other charges pending."

Sev bared his teeth as his hand slid into his pocket.

"Sev, don't," I gasped.

His head snapped to me, and for a half a moment, he wavered. He took an empty hand out of his pocket and rushed to my side. I barely felt his touch on my back. "It's fine, everyone's fine," he whispered.

Kelly dragged Bella past me, and I could have sworn I saw her roll her eyes at me. Pathetic, she'd called me once, and she was right. I could only imagine how worthless she thought me now. Or I might have if I hadn't been so preoccupied with keeping my breath steady.

The officer with the gun slid it back into its holster and hurried down the stairs after them. His departure helped somewhat, and I was able to stretch my focus away from what was directly in front of me. Aside from Bella being shoved into the back of the cop car, I noticed Fran where the yard met the road, poised on her bike, her mouth open and her eyes wide. She must have been the person who screamed. As soon as the car pulled away, she dropped her bike and raced up the stairs.

"What was all that about?" she exclaimed. "Are you all right, Mr. Carrow? Did you faint? How—"

Sev nudged her away from me. "Let's let him have some air, yes? Come on, Alex, go inside and relax. I'll be back as soon as I can talk some sense into Sheriff Kelly."

"Oh, I can stay with him," Fran squealed. "I'll take very good care of him, I promise."

Her words snapped me out of my frazzled state or at least gave me something new to be panicked about. I shrugged Sev off. "Don't be ridiculous. I'm coming with you."

"If you think you're up for it?"

"Yes. Let's go. Actually, wait. Fran."

Her eyes lit up. "Yes?"

"What's your babysitting rate?"

"Oh, uh, five cents an hour."

"Great." I jammed a nickel into her palm. "I'll give you the balance when I get back. Stay here and watch Pearl. And do *not* let the cat get out!"

I THOUGHT I might calm some in the time it took for us to hustle down to the police station, but I didn't. Rather, I was too exhausted to feel much of anything. I ended up collapsed on a bench inside the door of the station while Sev tried to argue with Kelly. I couldn't quite hear what was being said since they were behind a closed door. What I caught sounded increasingly desperate on his part. About a quarter of an hour into his attempt, he stormed out, and he went for a payphone on the wall. Well, at least he knew when to call for backup.

The conversation was carried on in Italian and was much shorter than expected. He slammed the receiver down. "Vacation!" he shouted. "Her lawyer is on vacation in Europe and won't be back until July!"

"You mean to tell me the Queen of Sin only has one lawyer?" I said.

He sighed. "I only know the number for the one, and Kelly won't let me talk to her." He paused. "Maybe he will let you. You're not a *foreigner*."

I didn't want to talk to Bella, but since it was Sev asking, I would try.

I stumbled my way to Kelly's office. It was well organized, down to the pens being lined up precisely across the top edge of the blotter. Maybe there was nothing to do here besides clean and get overinvested in his biases. He glared as I approached.

"Mr. Carrow," he grunted. "Let me guess. You want me to release Mrs. Ferri."

I shrugged. "Even you have to admit, holding a woman for slapping you is a bit much."

He folded his hands on top of the desk. "See, the thing is, I think I'm going to up the charge."

What? "Up the charge to what? She only smacked you."

"She only smacked *me*, but I'm beginning to suspect she killed Walter Trask."

I thought I had misheard, but there was no mistaking the cold smirk on Kelly's face. He thought he was winning. Hell, maybe he was. "On what grounds?" I demanded.

"I've had her in my sights for Manco's death, and now she turns up again. I'm one of those people who doesn't believe in coincidences."

"She wasn't even here."

"I'm not an idiot. You can kill a man, drive away, and come back the next day, acting like it's a surprise."

Fine, if he didn't want to play nice, I'd have to get creative. "Can I talk to Bella, at least? We can't get her lawyer on the phone, and we need to know who we should try contacting instead."

Kelly eyed me. "All right, only for two minutes. And no funny business."

I would have been pleased, except Kelly's quick acceptance of me meant Sev had been right about the foreigner thing.

Kelly led me beyond an iron door directly behind him. Inside were three cells, one on each wall. The walls were blocks of cement, and of course there were iron bars, but the cots had clean-looking pillows and blankets, and there weren't any dust bunnies or cobwebs. The room was, however, stiflingly warm. Bella sat on her cot in the cell across from the door, hands clutching the edge. She stared me down as I walked in.

"Two minutes," Kelly snapped before slamming the door closed behind me.

Bella crossed her arms over her chest. "Have you come to help or to laugh?"

While I was sure she had committed murder by proxy, Walter Trask wasn't one of her victims. And I *was* grateful she'd gotten us out of Westwick. I had to even the scales somehow.

"Sev tried calling your lawyer, but he's in Europe and won't be back until next month."

She snorted. "Why isn't Severo in here telling me this himself? Oh, I bet the sheriff thinks we will gossip about him." She affected his Boston-tinged accent. "'Speak English!'" She made a face and flicked a hand in what I was sure was some kind of rude gesture. "Men like him will get what is coming in the end."

"Well, I'd like to think so, but right now, he wants to put you in a noose. He's going to charge you for the murder of Walter Trask."

Bella's prideful face slipped. "Murder?"

"I don't know, he seems to think you killed him, ran off, and came back."

"Why would I come back?"

"Look, I didn't say he was right or even that he was smart, just that was what he's thinking. I know you didn't kill Trask. If you had, you'd be bragging. And you wouldn't have needed to come up here to do it personally. Why *are* you here anyway? I don't believe for one second you're running away. I may not know you well, but I know you don't run. And even if you were going to run, this is a stupid place to go, especially with all your money. So why Chickadee and not Rome or Paris or Shanghai?"

She watched me with those expressionless black eyes. "I did not lie to you. I am nervous. Two betrayals," she turned back, "three if I assume Mr. Trask's death is someone trying to attack me somehow. That is too many in a month. But you are right, I do not walk away from fights. As we speak, I have enough people who are working to restore order."

I cringed. It was going to be a bloody night in Westwick. Maybe bloody enough the police would have to focus on that and not on the deaths of the mayor, his wife, and his father-in-law for a little while.

"You still didn't say why you're *here*, specifically," I said.

Bella straightened, and I saw a glint in her eyes that might have been tears. "I don't know. There's nothing there for me now with Dario dead. Why would I go back to an empty home?"

I sighed. I couldn't begrudge her loneliness and grief—I was reeling from the same with Donnie and Martin gone—but of all the people to harass, she had chosen us? "And, what, you have no other family? Sev's suddenly your best friend?"

"I told you, I trust him. I trust *you*. If I go to Rome or Shanghai, who will help me there?" She nodded. "And Crista is a friend of mine from childhood. She will help too."

"You sure? Kelly seems to think you had something to do with her husband's death. If she thinks so too, she might not see the point in helping."

My insinuation finally got some reaction out of Bella. Unfortunately, the reaction was annoyance. "I had nothing to do with that. I don't even know what happened. He was missing. She called me, so I came up. He was found shot and rotted over a week later."

"Does anyone know what happened?"

She shook her head. "If anyone did, it was Trask. They were on a job together. I sent them to pick up crates of whiskey. Only he came back, saying they were separated when they were chased by the border patrol."

Interesting. "Right. Well, what do you want me and Sev to do? Do you have another lawyer we can phone or—"

"Leave me."

"Did you forget the whole conversation we just had? Kelly wants to charge you with murder!"

She didn't answer. Was something worse than murder?

"Bella, what aren't you telling me?"

She raised a shoulder.

"All right, fine. Don't say anything. But Sev isn't going to like you giving up," I said. "He's going to destroy himself trying to fix this. And I'm not going to let him do that. So, whether you want it or not, I'm going to get you out of here."

A smirk curled up Bella's face. "I knew he must like you for a reason."

The door opened and Kelly grabbed my upper arm. "Time's up, joker." And with one yank, he dragged me out.

Chapter Six

AS EXPECTED, SEV didn't take learning that Bella was going to be charged with murder too well and took the information that she didn't want us to get her another lawyer even worse. He swore in two languages, punctuating the rant with expansive gestures. I had to coax him outside and away from Kelly's earshot before he got us into trouble.

"Will you calm down for five seconds?" I hissed as soon as our feet touched the sidewalk. "Do you want us arrested too?"

"I don't understand," Sev protested. "I don't understand any of this."

"Yeah, well, I don't either, but yelling inside the police station isn't going to help anything." I lowered my voice. "She doesn't want to get out. Why wouldn't she want to be let out of prison? What's worse to her than hanging?"

"What?" He shook his head. "I have no idea."

I sighed. "Fine. We'll go back to the house and call someone in her little troop. They probably have a plan in case of something like this. And maybe they know why she's being so cagey."

Sev took a breath, and his shoulders settled. "You're right. I'll call Ernesto at the Ostia. He'll get the message to the right people. You think so clearly under pressure, *caro*. Where would I be without you?"

Not be in Chickadee, Vermont, for starters. "You were doing pretty all right as far as I could tell," I answered. "Come on. I don't want to have to pay Fran any overtime."

Part of me wanted to stomp straight to Crista's place and demand to know the exact circumstances surrounding her husband's death, but I knew confronting her would be either futile or dangerous. Possibly both. She'd had a whole year to go through the story, and if she *had* killed Trask in revenge, I would only be walking into a hornet's nest. Considering I'd almost gotten my head shot off for that kind of recklessness last week, I was in no mood to test those waters.

As we approached the house, Fran peeked out the front window. As soon as she saw me looking, she darted away. I sighed. That child was not subtle.

She popped up again at the front door, which she flung open. "What's going on?" she asked. "I don't understa—"

Pearl squeezed between her and the doorframe, one arm wrapped around a teddy bear I hadn't been aware she owned. Another gift from Bella, presumably. "Miss Fran says Mr. Trask is dead like Daddy and Martin and that Miss Bella is in jail."

Shit.

I looked to Sev, hoping he'd have a positive way to say this. He did manage to keep his near-perpetual half smile, but his gold eyes had the look of a cornered animal. At last, he took a step forward to usher them back into the house and said, "It's a misunderstanding. Bella will be let out soon. As for Mr. Trask, unfortunately, yes, he has passed away." He shooed Pearl inside before shutting the door behind us. "We should pray for him. Why don't you go to your room and start?"

She gave him a suspicious look like she knew he was trying to get her out of the picture but started moving up the stairs. She climbed slowly, and I watched her the whole way to make sure she didn't decide to eavesdrop. Only when I heard the door shut did I round on Fran.

"What the hell were you thinking, telling her all that?" I demanded.

Fran's lower lip trembled. "I'm sorry, I didn't think it'd be bad to tell her. She was going to find out anyhow—"

"She's right, Alex," Sev murmured. "Unless you want to lock Pearl in her room, she's going to hear about things."

I huffed. "She didn't need to know about Trask. She doesn't even know who he is. What does it matter to her he's dead. It's going to remind her Martin's gone." I stopped. Was it Pearl or myself I was worried about?

Sev must have seen something in my face because he patted my shoulder and headed for the kitchen. "I'm going to make more tea. Would you like any, Miss Gaines?"

"Oh, no thank you." She shuffled her feet. "I should go home. Mom was pretty upset Mr. Trask died, and I bet Dad's come home by now." She reached for the doorknob.

Something sparked in my messy brain. If Fran had been willing to gossip to Pearl about what had happened, maybe she would tell me too. And if she told me the right thing, maybe Bella would be out of before supper.

I stepped in front of the door, blocking Fran's way out. "Fran, I'm sorry. I shouldn't have gotten angry. She's a little young for murder, you know?"

Fran's eyes widened. "Murder?"

Fantastic, I'd put my foot in my mouth. "That's what Sheriff Kelly thinks. And well, I don't know anything about anything here, so I guess I believe him."

"Oh, well maybe it was! He's a rich man"—Fran lowered her voice and leaned in—"but not very popular. Everyone says they like him, but that's only because they all work for him."

"Everyone?"

"Well, not *everyone* everyone."

Right, now time to reel in the fish. "Who was close to Walter Trask?"

"Well, Judith, you know, they were stepping out together. And her dad didn't like him much. Um, he has a younger brother? Mr. Richard. He's kind of an odd fellow if you know what I mean."

"Any business partners?"

Fran squirmed and said nothing.

"Fran. This is important."

Her face screwed up like the words caused her pain. "No partners, but my dad works under him. If Mr. Trask is dead then the whole factory... But Dad wouldn't do anything to hurt Mr. Trask!" she wailed. "Never!"

That was more of a reaction than I had bargained for. Since I didn't want a weeping teenager on my hands, I filed away the information and changed the subject. "Anyone else? Anyone he had problems with?"

Fran sniffled and dabbed her nose with her sleeve. "Well, there's Ed."

"Ed who?"

"I dunno. He's Ed. He lives by himself up in the woods. He comes into town maybe twice a week to buy and sell at the store. Nobody really knows him."

"And what were he and Mr. Trask having a problem over?"

"Ed doesn't like people coming up into the parts of the woods he thinks are his. But there're good maples up there, so Mr. Trask was trying to, I don't know, buy the land? And Ed wasn't having it. Chased him off with a bowie knife once."

So, Kelly had decided to harass a woman who had been nowhere near the crime scene instead of a man who had threatened Trask's life once already. Amazing police work in this town, truly.

"Right, well, thanks. That's all very good to know." I hesitated. "Are you sure you don't want any tea or anything?"

Fran shook her head. "I should head home."

I stepped away from the door, and she scuttled past me without so much as a flirting wink. I sighed as I shut it after her. That had been too harsh. But information was information, and she had a lot of it. I traced Sev's steps into the kitchen.

He looked up from the kettle he was putting on the stove. "You upset her."

"I didn't mean to upset her. I just wanted to know who might've wanted to kill Trask. You want Bella hung, or you want the truth?"

"Of course I don't want anything to happen to Bella" He paused, and his eyes tracked across my face. Then he shook his head. Without looking at me, he went for the phone. "Ernesto will be able to help."

I watched in silence as he asked the operator for a Westwick line and started a conversation in Italian with, presumably, Ernesto. That itchy, lonely feeling started building in my chest again. Maybe this time, I would be able to smoke it away in peace. I went outside, careful to shut the door all the way this time.

PARTWAY THROUGH MY second cigarette, Sev popped his head out. "Tea is ready."

I didn't move from my place by the rail. "What'd Ernesto say?"

"Bella did not give us the whole story." He sighed and pulled out his own cigarettes as he took a spot beside me. "A shock, I know." He paused to light up. "Things are bad at home. Other gangs heard about Dario and everything else, and they moved in like wolves, thinking we're weak." A thin stream of smoke wisped between his lips. "Maybe we are weak. I don't know. In any case, there isn't anyone to spare right now. They're all dead or arrested or hiding." He turned to me. "I'm afraid it's down to us at the moment."

I probably should have felt some kind of pleasure at Bella's criminal empire crumbling around her, but seeing Sev's wilted posture, I found only pity. That had been his life too, after all. He knew most of the people caught in the crossfire even if they were only what one might call workplace acquaintances.

"I'm sorry," I mumbled.

He shrugged. "It is a dangerous business. We know what we risk."

Risky enough that Bella was in deeper trouble than she'd let on? "Do you think someone followed her? They knew she'd get out of the city and went to cut her off, so maybe she thinks she's safer with the police?"

He hesitated. "I can't imagine why she would. Anyone bold enough to chase her hundreds of miles wouldn't be very put off by two country policemen."

"What about Trask? Do you think someone knew he was on Bella's payroll and came up here to cut him out as part of this turf war?"

"I don't know why anyone would bother. He's one bootlegger in the middle of nowhere. I didn't even know he existed until she told me we'd be working together. Perhaps money. And if the reason was money, wouldn't it be better trying to bribe him away? What good is a dead smuggler to anyone?"

"So, someone here killed him?"

"I would have to assume. Or else it was an accident, and the branch fell on him like you said."

I *had* said that, but it had been more to distract Kelly than my actual theory. How many people were in town, a couple hundred? I could probably chuck a rock at random and hit the murderer by pure chance. But chance wasn't going to get Bella out of prison. I'd have to walk into Kelly's office with ironclad proof or else she was going to swing, and that was unacceptable. For Sev's sake, of course, and because I had the hazy feeling in the back of my mind she'd slapped Kelly to get his focus off us.

"What about Crista's husband?" I asked. "He was working for Bella too."

Sev shrugged. "I don't know anything about him except he brought us very good-quality gin once. I met him maybe three times total. Nice enough man. Or as nice as you can be in this business."

"And Crista? She's Bella's oldest friend or whatever."

"I remember her name being mentioned a few times, but Bella isn't very talkative as you've noticed. Perhaps I met her? If I did, I was very young and don't remember. Bella is fourteen years older than I am. Anyone she was friends with as a child was almost an adult before I was even born."

No leads. I sighed.

"Sev, I want to help. I do," I said, "but I'm going to have to ask people questions like I just did to you, and some of them are going to be nasty questions they're not going to want to answer, and it might get ugly. I need to know you'll be okay with that."

Sev stared at the tree line for a few seconds in silence before turning back to me. "I trust you, *caro*. Do what you need to do." He kissed me briefly and stubbed out his cigarette on the rail and went back inside.

I WENT BACK in some time later. Three cigarettes in a row hadn't helped. If anything, they made me feel sick as well as uneasy. Sev wasn't in the kitchen, but he'd left a cup of tea for me. The delicate porcelain looked almost comically small with my hand wrapped around it. I decided to put the cup down before I accidentally destroyed something else. The tea had gone cold anyway.

Turning back to the table, I saw the box containing the typewriter. It couldn't stay in the kitchen. As I lugged it into the living room, I heard Sev upstairs with Pearl. I couldn't quite catch what they were saying at first, only that she spoke after him much more slowly and carefully. Then I realized they were speaking Italian. Slow and simple but patient and calm despite everything. I smiled to myself as I unpacked the typewriter onto the desk in the parlor. I'd found a good man somehow amid all the Westwick corruption.

Someone knocked so softly I barely heard the taps even in the quiet of the house. Rubbing ink off my fingers with my handkerchief, I opened the door. Crista. She had a covered casserole dish propped in the crook of her elbow like a baby. A strong garlic smell wafted from it.

"I know I was supposed to come earlier this afternoon to cook dinner for you"—she smiled hesitantly—"but I heard Mr. Arrighi was the one who found Mr. Trask, and I thought maybe you would both like some time to be alone." She held the dish out. "So, I cooked at home. I hope you don't mind."

"Uh, yes. I mean, no; we don't mind." I jammed my stained handkerchief into my pocket. I took the dish and nudged the cloth covering with my thumb. A whiff of garlic and tomato escaped, though I couldn't identify the contents with such a small peek. "If you hang on a second while I put this down, I can get my wallet."

"Oh, no, no. Consider it a housewarming gift."

"Um, well, thank you." Now I felt awful about suspecting her of trying to steal Sev from me.

Her smile broadened. "You're very welcome. Enjoy," she said. "*Buona sera*, have a pleasant evening."

"Wait."

She paused mid-turn. "*Si?*"

I took a breath. If Walter Trask had been involved in her husband's murder, and she had tried to take revenge, I was about to drop myself into a viper pit. Looking at Crista, though, it was impossible to be afraid. She just stood there in a faded green dress, no weapon, no fists, not even a suspicious look. Plus, the top of her head reached my shoulder. How would she lift a branch and swing it hard enough to crack a man's skull?

"Did you hear about Bella?" I asked.

"No? What has happened?"

"Sheriff Kelly arrested her on, uh, well, assault, but he's holding her on suspicion of Trask's murder."

Crista paled. "*Madonna*. She didn't!"

"I don't think so either, but how well do you know Bella? Because she seems content to sit there with a murder charge. You're friends. Do you know why she might do that?"

"We are friends, yes, and she has always been kind to me, but she is a private person, I think is how they say it. She does not share when she does not have to."

Well, I couldn't argue with that. "Does she know anyone else here besides Mr. Trask who might know?"

Crista shook her head.

"Right." I sighed. "Well, I didn't want to have to drag this up, but Kelly also thinks she had something to do with, um, your husband Leo's death."

"No, ridiculous!"

"Exactly." I lowered my voice. "I know this is a lot to ask, but I want to go back to Kelly in the morning with hard proof, or at least reasonable doubt." I took a breath. "What happened to Leo, Mrs. Manco?"

"I don't know," she mumbled, not meeting my eyes. "He and Mr. Trask left one night. Two days later, Mr. Trask stumbled back, and Leo never returned. And Sheriff Kelly did nothing. He said Leo had abandoned me, which I knew wasn't true. So, I called Bella, begging for help. And she came, brought her own men to look. And they found him." Crista took a shaky breath. "He'd been shot with a rifle, but that was all they would tell me. We told Sheriff Kelly to look into Mr. Trask, and he did after a while, but his rifle bullets didn't match." She shrugged. "So, we do not know what happened. Perhaps it was the border patrol."

I nodded. So, not much different than what Bella had said. Could the story really be the truth? "While Bella was here, did she go anywhere while you weren't with her? Did she seem particularly friendly or unfriendly with anyone?"

"Unfriendly with Mr. Kelly. That is to be expected." Crista worried her bottom lip with her teeth. "There was a man though. He wasn't from here; he was renting from the Reeds." She gestured at the house. "For a hunting trip, he said. He was here perhaps a little more than a month, but he stayed the whole time Bella did. Left the day after. She didn't speak with him at all, but she..." Crista shook her head. "Now that you say it, I think she tried to avoid him."

Well, a mysterious man might be anyone. Rival mob. G-man. Hell, he might have been her ex for all I knew. "Does he have a name?"

"James Smith? Maybe Joseph?"

I suppressed a groan. That had fake name written all over it. The least he could have done was be creative. "Did he talk to anyone a lot?"

"I wouldn't know. My mind was elsewhere."

Right, murdered husband. "Understandable. Did the police have a word with him at all?"

"No. He left before they decided to do anything."

"And what did the Reeds have to say about that?"

"Not much, as I understand it. They weren't here, and when the police asked for his contact information to track him down, it all ended up in dead ends."

And yet Kelly still thought Bella had something to do with these deaths? Somehow, this town was shadier than Westwick. "I find it kind of strange Kelly wouldn't have hounded them about that."

Crista shrugged. "They're not here often, perhaps a few months every few years, and they're very wealthy. And Robert Kelly has family in the Boston police department.

Maybe if he were a good man, he might sacrifice his own job, but even a good man would have to think twice about ruining his whole family."

Ah, good old extortion. That explained at least some of Kelly's reticence. So, I'd have to track down the Reeds myself. "Who knows the Reeds well?" I asked.

"Mr. Trask did. He did business with them in Boston, or at least that's what I have heard. And Bella does. I don't know who else. When they stay, they are very quiet."

I nodded. Definitely shadier than Westwick. "Thanks. If you think of something else, will you let me know?"

"Of course." She took a step back. "Is there anything else?"

"I wanted to say I'm very sorry about what happened to your husband."

"Believe me, Mr. Carrow, no one is sorrier than I am. Now if you'll excuse me." Crista smiled faintly. Then she walked off the porch, leaving me with the dish and no real answers. "Please give Mr. Arrighi my regards."

Chapter Seven

AFTER ANOTHER RESTLESS night, I concluded that Alex Carrow was definitely not a morning person, but again, only after Pearl demanded I wake up at half past seven. I struggled my way through putting on clothes and slumped downstairs. Sev's voice drifted from the kitchen. Strange, especially since Pearl was still upstairs. Even stranger, it sounded melodic. Or it might have been if it hadn't been horribly off-key. I shuffled toward the back of the house.

Sev was dressed in a full suit again, the navy pinstripe that followed all the right lines. He hovered by the stove, his back to me. Daisy sat on the counter beside him, staring at the contents of a bowl. He was singing. Or trying to. "Daisy, Daisy, give me your answer do. I'm half crazy over my love—"

"Are you singing to the cat?"

Sev froze. He turned to me, his face turning a dusty red. "Would you believe me if I said no?"

"Caught red-handed, I'm afraid." I chuckled. I slid into one of the chairs. From her perch on the counter, Daisy glared at me and swished her tail. I rolled my eyes. "What're you doing all dressed up?"

He shrugged. "I thought I might go to the factory to see if the accounting job is still available. If Mr. Trask was working with Bella, maybe I can find something there that will help get her out."

Well, he had a point. An inside man would make things a lot easier. Or worse. Hell, there might even be trouble from him knocking on the door. Considering the looks Sev had garnered in our walk through town the other day, Robert Kelly wasn't the only person here who had an issue with "foreigners."

"Do you think they'll bring you on?" I asked.

"It's worth trying. The worst they can do is say no, and then I come home."

That definitely wasn't the worst they could do, but I didn't want to cut off his grand plan to save Bella, especially considering that was also my own goal. I'd have to keep all my paranoia to myself. Maybe I ought to go with him to keep an eye on things. My blocky six-foot frame might keep some people in line who might have otherwise tried a thing or two.

God, I was already so stressed I wanted to smoke. I could practically smell it. No, wait, I *could* smell it. Streams of gray were snaking off the pan on the stove. I jumped up.

"Uh, Sev? Whatever you're frying…"

"*Cazzo*," he hissed as he whipped back around.

Knobs were turned, but the smoke remained. I dared creep closer as he muttered a stream of what were probably swears in Italian. Whatever had been in the pan had charred beyond recognition.

"What were you *making*?" I asked. My voice came out strained as the smoke scraped my throat.

"Pancakes," he muttered as he dumped the still-smoking pan into the sink. "I thought I would be cute."

Ah. Well, that matched up with his ironic sense of humor. Though maybe this wasn't quite the time. "You're cute enough," I said as I pulled him toward me. "You don't need to go burning down the house to prove it."

Apparently, I'd said the wrong thing because he twisted his face away so my kiss landed on his cheek rather than his lips. "One of us *has* to learn to cook," he insisted. "Unless you want Crista having to come by every day?"

The image of Crista getting kissed while cooking flickered into my mind unbidden, distracting and horrifying me so much I barely heard Pearl rumbling down the stairs. I only just managed to step away from Sev as she appeared in the foyer.

"Something's burning," she said.

"Yeah, we know," I answered, waving the last of the smoke away with my hand. "Did you have breakfast?"

"No, but I have to go now, or I'm going to be late to school!"

Oh crap, I'd forgotten about school between the car accident, the murder, and Bella being in jail. What time was class supposed to start? Eight thirty? I looked at my watch. Eight fifteen. Shit.

"Okay, okay, we're going now," I said. I snatched an apple off the counter. "Here, this is breakfast, and I'll come around at noon with your lunch." I smiled at Sev. "See you tonight, I guess."

"Ah, actually." He looked to Pearl. "Can you wait on the porch for Alex, *gattina*? I need to talk to him about something."

"Fine. But I *don't* want to be late," she huffed.

Her hair ribbons flapped as she spun on her heel. The sass on this kid. Was that normal at such a young age? Should I be trying to do something about that? Sev seemed oblivious to the fact we'd been scolded, only focused on fishing in his pocket. As soon as Pearl stepped outside, he produced his knife.

"I know you are going to start looking around for answers today." He held it out to me. "Better safe than sorry."

I wanted to protest—the sight of the blade dragged up memories of Emma's slashed neck—but he had a point. My mouth tended to cause problems, and I knew nothing about any of these people. So, I tucked the knife into my own pocket.

Sev smiled. "*Sei troppo corrigioso*," he murmured.

He said that to me often. Very brave or too brave, depending; I had a feeling he meant the latter. But I didn't feel very brave. It was just that someone was going to have to do something, and it might as well be me.

"Thanks." I pulled him against me again. "Good luck at the factory, okay? If something goes belly-up—"

"It will be fine, *caro*." He kissed me. "Now get going. God help us both if Pearl is late."

SEV HAD BEEN right—I'd been planning on beginning my hunt for answers that morning, and I'd decided to start with Judith. She was Trask's fiancée, after all. She was bound to know something. So, as soon as I got Pearl to school, I went looking for her.

It was easy enough to find where Judith Howe lived. All I had to do was ask the first person I saw on the street, though there were so few houses I could have probably knocked on every door and found it within the hour as long as I didn't mind the wafts of sickly sweet maple smell clinging to everything. In any case, the house was on one of the streets crossing Main. It was made of brick and was largeish, though nowhere near as big as the ones belonging to the upper crust in Westwick.

Judith seemed only slightly surprised to see me. "Can I help you, Mr. Carrow?"

"I came to offer my condolences," I said.

She smiled politely. "How kind. You didn't even know Walter. Or me." She stepped back and gestured at her foyer. "Won't you come in and have some tea?"

Alarm bells started ringing in my head. This was too much like how Emma had coaxed me into a false sense of security. But I was here, and no one else was going to put the effort into fixing this. I mounted the last stair with a murmur of thanks.

The parlor looked something like ours except it had a hutch instead of a desk, and a striped area rug took up most of the center. The fireplace was solid and swept and unremarkable, but above it was a sheet dangling off whatever had been hung there.

"A painting?" I asked, my mouth moving too quickly for my brain to shut it in time. *Great job being rude, Alex.*

Judith paused in the doorway between the parlor and the kitchen. "A mirror."

"You're Jewish?"

She returned with a small tray of tea and picked over cookies. Undoubtedly, she'd had many people traipsing through since they'd found out about Trask. She placed the tray on the table and motioned for me to sit.

"My mother was," she said, "which means I am, at least in theory. I'm not much of a practitioner." She waved a hand at the mirror. "Though some details come through."

I nodded, wondering how many people hadn't known until they'd paraded through her living room as she'd mourned and if that would change their opinion of her. Funny thing, though, she didn't seem particularly upset.

She hadn't even been particularly sad back in the forest with Trask's body right in front of her. Grief could be different for different people, so maybe she was numb. Still, her impassiveness was suspicious. And why wasn't Kelly in here trying to corner the statistically most likely culprit?

"How did you meet Walter?" I asked.

A flicker of something shone in her eyes. "I was his secretary. The factory had grown, and I was the only one who knew shorthand at the time." A hint of a smile appeared. "I started college in Boston, and I came back here to take care of my father when my mother died and ended up asking for work."

Well, not an unusual story, in-office romance. I'd slapped together a few short stories on the theme for the pulps. "You're not the secretary now, are you?"

"No, that would be Mrs. Gaines. I felt it was unprofessional to keep working once Walter and I became serious. We were supposed to get married this summer."

"I'm very sorry."

"Oh, don't be sorry for me," Judith said. "I understand you're in mourning as well. Your sister and your brother."

Brother? Oh right, Martin. I'd forgotten I'd told Crista that detail. And if I told Crista, half the town probably knew by now. "Yeah. Yeah, I mean, we saw Marianne's coming, but Martin was so sudden." A wave of real grief floated across me and settled in my throat, giving my next words a strained quality. "Shot. Wrong place at the wrong time. That's when we decided to come here."

Judith sighed. "It is very unfortunate you arrived in time to see another murder, especially since there hasn't been one here besides Mr. Manco in some thirty years. Don't misunderstand me; I'm not like Sheriff Kelly. I don't believe you or Mr. Arrighi had anything to do with it." Her finger tapped against her teacup. "It would be very silly for you to kill a man you'd never met, wouldn't it? No motive."

Well, she'd started it already. "What do you think the motive was?"

She shrugged. "Walter was a wealthy man, and there will be people who will benefit financially from his death. His brother, for one. Mr. Gaines may, depending on legal factors."

Yourself, maybe? "Any personal grudges going around?"

"I suppose I should be happy you're the one asking me and not Mr. Kelly, but I will assure you and everyone in town I had no reason to want to harm Walter. He may have had his faults, but he was a good man."

I watched her. Nothing. No grief, no anger, not even insistence. Like her face was plastered over. Like she had trained herself to be still.

"You know, in my experience, when you have to specify someone was a good man, they usually aren't. And I'm not trying to badmouth your fiancé. I'm including myself in that."

"How unfortunate you feel that way."

Geez, she cut me off at every angle. What if I came at her from somewhere she didn't expect? "I hear he was mixed up in Mr. Manco's death."

Judith sighed. "Mr. Kelly says otherwise, but I understand why you might not want to believe him. Particularly if you're friends with Crista. She never quite forgave Walter for making it back alive." She lowered her voice. "Did she tell you what happened?"

"Just that they both went out and Leo didn't come home. Why, what happened out there?"

"I couldn't say about how he was shot, but Crista was in the family way at the time." Judith softened a little. "You should have seen her, Mr. Carrow; she glowed. And so happy! But all the stress of her husband being missing and then knowing he was dead…"

I could see where this was going, considering I hadn't seen any signs of a toddler around. "It must have been very hard to lose her husband and then her baby."

"She was inconsolable. She's mostly herself now, but it's like someone took a piece out of her and didn't put it back right."

Interesting. "Do you know what Mr. Trask and Mr. Manco were doing out there in the woods?"

"Hunting, Walter said. Though I believe it came out later that Mr. Manco was a bit of a scoundrel. Walter said he disappeared, and after searching for him some, he came home. They found Mr. Manco about a week later. Shot by government agents while smuggling." Judith nodded to herself. "And rigging the factory books to hide it as well. I believe he worked for Mrs. Ferri, who Bobby has in custody right now, as I heard."

I ignored the part about Bella in favor of the hunting angle. Crista had mentioned a mysterious hunter showing up around that time. "I heard there had been a man renting the place I'm in now who went by the name of James or Joseph Smith. Came for the hunting. Were they out with him?"

"I don't believe so. I do remember him though. He kept to himself. The only time I spoke with him was when he came in." A faint smile spread across Judith's face. "He came into the police station to complain about Ed."

"What had Ed done?"

"Threatened to shoot him, I think. Ed doesn't like people. He spends most of his time in the forest. Only comes into town twice a week or so to sell fur and clear business."

"Funny thing, to laugh at someone being threatened."

"Ed wouldn't really have hurt him." She hesitated. "He's different, and different here isn't ideal."

I shrugged. "Maybe it's better?"

Her eyes narrowed slightly. "My father says something very similar. Have you been speaking with him?"

"No. I don't even know who he is."

"Did you call for me, Judy?" A man's voice rattled down the stairs, followed by heavy footsteps and wheezing.

The person belonging to the voice appeared at the base of the stairwell, stark eyes sunk into a skull as bald as a cue ball. I vaguely recognized him as part of the crowd that had gone looking for Trask. He blustered forward to shake my hand, trying to cough discreetly into his other elbow as he moved.

"George Howe, nice to meet you. Mr. Carrow, I expect. You don't look I-talian enough to be Mr. Arrighi."

My eye twitched as he pumped my arm. "Yes, Alex Carrow. Pleasure. I was on my way out."

"Ah, well, let me walk you out. I was about to head down to the post office anyway. I appreciate you coming to see Judy in her hour of need." He nodded at his daughter, and she returned his words with a shy smile. "Bit of a shock to her. And to all of us."

"Are you sure you're all right to go?" asked Judith. "You know the doctor said to rest as much as you can—"

George waved a hand to silence her. "It's not even half a mile. If I can't walk half a mile, I might as well be in the ground already." He turned back to me. "Well, come on now. The day is wasting away."

He put a broad boney hand on my back and guided me out the door, a little too firmly to be friendly. I let my hand drift into the pocket where Sev's knife was hidden and hoped George couldn't feel my pounding heart through my clothes.

As soon as the door shut, he released me. "Got some nerve, moving in on my little girl before Trask is even in the ground," he rumbled. His breath came short and stunted.

"Believe me, sir, I wasn't doing anything of the sort." *I was only seeing if she'd murdered her fiancé.* "I wanted to make sure she was okay after yesterday."

To my surprise, George looked almost disappointed. He jammed his hands in his pockets. "Too bad. You're a good-looking fellow, and I hoped she might take a liking to you."

"Sorry, you *want* me to flirt with your daughter?"

"Well, better you than Walter." He shrugged. "Everyone knows I never liked him, so might as well tell you flat-out now before it hits your ears some other way."

"Oh. Any particular reason? He was quite rich from what I understand. Wouldn't you want your daughter to be well supported?"

"Some things ain't worth the money, which you'll figure out in due time. Not sure Judy has yet though." He cast a glance over his shoulder and hustled me down the walk. The swift motion made him even more breathless. "Walter had money, yes, but I never quite bought it was all from that factory of his. He disappeared a lot, saying he was looking at his trees. He'd be gone for days. It don't make sense to have trees so far off. He was up to something, no doubt. He was older too. Probably has a wife somewhere and snuck off to see her."

I nodded. The more likely reason was he had been shuttling liquor across the border, but it was also possible he'd been having an affair. Mayor Carlisle had kept a young woman on the side, and his philandering had caused the whole damn mess back in Westwick.

"What I don't understand," George continued, "is why. Judy is a beautiful girl. She could have any man in this damn town. Hell, she could have any man between here and Boston, and she chose that slimy little weasel."

"I'm afraid I don't know, sir."

"No, of course you wouldn't know. I just wish she would learn some sense and try to be happy for a change." He clapped a hand on my shoulder. "Sorry you have to see the worst of us in your first week. I hope your time with us gets better from here." He left me on the sidewalk and started heading for Main Street.

"Actually, sir? Before you go, can you tell me where I can find Mr. Trask's brother? I ought to give him my condolences too."

"Heh, well, ol' Rich is even worse than Walter, but I guess you're right: he ought to have some sympathy." George pointed to the northeast. "Most likely he'll be wandering around the library."

"The library?"

"Mr. Parrish is about the only person that won't throw him out. Says being in the library is a public right. Too nice for his own good, that Mr. Parrish. Anyway, have a good day, Mr. Carrow." George nodded and continued on his way, coughing.

I stood there for a moment, watching him leave. Pretty odd someone would up and announce his hatred for a man murdered only two days before. If he had meant to draw suspicion to himself, he'd failed hard. If anything, his talkativeness made me want to keep a closer eye on Judith. Fathers did all sorts of things for their children. Logan had killed six people at Emma's insistence, after all. It wouldn't be too shocking if George Howe would be willing to hang for his daughter's crime.

But I didn't actually have anything on her yet, and if George and Fran were right about Trask, there was a lot more going on than anyone had yet admitted to.

Chapter Eight

AS MUCH AS I wanted to go straight for the jugular and hunt down Richard Trask next, I still needed to get Pearl something for lunch. Plus, getting my pants fixed was probably a good idea, and I might as well get Sev's gray suit cleaned while I was at it. Trouble was, I couldn't do any of those things on my own. No one had ever trained me in domesticity. Back in the city, it was so easy to walk down the street and find a cleaner and a tailor and a deli, but here?

I swept home, jamming the leftovers from the night before into a lunch pail that had been left out on the table. Presumably Sev had found it in his excavations of the cabinets. Thank God he was better at running a household than I was. I'd spied what looked like a dry cleaner's on my now-frequent walks through town, so I grabbed the clothes, too, hoping to drop them off before handing off Pearl's lunch and probably embarrassing her in the process.

The store was indeed a dry cleaner's. It wasn't a big place, barely big enough for me, the counter, and the woman behind it. I tripped on the small step leading up, nearly dropping my awkward burden. She snatched the clothes away from me, so they didn't fall on the ground.

"How may I help you, sir?" she asked. A French accent. I froze, remembering Birdie and all the trouble she'd caused in Westwick.

Except this woman wasn't Birdie, didn't look a thing like her, barring the young face. Instead of bobbed red hair, this woman's was black and set in a neat braided bun. Nor were her eyes blue, but a deep brown, set off by tasteful red lipstick. And now that I was looking, she'd also been in the group that'd gone looking for Walter Trask.

"Hi, sorry," I said, trying to look like I hadn't been staring at her. "Is there anything you can do about these?"

She inspected the sweat, dirt, and grass stains on Sev's suit and tutted. "Yes, I've seen quite a lot of this today after all the commotion in the forest. Poor Mr. Trask. Horrible thing to happen to a man." She ran her hands across the fabric. "This is very nice material," she said, almost to herself. "Silk and cotton?"

"I haven't the slightest. It's my brother-in-law's."

"Oh, oh yes. Nice to meet you, Mr. Carrow." She smiled at my confusion. "My apologies. New people, always news. My name is Maude Lamar." She held out her hand to be shaken. "I was new myself about five years ago. *Quebecoise* since I know that's the next thing people ask. Born in Montreal."

"That's quite a bit away."

She shrugged. "It's all the old French fur routes, isn't it?" She picked up my torn wool trousers. "I'm afraid I don't do repairs. You may want to ask Mrs. Manco."

"Really? She's already cooking for us."

"She does all sorts of piecework. I don't think she'd mind sewing some. In fact, I'm sure she'd be happy for the extra income." Maude smiled. "It's difficult for single women to earn a living. Even with my own business, I can't say it's easy."

She waved at the shop, and as she did, something caught my eye. Almost the entire back of her left hand was a mottled red. Something about it struck me as familiar, but I didn't know why.

"Are you all right?" I asked, gesturing at the mark.

She looked at her hand and let it drop behind the counter. "A chemical burn, very old. This is not the safest career. To have such a burn is embarrassing now. It makes it look like I don't know what I'm doing."

"Well, I trust you since you know what kind of fabric something is just by touching it."

"Thank you, Mr. Carrow; you're very kind." She took the suit and hung it on the rack behind her with maybe a dozen other items. "I don't think I can do this overnight when there are so many others, and it's such a nice piece I don't want to rush. Is Monday all right for pick up?"

"Oh, yeah, that's fine."

She wrote out a ticket, smiling the whole time. It was almost a relief to talk to someone normally for a change. Still, something nagged at the back of my mind. *Calm down; you're being paranoid.* But why wouldn't I be, considering everything that had happened in the last few weeks? It was like I'd become a magnet for terrible things. But it wasn't like dry cleaning could go awry, right?

I arrived at the school as they were letting out for morning recess, and as I suspected, Pearl wasn't too happy about me handing her lunch in full view of her peers. I would have the knack of this parenting thing by Monday though. Definitely. Probably.

I started back for the house, trudging through the sticky, sweet-smelling heat. I paused in front of the syrup factory. Peculiar venue for bootlegging, but that was part of the appeal, wasn't it? Who would think to look there?

Plus, there had to be some kind of chattering over the border, maybe even imports. Bottles of booze stuck into random crates of syrup would be hard to find. Maybe no one would have noticed at all if Leo Manco hadn't been killed.

"Ah, Mr. Carrow."

Oh, Christ. I turned to face Robert Kelly, who was trudging his way up the street. "Yes, sheriff, what can I do for you?" I asked with a minimum of sarcasm.

"Saw you down by the school," he answered as he stopped in front of me. "Your niece, right?"

I didn't know where this was going, but I was fairly sure I didn't like it. "Yeah, what about her?"

He shrugged. "Nothing. Just thinking that Mr. Arrighi is a devoted man, taking care of a child who isn't his."

Of course, he was going to aim for that. Because honestly? I knew how suspicious this looked. That meant I'd have to do some damage control fast. "He loved my sister," I snapped. "And he loves Pearl like she's his own child."

Kelly shrugged. "I'm looking out for the girl. There are some sick people in this world, you know."

"I can look out for her fine, thanks."

"I'm sure you can. I'll be keeping an eye just the same." He waved and started walking away again. "We keep a watch on one another here in these small towns." He didn't turn back or say anything else, only strolled away from me like he *hadn't* insinuated Sev was some kind of predator.

Fuck this town, and fuck its sheriff. Maybe we should leave and convince Bella's little criminal friends to get her out. Lawyer or not, they could do *something*.

But then what? We had nowhere to go. Cops in Connecticut were still looking for us, and maybe Kelly if he decided he wanted to chase his imaginary lead. Without Bella, Sev and I would be as good as dead. And what would happen to Pearl?

As I pondered the impossibilities of making a run for it, the door of the factory opened, and I took a step back to avoid colliding with the person coming out. To my surprise, the person was Sev. He saw me and smiled weakly.

"I saw him out the window," he murmured, tilting his head in Kelly's direction. "Is everything all right?"

"Yeah, he's being a jerk. Don't worry about it. Go on back in."

Sev shrugged as he pulled the door shut. "I was on my way out anyway."

"Oh. Didn't go so good?" I asked.

He hesitated. "I think it depends on what you think is good. Come, we can talk at home."

He pressed a hand against my back, and for a moment, I relished in his touch, but it turned into an insistent push. He had a very strange look on his face, one I'd never seen before, so I changed tack at the last second.

"I brought Pearl her lunch and your gray suit to the dry cleaner's," I said.

"*Bene*," he said stiffly. "Thank you."

Unease started creeping up my spine, so I didn't say anything else until we were safely inside the house. The smell of maple followed us, and I realized it was Sev—the scent had permeated his hair and clothes, displacing the more comforting tobacco and roses. He ran a hand over his curls, making the cloying sweetness surrounding us worse.

"So, what happened?" I asked as I draped my torn trousers around the finial of the banister as a reminder to have Crista look at them.

He sighed and drifted into the parlor where he sank onto the couch. "Well, I went, and I asked to speak to Mr. Gaines since he is assistant director or whatever the position is." He waved a hand to gloss over the irrelevance of the exact wording. "He was not there yet, and I was told to wait in his office."

I sat next to him and nodded. So far, pretty normal. In fact, the story was already better than my worry the door would be slammed in his face, or worse, that he'd be chased off with racial slurs. But his expression was all discomfort, and I knew the rest of the story wasn't going to be good.

"So I waited," he continued, "and his wife, Louise, comes in and says she was Mr. Trask's secretary, and while they had been told I was coming, with him gone they are not looking for any extra help and all the other things they say to make you go away. Her husband arrives as she is saying them and pulls her into a different room." He paused. "They ended up yelling at each other, and I heard them through the wall."

"What did they say?"

Sev shook his head. "I don't think they are very good people."

I blinked in shock. Sev liked everyone—me and Bella included. What could they have said to put him off? "Like murdered Walter Trask in cold blood kind of not good?"

"Mmm, well if they did, they didn't shout about it, unfortunately." He closed his eyes briefly. "It was about me. Mrs. Gaines said some—" He cleared his throat. "—choice words; words I hadn't heard since I was a boy about where I come from."

So, I hadn't worried for nothing. "I'm so sorry." I pulled him closer to me. At this nondistance, the maple smell faded, and I found him again under all the heavy sweetness. Even here, he smelled like home. "I don't know if that helps, but I am. Fuck her. You didn't want to work for someone like that anyway."

"That's the thing. Mr. Gaines, Oscar, won the argument, mostly by being louder. I think he knows about whatever Bella had arranged, but maybe not the whole thing. Anyway, the fight ends, and he comes back in and says they can keep me for three days a week starting Monday. And I said yes."

"What! After everything she said?"

Sev shrugged. "If we are going to help Bella, I need to find out what's going on in there. I can't do that if I stay home. Besides"—he glanced away from me—"the money Bella lent us will not last forever."

Right, the two hundred she'd given us when we'd fled Westwick and the extra hundred given with the false papers. To me, her gift had been almost more money than I'd ever seen in one place, and since Bella also paid the rent on this house, I'd been confident it would last nearly forever. But no, Sev was right. We'd dumped a lot into food, and Crista would need to be paid for her housekeeping, eventually, and if I'd learned anything in the years living on my own, major expenses popped up at the worst time. Plus, I wasn't earning *anything* at the moment. What meager royalties I would have gotten from the one novel and handful of short stories I'd published were no longer coming to me. Alex Dawson had written them—not Alex Carrow—and as far as anyone beyond Sev, Bella, and Pearl was concerned, Alex Dawson had disappeared.

I pulled Sev against me again. "Well, if she gets to be too much, tell her to shove her head up her own ass and walk on out of there." *And I will personally help her along.*

He laughed. "Well, if it comes to that, I think I will be more diplomatic." He leaned his head against my shoulder. "I don't like making people angry because I can."

"No, you don't, do you?" I looked at him. "I like that about you, you know? You're so nice. Nicer than me, anyway."

A smile crept up his face. "You are nice, just a different sort of nice. You don't like when people are pushed around." He leaned in and kissed me. "Now, tell me more about the things you like about me."

"Oh, well, you're handsome. And smart. And patient. And you make me laugh even when I don't think I feel like laughing. And you calm me. And—"

The rest of my list got cut off by Sev's mouth on mine. I clung to him greedily, sure something or someone was going to storm in and ruin everything. He seemed equally as frantic like he, too, was afraid of time being cut short. We groped our way to the bedroom, where I nearly cracked my head on the brass headframe as he pushed me backward onto the blankets. He fell with me, laughing, setting off the bells in my head.

He stopped, a confused expression on his face. "Is there something in your pocket?"

I tried to pull him back down to me. "Just happy to see you."

He sighed. "It's uncomfortable."

"Fine."

I reached into my pocket, and my fingers closed around his knife. I'd forgotten all about it. *Whoops.* I brought it out and showed him.

"Didn't need it," I said.

He pushed the blade back toward me. "Hold on to it, *caro*. If I need it back, I will tell you."

"Are you sure?" I turned it over in my hands.

"Positive." He took the knife from me and tossed it onto the side table. "Now, where were we?"

Chapter Nine

"HOW DO YOU do that?" I asked.

Sev paused. "Do what?"

"Get your clothes and everything so fast."

He laughed and continued brushing out his suit. He'd already changed into something more casual and combed his hair. Meanwhile, I was still searching for my other shoe, which was not under the bed where I thought I'd kicked it.

"I suppose it's practice," he said.

Somehow, I hadn't expected that answer. But why shouldn't I have? There was no way I was the first person he'd been with. I probably wasn't even the first person he'd been in love with. I couldn't even say that about him, and I was a lot younger. And yet the idea left me with a sour taste in my mouth. I wanted to know who and how many and how much more he cared for me over them.

A knock on the front door snapped my thread of thought. Sev moved faster than I did, sliding against the wall and flicking aside the curtain. His shoulders relaxed.

"It's Crista," he said.

Crista? What was she doing here? I gathered my remaining bits of clothing and bolted up the staircase with them before Sev opened the door.

I caught pieces of his welcome and her response, and of those, I understood almost nothing since it was in Italian. I shuffled the rest of my clothes on and skidded back onto the upstairs landing. Sev was already walking toward the kitchen, and Crista stopped and smiled at me as I tried to descend the stairs like a normal person.

"Ah, there you are. Miss Lamar said you were home." She touched the trousers still draped on the railing. "I should fix these?"

"Please?" My brief conversation with Sev about our funds flickered into my mind. "What's your going rate for mending?"

She waved a hand. "No, no. For Bella's friends, it is free."

I wasn't quite sure how ready I wanted to be called Bella's friend, but I knew how good it was to save a penny or two. "Well, thanks."

"I like to help where I can." She began examining the tear. "If you will excuse me for saying so, your hair is..." She gestured at the back of her head.

I became aware of how mussed my hair was. "Oh." I tried to brush it down with my hand. "I, uh, took a nap."

"Ah. Well, I am glad someone has found the time to rest," she said as she folded my trousers over her arm.

Had I just been insulted? I wasn't sure. She walked toward the kitchen, saying something in Italian. Sev's voice answered her, and she giggled as she crossed the threshold and out of sight.

I needed to smoke.

Out on the porch, the ever-present heat felt extra stifling after our unplanned exertion. We needed to get out of this stupid town, away from the warmth and the stares. And, yeah, maybe even away from Crista.

There was something off about her I couldn't place. Or maybe my unease came from something she had said, going around telling everyone about us. Maybe it was the fact she remained here alone when there was nothing to recommend the place. Surely, there was some family, some friends to stay with? Some better job than random housework? She had to be staying for some reason.

The door behind me opened, and I turned, expecting Crista back. Instead Sev appeared. He smiled as he slid his own cigarettes out of his pocket. "Great minds, yes?" he said.

"Yeah." I glanced at the door again. "Isn't Crista going to go home?"

"I told her she might as well stay. She was going to have to come back in an hour to cook anyway."

"Do you think it's okay to leave her alone in the house?" I asked.

Sev gave me a confused look. "I imagine she won't set anything on fire. She's not like me with the stove."

"No, I mean"—I lowered my voice—"you don't think she'll snoop around or steal anything, right?"

"Even if she did, what are we hiding?" He held up a hand to stop my protests before they started. "Among our things. There's almost nothing to go through anyway, and nothing worth taking." He huffed. "You should be ashamed for thinking such things."

Should I? On the one hand, Crista hadn't done anything to deserve my distrust. On the other was that nagging feeling... "It's not *her*, specifically," I said. "I grew up down by the train tracks at home in all those slums. You left your window open for a minute, and by the time you turned back around, all your furniture was gone."

"You're exaggerating."

"Only a little. It isn't really safe there. Go ask Pearl if you don't believe me."

Sev went quiet, probably trying to piece together what I'd said. His version of crime was genteel silk suits and sequined dresses, singers and champagne, a wink and a stack of bills passed under a table. Even the bloody aspects were full of romance. It made a much better story to be killed in a drive-by with a Tommy gun outside a restaurant than to be beaten to death in an alley because someone wanted your holeless shoes.

"Well, in any case, Crista would not," he said. "You don't need to worry about every little thing, Alex. It will make you crazy if you try."

Spoken like someone who hadn't had to worry about money or food or rent most of their life. But he had a point. "Yeah, I know." I sighed. "A lot of stuff's gone wrong, and I keep expecting more."

Sev nodded. "I know. Here. You forgot this," he said. The knife appeared in his hand briefly before he slid it into my pocket. "You'll give Pearl a bad example, not picking up your things."

I shrugged. "If that's the worst thing I show her, I'll consider it a job well done."

"Well, if she is here and not in the slums at home, then that is already a better job." He patted my arm and smiled again, his eyes tracking over me. They settled on my hair, and he chuckled. "You need to do something about your hair. It looks like you rolled out of bed."

I threw a look over my shoulder to make sure Christa couldn't see. "How about this option: We go back to bed, and I worry about it later?" I whispered against Sev's neck.

He laughed and squirmed so he was out of easy reach. "Great minds again. But unfortunately"—he stubbed out his cigarette—"we have a guest, and one of us is going to have to get Pearl from school soon." Discreetly, he ran his hand across my back. "There are many tomorrows, *caro*. No need to burn it all up at once."

THE FIRST TOMORROW was, of course, Saturday. I felt more than a little ashamed I'd let myself get carried away the day before. And I couldn't imagine Bella was too pleased she'd been stuck in prison an extra twelve hours because I'd decided spending the afternoon with my boyfriend was better than gathering evidence to get her out. So, first thing in the morning, I went for my next target—Richard Trask, Walter's brother.

Stepping into the library was like stepping back in time for me. I'd spent a lot of my childhood in them due to my general dislike of other children and my refusal to spend more time with my drunk bully of a father than was absolutely necessary. Got teased a lot for it—people tended to think I ought to be playing football instead of sticking my nose into books. Not that I regretted it. Books were better than people, after all, and the library was free and safe. And, of course, books had fueled my career choice. Nope, I had no bad thoughts about libraries. At least so far.

The sun beamed through the large front windows in what would have been excellent reading light in the winter, but in the heat, it caused the temperature in the room to soar. I shuffled my jacket off and draped it over my arm as I inspected the rest of the interior. It wasn't large, only the front reading space partitioned from the actual stacks behind it. In front of both sets of windows were long tables with simple hardback chairs for working. Across from the entrance was the check-out desk smack between two arches leading to the rows of books beyond. Arthur Parrish sat at his oversized librarian desk, scribbling something into a notebook.

"Hello, Mr. Parrish?" I whispered.

His head jerked up, sending his glasses sliding down his nose. He pushed them up with two fingers and smiled. "Hello, Mr. Carrow, nice to see you again. Have you come to open a library card with us?"

He practically beamed as brightly as the sun in the windows. And why would he not? Fresh blood in a place like Chickadee probably didn't happen very often. There wasn't even anyone in here, and it was a Saturday. I decided I might as well let him lead me a little bit before I started asking if he'd seen Richard Trask around.

"Um, yeah. I figured we're going to be here a while, and I know I go through about a book a week."

"Wonderful!" He started scrabbling in the desk for the proper forms. "I understand there's another logophile in your household. Mrs. Manco said she spotted a typewriter in your front room."

Why did Crista feel the need to chatter about me to strangers? "Another what?"

"Oh, forgive me." Arthur slid the paper and a pen at me. "A word lover. I assume it's you if you're reading a book a week. Though I'm sure Mr. Arrighi does as well."

There was something in his tone I didn't quite like. "Sev—I mean, Seb reads too." Dammit. I busied myself filling out the paperwork with all my false information so he wouldn't catch a glimpse of my reddening face.

Either he didn't notice or didn't care about my defensiveness. "Is there any particular genre you're interested in?" he asked. "We have all the classics but very few contemporary pieces, I'm afraid. Though I'm sure your niece would be very glad to know we got a collection of children's books donated recently."

I stopped paying attention. He was so chatty for a librarian! Was there something in the water here that made people not shut up? I flourished the signature a bit too broadly on my fake name and shoved the materials back at him.

"I have a question unrelated to the books," I said. "Do you remember the guy who was renting out the Reeds' place when Mr. Manco was killed?"

"Oh." Arthur rocked back in his chair like I'd ripped the title page out of his favorite novel. "Oh yes, James Smith. Quiet fellow, kept to himself. He didn't come in here, though, I'm afraid." Arthur sighed. "Many people here are not enamored of the written word. The Howes come in, of course."

Oh, my God, why is he still talking? "Also," I said, interrupting Arthur's monologue about Judith's reading list, "I wanted to offer Richard Trask my condolences on the loss of his brother, and I was told he was here often."

"Yes, he is here. He's here quite often." Arthur leaned forward again and lowered his voice even more. "But I don't think he's in much of a condition to speak with anyone at the moment."

That sounded suspicious. "Regardless, I'd like to meet him. Now."

I straightened and squared my shoulders. I was a big guy, and most men did not want to mess around with a big guy. Arthur was no exception, and he scrambled out from behind the desk.

"Very well, follow me," he squeaked.

He slipped into the room with the books and dove straight ahead. I glanced at the shelves. They weren't quite as sparse as they could have been, but some sections seemed underpopulated. We passed by them too fast for me to feel proper disappointment and soon reached the back wall where there was a gap between shelves. Instead of another case, there was a cushioned bench with a bundle of fabric on it. No, not fabric. It was a man curled up asleep.

"I'll leave you to it," said Arthur as he took a cautious step backward. "Just so you know, he doesn't like being disturbed." He scuttled back to the front room.

Well, at least I'd been warned. I grabbed what I assumed was Richard's shoulder and shook him.

He exploded outward with a yell that echoed in the otherwise silent library, arms and legs striking me. I held my ground—I'd taken much more forceful hits in my life. After a few seconds of his thrashing, I pushed him back onto the bench. He settled into a sitting position and stared up at me with bloodshot eyes.

Mess didn't even begin to describe Richard Trask. No tie or jacket. Just a wrinkled flannel shirt untucked from oil-stained work trousers. His black hair hadn't seen a comb that day, and his cheeks hadn't seen a razor in several. Below the stubble, his cheeks were flushed. I recognized the spidery nature as a sign of a drunkard. And now uncoiled, I smelled the whiskey on his breath. Memories flickered, all of them unpleasant.

"Who are you?" he croaked.

I wanted to punch him in the mouth and tell him I was the nightmare of all alcoholic assholes, but the image of Sev's concerned face rose in front of me. To him, I was a better man than all those mob goons he'd spent his life with, the ones who thought violence was the answer to everything. Fine, I'd do this as gently as possible.

"My name is Alex Carrow," I said quietly. No need to shout and make Arthur more nervous than he already was. "I want to talk."

His eyes darted around me, looking for a means of escape. "About?"

"Your brother, Walter, is dead."

"Oh, like I could forget that." He made a sound like giggling, except it was tinged with bitterness. "Listen, I don't know who you are, but you must be new in town or else you'd know me and my brother never got along."

He patted his pockets, and my hand automatically went to my own. My fingers closed around Sev's knife, but I released it as soon as I realized Richard was only going for a flask. I rolled my eyes at my own jumpiness.

"Why didn't you like your brother?"

He took a swig from the flask and closed it again. "I don't have to tell you nothing. I don't know you; you don't know me. You oughtn't be prying into the lives of strangers. Did Bob Kelly put you up to this? Wouldn't put it past him. Snotty little stuck-up know-it-all."

As much as I enjoyed hearing Kelly being insulted, I didn't want to spend all day coaxing answers out of someone who didn't want to give them. Maybe if I started bribing the flies with honey instead of vinegar? "I don't have anything to do with Sheriff Kelly." I gestured at the other half of the bench. "Can I sit?"

"Can't stop you. Public space."

"I wanted to say I was sorry for your loss."

Richard snorted and crossed his arms over his chest. "Yeah, and my ma was the Queen of Sheba." He turned to look at me. "You're the first person to say that to me, you know."

Christ, really? Even Logan had offered condolences when Donnie died, and he'd been the one who killed him. "Then I'm sorry for that too. My own brother, Martin, died a little while ago, so I thought maybe you needed someone to talk to."

Richard gave me a suspicious glance. "Yeah, but you *liked* your brother, didn't you?"

Like wasn't even strong enough of a word. Martin had been my best friend, sometimes my only friend. He *had* been like an older brother to me, and every time I said it as a lie, the reality of it became more obvious. "He was the kindest man I ever knew," I said. "And he didn't deserve all the terrible things that happened to him."

Richard nodded and fiddled with the flask cap. "Yeah, can't say that about Walter. Well, I know some of it wasn't his fault. He was always better at *stuff*. Smarter, faster, better looking. Had a way with the ladies most everyone would envy. You get a big head when you're already on top."

So, Trask had been arrogant. Not unexpected. It would take someone with a lot of confidence to run a business and hustle booze over the border. But a lot of people were arrogant, and they weren't getting murdered all over the place. And baby brother Richard didn't seem to be the raging kind of jealous that gave people blunt force trauma. At least, not in this moment.

"Well," I said, "what *did* you like about your brother?"

"Dunno. We didn't speak to each other much since our parents died." Richard continued twisting the lid. "A couple weeks ago, he came here and said he wanted to talk about money." The cap squeaked as he unscrewed it completely. The smell of whiskey drifted into the air, displacing the smell of paper. "He said he felt bad our parents had left everything to him, and I got mad 'cause if he really felt that way, he could've given over my fair share at any time in the last five years, and he didn't. And I told him so, and he stormed out. I haven't heard a word from him since. And now look what happened."

I nodded in what I hoped looked like a sympathetic manner. Money and Walter Trask kept coming up together, though this was the first I'd heard anything about him wanting to give it away. Richard might have been lying, but if he'd made up Walter's attempt at charity, why bother saying anything at all? Like he'd said, I was a stranger and didn't have any business nosing around his family life.

"Did he say why he wanted to give you the money now?"

"No, I didn't give him the chance. Kind of kicking myself about it now. Might've included me in his will or something if I'd been a little nicer."

"Do you know who the current beneficiary is?"

"Nope. No one here does that sort of fancy legal stuff; he had to go out to Burlington to get it done. It's all locked up with his lawyer there. I suppose the stuffed shirt'll be down on Monday to tell us what it said."

So, I'd have to convince the lawyer to talk to me. If he wouldn't, I'd have to wait until after Walter's funeral and see what kind of ripples the reading made, and that would be days, maybe even a week or longer. What would happen to Bella in the meantime? I couldn't risk the wait.

"You have to have some idea," I insisted.

"I just said we didn't talk. What makes you think I'd know?"

"Well, you said he wanted to give you money. Did he mention anyone else he thought of giving it to? Or why?"

Richard squirmed, and the flask went to his lips. In the movement, I saw both my father and Pearl's father—the action of a selfish man who didn't care about family, didn't care about anything beyond where to get the next drink.

I pulled his hand down. "Maybe look at me when I'm talking to you?"

He ripped his arm away from me, and before I processed what he was doing, his other arm swung around. His fist connected with my temple, sending sparks across my eyes. The blow didn't hurt so much as it was a shock. It shook loose memories I'd buried after my dad died of knuckles against flesh more times than I could count. But this time, oh, this time, I was a grown man, and I had no fear of Richard Trask. With one well-placed hit, I sent him sprawling onto the floor with a bloody nose. He screamed a curse at me as he clutched at his face. The flask of whiskey glugged its contents onto some books knocked over in his tumble.

Shit.

I bolted. Arthur Parrish's confused face appeared in the doorway, but I ran past. I burst outside, my heart thumping too fast. My altercation was going to be the talk around town in a matter of hours, and God knew what kind of consequences that would bring. Maybe arrest. Maybe someone would put some more pieces together and call the Westwick cops on us. And with Bella in jail and sundered from her network, there would be no hiding this time.

I paused. The commotion hadn't followed me, and the residents of Chickadee didn't seem too interested in me despite my clearly frantic state. I didn't want to take more chances. I slid my jacket on and walked as quickly as I dared back to the house. With every step, my heart tightened; I was going to have to tell Sev what I'd done.

Chapter Ten

I CLOSED THE door to the house too forcefully, and it rattled in the frame.

"Alex?" Sev's voice floated from the kitchen.

"Yeah."

"Good. I'm glad you're home." He stepped into the hall and came toward me. Car keys dangled from his hand. "I need to go out, and I didn't know how you felt about having Fran babysi— Are you all right? You're red again."

I rubbed at my eyes. This was going to be so difficult. "I'm fine."

"I don't think so." He squinted at me and brushed hair away from my temple. I winced as his fingers touched the sore spot. "What's this red mark?"

"I got hit." I pushed him off me. "Here's the thing—"

"I thought you were going to the library. How did your face get hit?"

"I'm trying to goddamn tell you, okay?" I was so anxious to get it over with, the words spilled out. "I went to the library to find Walter Trask's brother, Richard. And we were talking, and I must have said something that upset him because he punched me."

"Alex—"

"And I punched him back, and I think I broke his nose, and Arthur Parrish saw me do it but not Richard punching me, so I don't know if anyone can vouch I was defending myself. But Richard Trask has a reputation for being a nuisance, so maybe Arthur will assume he started it, but I don't know, and I don't know if either of them are going to call Sheriff Kelly and—"

"Enough! *Basta, calmati.*" Sev sighed and ran a hand over his hair. "Well, if he has a reputation, I'm sure if someone calls the police, they will take your side. But Alex, you have to learn to control your temper better. It's going to get us in trouble, and we *cannot* get into any more trouble. One call and—"

"I know. I know! I'm sorry. But it's fine. Right? It's fine. It's fine, and I will take care of it." I couldn't look him in the eye, so I looked down. My gaze caught on his keys again. "Maybe you should go; go do whatever you were doing, so if the police come, you're not in their sights. Where were you going, anyway?"

He collected the keys into his fist like he had been caught doing something he wasn't supposed to do. "I'll be back in a half hour, an hour at most."

Where could he possibly be going? It wasn't like there was anything of worth within a half-hour drive, and we didn't know anyone nearby. "Come on, seriously."

"It's not like I'm going carousing. I'm going to the mission."

What? "It's Saturday, you know. Church is on Sundays."

"Yes, I know," he snapped. He took a breath. "I'm going to confession," he murmured. "I—"

"What! After what you said to me about watching our backs, you want to tell someone what we did?"

He lowered his voice and motioned for me to keep my own down. "It's not to the police; it's to a priest. It's something Catholics do so God can forgive us. You do penance to make up for things. You pay for your sins."

Right. Something in my memory flickered about having learned about that once and tossed it aside as something unimportant. While I tried to track the recollection down, I almost missed the rest of Sev's insistent whispering.

"Before I met you. And then I couldn't with everything happening so fast, so this is the first chance I've gotten since I killed…"

Since he'd killed Emma Carlisle.

We both stood in silence for a moment. Yes, he'd killed her, but he'd done it to defend me. She'd been a murderer even if her father had pulled the trigger. She'd killed Donnie and Martin and Bella's husband and others. As far as I was concerned, there was nothing to feel sorry over.

"I hope to God you never know this guilt," he continued quietly. "I—"

"But you *can't* tell them," I hissed. "They'll get the cops."

"They can't tell though," he insisted. "It's forbidden."

"Right, you expect me to believe that?"

Sev crossed his arms. "Well, you should because it's true."

"Fine. It's true. But they wouldn't even have to say anything. Just make a couple vague statements. 'Huh, I heard you had a bunch of murders down there and are looking for the culprit. Did you ever think of visiting Vermont in the summer? It's beautiful. Maybe you'll find something.'"

"Stop. You don't understand."

"You're right. I *don't* understand. So maybe you should explain to me why you have to go tell a stranger you killed someone?"

"Hush, Pearl is right in the kitchen." He closed his eyes for a second, gathering his thoughts. Somehow that annoyed me more than if he'd started getting louder with me. "You tell them your sins," he said slowly, patiently. With infuriating kindness. "There's *that*, and there's you, and—"

"Wait, wait, wait. How did I start figuring into this?"

Crimson spread across his cheeks. "It's not *you,* specifically." To my twisted delight, he finally seemed to be getting flustered. He lowered his voice even more. "It's the sex. We're not supposed to—"

"Are you saying you feel guilty about *me*?"

"No! No, that's not it at all! I love you. It's just—"

"What a fantastic religion you've got there. You have to beg forgiveness for loving."

His eyes narrowed, and I knew I'd crossed a line I hadn't been aware was there. Face livid, he opened his mouth. But instead of shouting, he simply said, "I'll be back in about an hour."

He swept past me. I chased him for a few steps, the urge to have a fight carrying me forward. He yanked open the door and left it ajar as he hurried down the porch stairs, the keys in his hand jingling with discordant cheerfulness.

"Sev get back here!" I shouted.

He turned partially, and I glimpsed the poisonous look on his face before he continued to the car. It was only when he reached it that I realized Crista was standing shocked and hesitant at the end of our front walk. I groaned. Exactly what I didn't need. She flinched as Sev slammed the car door and shied away from the drive as he backed out too quickly.

"Should I come back later?" she asked.

As much as I wanted to tell her to go to hell, I needed her help to get something edible on the table at a reasonable supper hour. Undoubtedly, Pearl was very sick of boiled eggs.

"No, you're fine. Come on in," I grumbled as I stepped out of the doorway. I began walking down the hall. "Pearl, Crista is here!"

No answer. Odd. It wasn't like she couldn't hear me. It wasn't a big house. I stepped into the kitchen. To my surprise, there was no Pearl, only Daisy wandering the counters. She couldn't have gone upstairs without me seeing. She must have gone outside. I marched to the back door and swung it open. Not on the back porch either. I scanned the yard. Still nothing.

"Pearl!" I yelled as I stepped off the porch.

A scratching noise near my feet gave me pause. I crouched to peek into the crawlspace under the porch. Sure enough, Pearl was huddled against the foundation. She watched me warily.

"What are you doing down there?" I demanded.

She whimpered and pressed her back against the wall.

"Pearl, get out of there." My voice sounded rough on the command, and with a sinking feeling, I realized she was hiding from me.

"Look, Pearl," I said reassuringly, "just because I'm mad doesn't mean I'm going to hurt anyone."

She continued regarding me with silent fear, green eyes bulging, only moving to place her teddy bear between her and me. Whatever I did, it would bring no comfort to her. What was left of my anger washed away in a sea of guilt.

"If I go away and have Crista come, will you come out?"

Pearl stayed frozen.

"Right." I sighed and straightened and came face-to-face with Cristina herself. Standing on the stairs, she was a good foot taller than normal, and I could look her in the eye. Except I didn't want to. Keeping my focus on the door behind her, I said, "I think she wants to talk to you."

In a daze, I wandered back to the living room. What had I done? Both Sev and Pearl were upset with me, and I had no idea how to fix it. The world pressed around my ears, the stuffy heat choking me. I needed to get out, go anywhere, as long as it wasn't here.

But there was nowhere to go. I couldn't very well wander around the town after what I'd done, and the woods... Actually, the woods were probably all right, at least during the day. We'd been in them for hours yesterday, and nothing bad had happened. Well, nothing besides the obvious. And I knew the path now, so I wasn't likely to get lost. Maybe if I took a little walk and reexamine the crime scene? Kelly might have missed something in his rush to harass people.

I went out the front door and took a wide arc around the house in case Crista and Pearl were dawdling outside and approached the tree line. City born and raised, I paused before following the path in. The trees were by far the tallest things in the area, many of them a good four or five stories high, and everything below their branches skulked in shadow. Still, I was more afraid of myself than I was of any imagined big bad wolf, so I dove in, following the dirt track leading into the depths.

It didn't take long to find the scene of Trask's murder. Kelly had run a rope around some of the trunks to keep people off the exact spot. Laughable and not nearly enough to stop me. I slipped under and walked to the center, foliage collapsing under my feet with every step. There, the indentation the body had made; there on one end the blood. The branch was gone, maybe even tagged and stored somewhere in the police station, though I doubted they'd get any useful prints off bark.

I looked around. Trees. Brush. Nothing else. So much for justifying my running away like a petulant child as a clue-finding expedition. I sighed and tried to slide back under the ropes. My foot caught on a root, and I stumbled forward, catching myself on a trunk. Something squished beneath my hand. Threads of sap clung to my skin. I groaned and reached for my handkerchief to wipe it off.

Sap and leaves. Whoever had killed Trask had probably gotten covered in them. It was almost stupidly obvious. Except most of the town had been in the woods that day, and they'd all gotten all sorts of debris on them if Maude's long list of dry-cleaning clients was any indication. Had that been the plan, to have a bunch of people traipse around the crime scene? Fran hadn't said who organized the search party. Maybe they'd planned it as a cover-up.

"Hey, what're you doing out here?"

I froze, the unexpected voice making my heart thunder in my ears and all the hairs on the back of my neck stand on end. I turned toward the source.

He was 90 percent white beard and 10 percent black boots, with blue eyes in a sun-roughened face. His frame was thinner than mine but more muscled. He had a rifle slung over one shoulder and a bowie knife stuck in his belt. Seeing the gun, what courage I had left took off to hide behind the nearest rock. I contemplated yelling for help, but honestly, who was going to hear me all the way out here?

"H-hello, my name is Alex," I said with a distinct and unintentional tremor in my voice, "I was just looking—"

"You're on my land," said the man.

"Oh, I didn't realize." I took a ginger step backward. "If you tell me where your property line is, I will get right off, Mister?"

"There ain't no mister. It's Ed."

Ed? The guy Trask had been having a land dispute with? The one who chased him with a knife? "I'm sorry. I thought this was Mr. Trask's property."

A gravelly noise came from Ed's throat, and I wasn't sure if it was a sign of contemplation or aggression. "Mmm, well, he's dead, so the land is mine now. This is all mine out here."

"All of it?"

He nodded. "If not in name, then in right. I'm the one living on it, aren't I?" He tromped around me placidly like he hadn't scared the hell out of me ten seconds ago. "Judging by your shoes, you don't take hikes often. What'cha doing out here anyway, boy? Are you a reporter looking to make a dime off a dead man?"

Vern's smirking face flashed in my memory for a moment. "No, I'm just looking. I heard mixed things about him."

"Yeah, well, we're all a mix, aren't we." Ed continued hiking away.

With a gust of nerve, I called after him, "What're *you* doing out here?"

He turned back, and for a brief moment, I was sorry I'd done anything to draw his attention again. "My land, I said." He inclined his chin to our right. North? East? I had no idea what direction. "Got a place yonder. Not that I recommend you visit. It isn't a place for big-city pretty boys. Yeah, I know about you already. Boston lightweight."

I thought about asking *how* he knew about me, but the whole town was a grapevine of rumor. It would be odd if he *didn't* know I was new. I opened my mouth to try to continue the conversation, but nothing came out. I was too fixated on the rifle. Ed ignored me and continued his trek to nowhere.

I took a step back and then another. I wasn't scared. No. It was that I'd left Crista to watch Pearl without asking, and Sev had said he would be back in an hour, and it had to be close to that now. If he came home and we had to move, then we needed to move fast. Even if by some luck we didn't have to flee *again*, I ought to be there with, well maybe not apologies, at least something nice like a cup of tea. I was definitely not retreating—looking over my shoulder every couple steps—because I was nervous.

Ed didn't follow me, or if he did, at least I couldn't tell. Still, I felt uneasy until I made it back to the yard. Neither Pearl nor Crista was visible, but I made a check under the porch just in case. Now I had to go back in and make my amends.

I opened the back door. Crista stood by the stove, stirring something that smelled of onions. Pearl watched me from a seat at the table, Daisy giving me scornful looks from her lap.

Crista glanced up before returning to her pot. "Ah, you're back."

"Yeah." I shuffled into the kitchen. "Sorry about disappearing there. I needed to take a walk."

She nodded, still not looking at me.

The silence gutted me. "Is Sev home?"

She shook her head.

Christ, it was like I'd had the fight with her. I sighed and went to Pearl, crouching so I looked her in the eye. "And I'm sorry I scared you. I know you don't like when people yell. But I would *never* hurt you, okay? Never in a million years."

Pearl's eyes tracked across my face. Searching for the lie, maybe. But it wasn't a lie. Whatever terrible things I was destined to do, hitting her would not be one of them. She must have seen the promise on my face because she relaxed, and a slight smile appeared on her lips.

"Okay, I know," she said.

She reached out to me, and I got an awkward hug with Daisy grumbling between us. The cat jumped down and meandered toward the living room. Pearl giggled and got up to follow her. I stood again and caught Crista looking. She too seemed to carry less tension.

"Not all men are so kind," she said quietly.

Heat rose in my face. While I wouldn't strike Pearl, my earlier outburst with Richard Trask showed I was willing to take a swing. What would Crista think when she heard about *that* little episode? And she would hear soon. If I wasn't arrested for it, I was going to be ostracized over it, and in a small town like this, that was like being the living dead.

"Well, you know, she's a kid, and it didn't have anything to do with her."

"May I ask what you and Mr. Arrighi were arguing about?"

"Oh, you know, a question of dogma." I rubbed my increasingly sweaty palms against my thighs. "Is it okay if I leave you here and go work on something in the parlor?"

"Of course, Mr. Carrow. It is your house, after all." She went back to cooking.

I slunk away. My house. Hysterical. Another lie on the pile, another secret to bury. Another thing to choke me in the middle of the night. Maybe Sev had the right idea. Maybe if we all said the truth out loud, it would hurt less.

It might even cut down on the murders.

Chapter Eleven

I PECKED SLOWLY at the space bar of the typewriter to match the motion of the second hand on my watch. I was desperate for a cigarette, but I was too afraid to move.

Tchk tchk tchk.

It'd been almost an hour after I'd sat down to pretend to work, and that had been a good forty-five minutes after Sev had stormed off. Crista was still in the kitchen, making what seemed like enough food to last us a week.

Half hour he'd said, an hour at most, and now the time was approaching two. Something might have happened. Arrested, maybe. Or maybe the gangs making the sweep of Westwick had decided to chase Bella and her family all the way out here. Or maybe whoever Bella was afraid of was lurking around. I still had Sev's knife. If he had ended up in a tight spot, he would have had nothing to defend himself with. How would I even know? How could I even get to him?

Tchk tchk tchk.

What if Kelly came to arrest me for assaulting Richard and set a trap for Sev for when he got back? And then phone calls, an armed escort back to Connecticut. What if we both ended up in the electric chair, never having seen each other again?

Tchk tchk tchk.

The rumble of a car engine on the street cut through the ambient noise of the house. I jumped up so fast I slammed my hip into the desk. Cursing at the pain, I ran to the door.

It wasn't our car. A truck had pulled into the drive of the Gaines's place. A man hopped out, average build, graying hair. A very pointy chin and nose gave him a birdlike look. Mr. Gaines, I had to presume. He noticed me watching and turned, looking me up and down. Without saying anything, he headed into his house.

With Trask dead, the factory was probably going to fall to Mr. Gaines. Everyone said so. Ownership of a business was motive enough. I'd seen people killed for less. And now he was cornered enough to justify talking to him.

I took a step back into the house. "Crista?" I called.

She stuck her head out of the kitchen. "Yes?"

"You're going to be here for another half hour, right?"

"I can be. Why?"

"I have to run out for a second, but I'll be right back."

I shut the door and hustled over to the Gaines's house. About to knock, I paused. Did I want to deal with Fran right now? Well, her parents were there. They'd put a stop to her ridiculous flirting. Maybe even forever. I rapped on the door.

A woman with the same ash-blonde hair as Fran answered. She was flushed, and her eyes were red-rimmed. She sniffed into a handkerchief. Allergies or tears?

"Mrs. Gaines, so nice to finally meet you," I said with as much cheer as I could muster. Her cruelty to Sev was hard to get over. "I'm Alex Carrow. We moved in on Wednesday. I believe you met my brother-in-law yesterday."

She shook my extended hand like I'd offered her a rotting fish. "Nice to meet you." Her voice had a deep tone I hadn't expected. "Fran has told us so much about you already."

Yeah, I bet she had. "I would have come by earlier, but there was so much commotion with Mr. Trask passing away."

She sniffed again. "Oh, yes, terrible business."

One second, two seconds. She wasn't inviting me in like I'd expected.

"Mr. Carrow!" Fran's beaming face appeared behind her mother's shoulder. "How nice of you to call. Come in!"

She grabbed my hand and pulled me inside. Good luck or bad luck?

The room was painted bright yellow, and the furniture had a satiny sheen. A well-woven carpet covered most of the floor. Lined up on the mantelpiece were fancy plates, not the kind used for eating. So, the Gaineses did have money or at least wanted to look like they did.

Fran deposited me in a plush armchair and scampered off, squeaking about how she would get tea. Mrs. Gaines paced into the parlor, squinting at me. I got a better look at her as she sat in another chair. While she wasn't adorable like Judith or elegant in simplicity like Crista, she had sharp, proud features that gave her a regal bearing. Too bad she was rotten all the way through.

More noticeable than her features was her dress. It was very clean, maybe too clean, and there were no signs of any fading or repairs. Clearly it was either new or rarely worn. Likely the latter, if she was in the factory all day. I wondered how Mr. Gaines felt about her being away from the house all day. Not that the house seemed to be in bad shape, but some men had a hard time with their wives working. Unless, of course, there were money issues, and she'd been working to help keep them afloat. Low funds would certainly emphasize the business as motive for murder.

"Oscar," Mrs. Gaines called, "we have a guest!"

"Be there in a second, Louise," came the reply from the room to my left.

Mr. Gaines appeared after a series of creaks. My assessment of him from the porch as a grumbly pigeon of a man was only reinforced by the hesitant, jerky way he walked. He brushed some dirt off his dungarees as he stepped into the parlor.

"Give a man a minute to change out of his gear, why don't you?" he mumbled as he passed in front of his wife to shake my hand. "Nice to meet you, Mr. Carrow. Sorry I snubbed you a minute ago. You know how it is, don't want to talk to anyone as soon as you get home." He took a step back. "Normally, I don't make rounds of the groves on Saturday, but what with Walter gone and all someone's got to."

Louise leaned around her husband. "And what is it you do, Mr. Carrow?"

"Wait a minute, woman! Don't you see I'm talking to the man?"

She gave him a poisonous look.

Fran pranced into the living room with a tray sloshed with tea from already-poured cups. She cast a nervous glance at her parents before setting it on the table. She lifted a dripping cup and pressed it into my hands and smiled encouragingly.

"Fran!" her parents shouted almost at once. She flinched back, her face scrunched. Great, now I felt bad for her.

Louise took over again, adjusting the tea set into what I assumed was a more pleasing pattern to her. "What I mean is we're so happy to get to speak with our new neighbor." She tugged the back of Fran's dress until the girl sat with a huff. "We've already heard so much about you, but you know how gossip is. You can't trust a single bit."

Oh, irony. "Ah, well, I'm a writer, and Sev is an accountant, as you know. We're from Boston. Um, unfortunately, we've had several recent deaths in the family, so we thought we might change the scenery for Pearl's sake. Not sure what else there is to tell." I put the cup back on the tray and tried to discreetly dry my hands on my clothes. "I did also want to come over and offer my condolences on the death of Mr. Trask. I heard you both worked for him."

Oscar cleared his throat. "Well working *for* him isn't quite right. We were more like full partners, he and I. And I'll keep the business going good and proud." He shot a look at Louise. "And I'll find myself a proper secretary."

Louise sniffled into the handkerchief again. "Are you saying there's something wrong with my skills, darling?"

"No, I'm saying"—he looked at me out of the corner of his eye—"some other people might be able to use the opportunity. Just think, with Walter gone, what's going to happen to little Judith there? No husband, no work."

At Judith's name, Louise's face darkened. "You're not responsible for her future. You have your own girl here." She gestured at Fran. "If you want to give a young lady some assistance, you could give your daughter some experience in the workforce."

"But mama, I don't want—"

"Frances is no good. She can't *read*, Louise! What am I gonna do with a secretary who can't read?"

Fran's face paled. She glanced at me and started chewing on her lip. Poor thing. She had started the conversation with such high hopes. Neither of her parents seemed to notice.

That was quite enough for me. Fighting like I wasn't there was one thing, but dragging their kid under with them was out of the question. I stood up. "Excuse me. I just realized I need to run an errand before tomorrow. Thank you for the tea."

Fran jumped up as Oscar and Louise continued sniping at each other. "I'll walk you out."

I didn't want to let her, but if it got her out of that house for a few minutes, at least it was something. As soon as the door closed behind her, she began to cry.

"Oh, no. Christ, here." I stuffed my handkerchief into her hand. "I'm sorry about what they said about you in front of me."

"It's not my fault," she whimpered. "The words jump around the page."

"I know. I know. I didn't say it was. And I don't think any less of you."

"But you said you're a writer, and I can never read what you write and—"

"It doesn't matter," I said as I coaxed her off the porch. I didn't want her to stalk me through my writing anyway. "You have lots of other stuff you can do. You don't want to be indoors reading all day anyway. You've got such a nice bike. Wouldn't you rather ride out in the sun?"

"It is a nice bike," she sniffled. She ran a hand across the handlebars. "And it is very fun. But they bought it to try to make up for something."

Oh Lord, not another abusive household. "What'd they do?"

Fran looked at me, swallowing a few tears before she whispered, "They're getting a divorce. They decided about a month ago. They avoid each other as much as they can while the lawyers do up the papers."

"Ah. Well, I'm sorry for that too." I patted her arm. "You know it's not your fault, right?"

She nodded. "I know. They've been fighting for a long, long time, and it got much worse about six months ago, a little after Mom started working for Mr. Trask."

"Do you know what about? Does your dad not like your mom working?"

"I don't know, but it sounds like something happened and that Mom was the one who did it, but she's always saying Dad drove her to it. But neither of them killed Mr. Trask though. I swear. Mom was in the factory the whole day; you can ask anybody."

Interesting. She'd leaped to her mother's defense and not her father's. But I wasn't going to get anything more out of her with her sniveling like this. Since I wasn't in the mood to coddle her, it would have to wait.

"I believe you. I do. And no one is going to arrest your parents." *Yet.* "Why don't you go clean yourself up and take a ride before supper, huh? Get all the bad stuff out of your head."

She gave me such an adoring look I knew I'd only made her infatuation with me ten times stronger. But what else was I going to do? Let a girl bawl her eyes out while her parents were at each other's throats?

Just as I was wondering how I was going to ditch her, another car pulled onto the street: the rickety ancient Oldsmobile. Sev was home.

"Right, well, good luck," I said quickly. "And, uh, if you ever need to leave for a few minutes, you can come by our house, okay?"

"Oh, thank you, Mr. Carrow. I—"

I didn't hear the end of her sentence since I was hurling myself at the car. I grabbed at the door handle as Sev stepped out, and I nearly got smacked in the face. He blinked in surprise and gave me an odd look.

"Hi," I said. *God, Alex, are you ever* not *going to be awkward?*

"*Ciao*?" He edged past me and started for the porch stairs. I trailed after him like a puppy, trying to ignore Fran's continued presence in the yard.

"You said you'd be gone less than an hour," I said.

"I did," he replied as he reached for the doorknob.

"It's been two."

He didn't answer as he stepped inside and hung his hat on one of the hooks in the wall. Crista stepped out of the kitchen door. She grinned.

"Mr. Arrighi, so nice to see you back."

He broke into a brilliant smile, enough to tighten the crow's feet at the edges of his eyes. "Crista, you're still here?" He stepped forward with a gust of energy. "I know we're men, but we're not helpless around the house."

She giggled and spoke again, this time in Italian. He answered, and the small talk became a full conversation, complete with hand gestures and laughter. She turned to go back into the kitchen, and he moved to follow.

Being stabbed by Pearl's father had hurt less than this.

A familiar, hot feeling not unlike the one that often prompted me to throw punches blazed down my spine. Maybe he ought to know what it was like, desperately wanting to talk and not being allowed to. To wait, panicked, while I disappeared for hours.

It was doable. The door was right there. Only trouble was, I was restricted to walking distance since I hadn't the faintest idea how to drive. So where could I go? It wasn't like I could stay with anyone, and the library was still off-limits.

Fine, I'd pout in my bedroom like a child.

I slumped up the stairs, too frustrated to even stomp. What had I gotten myself into? And it wasn't even all the murder stuff—that wasn't actually my fault—it was the running off into the sunset with someone I'd met less than a month ago and thinking it'd be happily ever after. The stories never did say what happened after the royal wedding, did they? Probably a lot of arguing and plotting infidelity. So much for fairy tales.

I tossed Sev's knife onto the nightstand before flopping into my bed. I buried my face against the pillow, determined to smother my own tears. Fuck Sev. Fuck Trask. And Kelly and Bella and Crista and Fran and everyone else in godforsaken Chickadee, Vermont!

Chapter Twelve

I WOKE UP blurry and blinked at the darkness surrounding me. It had been midafternoon when I came up here. I must have been out for hours. Squinting at my watch in the thin moonlight, I learned the time was eleven fifteen. Well, at least I'd slept nightmare free for the first time in a while.

My painfully empty stomach had woken me. I hadn't eaten lunch or supper, and I was starving. I'd skipped plenty of meals before, but that had been out of desperation, and now with a stocked kitchen a floor below me, there was no reason not to eat.

I peeked in Pearl's room on my way down. She was sleeping peacefully, and Daisy too. Thank God. How did parents do this all day, every day, focusing on a tiny person's well-being while handling everything else in their lives?

The stairs creaked as I went down, and I cringed. The last thing I wanted to do was let Sev know I was up. But the lights didn't seem to be on in the parlor, and I didn't see any spilling from his door. I nudged it open a crack, just to make sure he was asleep.

He wasn't there.

I turned and saw the whole of the empty parlor. I went down the hall into the kitchen to see if he had gone to the bathroom. No. My heart squeezed tighter and tighter as I ran back to the front of the house.

He wouldn't just up and leave in the middle of the night, right? That was the kind of shit I wrote for the pulps, not something real people did. Or what if something had happened; one of the people out for Bella had hunted him down and me with his knife upstairs? I yanked open the front door.

He was sitting on the porch swing, smoking and staring out at the street. The white of his shirt almost glowed in the moonlight while everything else about him ranged from a dusty gray to a pitch-black. Even his eyes, gold in the light, were an unimpressive charcoal. Only the end of his cigarette sparked a bright orange. I wasn't sure if I wanted to kiss him or kill him.

"What are you doing out here?" I asked.

He shrugged. "Couldn't sleep. And it's cooler out here."

Well, he was right about the cooler part. A continuous breeze tousled his curls and chilled me, though I wasn't quite sure if the tremor in my shoulders was from that or from all the panic flowing out of them.

"You could have woken me up for supper, you know."

"I did go up, but you were sleeping so quietly I thought you maybe needed the rest." He glanced at me before looking away again. "I know you're having nightmares."

How he knew that was a mystery since we hadn't been sleeping anywhere near each other in over a week. Not the current problem though. "Still. It would have been nice to talk. You had me scared almost to death before, you know."

He nodded and edged to the side. I took the seat next to him, and the swing jolted at my weight. He continued to avoid my gaze.

"So, where'd you go?" I asked.

He took a breath and exhaled the smoke through his nose. "I started for the church, but as I drove, I thought about what you'd said, and I needed to think some more, so I kept driving. I didn't realize I'd gone so far until I saw a sign saying the distance to Boston." He looked at me out of the corner of his eye again. "I didn't mean to frighten you."

Part of me was still furious, but I knew very well I'd chased him off in the first place. At least he'd come back in one piece. "So, what are you going to do? About the confessing thing."

He took another drag on the cigarette. The burning end cast odd shadows across his face. He shrugged. "There's nothing I can do until next week."

I waited for him to say something else. Another gust of wind sent a shiver down my back. The silence weighed on me as a cocktail of guilt and embarrassment roiled in my stomach.

"I'm sorry, you know," I whispered. "About what I said."

He nodded but otherwise didn't answer.

"So, are you gonna come in or...?"

"I will, just not right now." He patted my knee. "I'll be in soon, I promise."

The quiet way he said it nearly ripped my heart out. "Okay. But, you know, come find me if you want anything."

He nodded again and went back to staring at the darkened streets of the town sprawled in front of us. Feeling too awkward to stay and push anything or even find the food I'd intended to eat, I went back to my room and stared at the ceiling until I fell back into a, thankfully, dreamless sleep.

I HAD TO choke my panic down when I woke up to an empty house. I knew Sev had promised to take Crista to church, and a note on the kitchen table announced he'd taken Pearl with them. I wasn't sure how I felt about that. Had he brought her with him so I could be left to sleep? Had she asked to come? Had he dragged her there in a fit of spite? I put the note down. No, not spite. Unlike Bella, he would never make Pearl a leverage point.

So, I would be alone for a few hours. I could write or gather my thoughts about where my relationship was going or any number of rational things. But Bella was still sitting in Kelly's cells and me lounging around wasn't going to get her out. And the longer she was in, the twitchier Sev was going to get. So, I washed up faster than I'd thought was possible and marched back out the door. The destination, the police station.

It wasn't that I was worried about Bella... Fine, I was a little worried about her. When I'd left her, she hadn't struck me as stable emotionally. And why should she have been? Her husband was only a few days in the ground, and she was locked up on false charges.

Charges that probably wouldn't even make it through indictment, now that I'd had some time to think.

So, why would Kelly even bother? He'd shown up at the house with armed backup only about a half hour after we'd seen him, which meant he had been planning on dragging me or Sev or both somewhere against our will. To me, the action said he needed a scapegoat more than a culprit, preferably someone who wasn't from town. Had

Bella just been the unlucky one? Or had she provoked him on purpose to keep his eyes off us?

Well, she was a criminal. I had to give Kelly that. And she was hiding Lord knew what about the Reeds and possibly even this mysterious James Smith character. The trick, though, would be convincing her to tell me the truth.

The police station was open, thankfully, but Kelly wasn't there. The desk was occupied by the bald officer, the one who had almost shot Bella for daring to defend herself. He was reading a newspaper. As I got closer, I realized there was something behind the paper. A girly magazine maybe? The woman in the picture I saw definitely had less clothing than was generally considered appropriate.

His head shot up at my approach, and he closed the newspaper, careful to fold the pornography inside. "What'd'ya want?"

"I'd like to see Mrs. Ferri, please," I said.

He chuckled. "What do you think this is, a movie palace? You show up and say what you want to see?"

Thank God I'd gotten some solid sleep because otherwise, his snide comment would have sent me over the edge, and I'd have been with Bella in the cells whether I liked it or not. "Come on, officer...?"

"Wallace."

"Officer Wallace, please. She's family." He raised an eyebrow. Fine, pathos wasn't the way to go. So, I added, "And I have some important information from her lawyer who will be here tomorrow from Boston." I leaned forward a little and dropped my voice. "You don't want to get in trouble with a big-shot lawyer, do you?"

"Not my problem. I don't make the rules. That'd be Bob Kelly's job."

"Fine. When does he get back?"

"He's off Sundays. Don't worry, he'll be in tomorrow to talk to your little lawyer friend."

I took a breath to bring my flaring mind back to a more peaceable place. "Maybe try to call Sheriff Kelly. What's he doing anyway? Having Sunday dinner with the wife?"

"Dunno what he does on his time off. Isn't my business. Now, get on. I have very important things to do."

"At least tell me where I can find him. I know he has to live in town or near enough."

"I said, get out."

In a fit of something that might have been cleverness or maybe simple spite, I snatched the newspaper and magazine off the desk. I let the newspaper scatter and flipped through the pages of the magazine. Yep, porn. "Tsk, tsk, Officer Wallace," I said. "And at work too."

"Give it back," he snapped, his face going red.

"Well, as much as I hate to come between a man and his reading material, I think I'm going to hold onto this. Maybe bring it to the attention of the town council or whatever you've got here. The city pays you, right? The state?"

Wallace continued staring at me and reluctantly stood. "Fine. But I'm standing next to you the whole time."

He unlocked the door and walked me in. It was still roasting hot, even so early in the morning, and it stank to high heaven, which was new. Sweat and piss. Not unlike the gymnasium Pearl's dad had frequented.

Bella lay on the bunk, tracing the edges of the stonework with her fingertips. She sat up when she heard the screech of the door, and my breath caught. She looked *bad*—drooping like a wilted flower. Her skin was a couple shades paler than it had been on Friday, which emphasized the discolored rings under her eyes. No one had even given her a comb, and her hair had frayed in the humidity.

"Are you all right?" The words came out of my mouth automatically before I remembered she had brought us to this rotten place.

She ran her hand against her sweaty forehead, somehow making the action look graceful. "I have had better days, Mr. Carrow."

I turned to Wallace. "You can't leave her in here," I snapped. "She'll get heatstroke."

"I *said* I don't make the rules, I just enforce 'em." He shrugged, but I noticed his hand went to the pistol on his hip. "Now, say your piece, and we'll let the lady return to her nap."

The hair on the back of my neck prickled, but I was determined. I turned back to Bella. "Do you know who James Smith is?"

Her thundercloud eyes skimmed over me. "No. Should I?"

"He was here around the time Leo Manco was killed."

Bella shrugged. "So why ask me?"

Because you're obviously hiding things. "Thought maybe you'd have an outsider's view."

"I did not speak with him. But maybe Mr. Wallace has."

She nodded at my escort. He didn't say anything.

"What about the Reeds?" I asked.

"Again, I do not live here, so I do not know."

Maybe she was holding back because of Wallace. How could I get rid of him? He wasn't like the well-meaning secretary in Rutherford's office, who I had tricked with a few fake coughs and an apologetic face.

"Mr. Wallace." Bella's unreadable eyes tracked to the cop. "I see you haven't broken your habits." She gestured at the magazine still in my hand.

He blanched. "Not mine."

She almost smiled. "I happen to know Mr. Carrow very well, and I know he isn't the sort to amuse himself with pictures of women on a Sunday, so I can only make assumptions."

Wallace bristled.

"But maybe I am mistaken," she continued. She nodded at the porn again. "Perhaps I'm seeing things because I'm overheated. Would it be too much trouble to ask you for water?"

He squinted at her. "Fine." He slunk off, presumably to a sink somewhere. I had maybe a minute, at most.

I took two steps into the cells. "Who are the Reeds?" I hissed. "You rented the house from them, you have to know *something*."

"Why does it concern you so much?"

"Because they rented the place to someone named James Smith, who probably killed Leo Manco, and if he killed Leo Manco, then Kelly can't tack that onto you. And if he killed Manco, he may have killed Trask, and if he did, then you're out of here."

"Who said I wanted to get out? I must pay for my sins at some point, why not now?"

Because as much as I was sure she'd done plenty of awful things, she hadn't done this. "Because I promised Sev I'd get you out, and I'm not disappointing him. Now what aren't you telling me? What has you running scared? Is it the Reeds? Is it this James Smith guy? Someone else?"

"Do not worry about the Reeds or Mr. Smith. They are meaningless to me."

"You said that about Carlisle and look what happened. You need to help me help you. If you don't get out of this, they could hang you!"

Before Bella said anything else, Wallace appeared at my elbow. He shoved a half-full paper cup through the bars. Bella took it with as much poise as she would accept a glass of wine at a dinner party. Her gracefulness didn't last though. She gulped the liquid down almost as soon as it passed into her hands. Wallace glared at me.

I cleared my throat. "So, as I was saying, your lawyer, Mr. Lieberman, will be here tomorrow to get you out," I mumbled.

Bella's brow furrowed but otherwise gave no sign of acknowledgment that the words coming out of my mouth were utter bullshit. Smart lady. "Good," she answered. "I look forward to meeting him."

Wallace nudged me. "There you go. All done." He tipped an imaginary hat to Bella. "See you later, ma'am."

Five seconds later, I was back in front of the desk. Wallace put his hand out. "You got what you wanted, now give."

I leaned away from him, keeping the magazine clutched in my fist. "She can't stay in there," I repeated. "It's hot as hell, maybe more."

"And I *keep* telling you, it isn't my problem." He lunged for the magazine. I held it away.

"I'll give it back if you tell me where I can find Kelly. *Today*."

"I don't know! Check around Judith Howe's place maybe."

What? "I thought he had the day off. What's he doing talking to people about Trask's death?"

"Like he gives a fuck what happened to Trask—" Wallace closed his mouth, his eyes widening with the realization he'd said too much.

Not that I hadn't figured. Kelly wouldn't have been rounding up random people if he was interested in catching the real murderer. But Judith was new. And yet not surprising either. I'd seen how he folded when she chastised him at the crime scene. She was, after all, very beautiful, and now conveniently single. Coincidence?

I tossed the porn onto the desk. "I'll check Miss Howe's house." I inclined my head to the steel door of the cells behind him. "I'll make sure not to mention this exchange to Kelly if you crack that open so Mrs. Ferri can catch a breeze, at least."

Wallace, still red as a tomato, glared, but got up and opened the door to the cells by the tiniest bit. I could practically hear Vern chuckling at my resorting to blackmail.

Chapter Thirteen

I KEPT MY eyes out for Kelly during the short walk to Judith Howe's house, but I didn't see him. Wallace could have been lying, but I felt Kelly was brighter than to go harassing a woman mere days after her fiancé died.

I saw a figure at her door as I approached. To my surprise, it was Arthur Parrish knocking—evidently futilely—a book wrapped in ribbon in his hand. After a few seconds, he gave up and hurried back across the lawn, head down and muttering. He nearly bumped into me on the sidewalk and about jumped out of his skin.

"Oh, Mr. Carrow," he gasped, "you shouldn't sneak up on people, especially with this murder business."

"Sorry." I glanced at the house. Something in the front window fluttered. "Going to see Miss Howe?"

"I was, but she isn't home. At church, I imagine." He tugged on the bottom of his vest. "I'll come back some other time."

I put a hand out to prevent his escape. "So, this might be a silly question, but where does Richard Trask live? I'd like to apologize to him for what happened yesterday."

"Oh, well, I'm sure he's forgotten by now. And he's had worse done to him. By Walter even. Men like Richard." Arthur shook his head. "Difficult is the kindest thing I can say."

"And you let a difficult man sleep in your library?"

"Well, I can't stop him. It is a public establishment. And even difficult men need somewhere to go. There aren't any government resources out here, breadlines and shelters and such, like there are in the city." Arthur shifted his weight. "Back to your question, if he lives anywhere, it *is* the library. There's a back door, for fire safety, you understand, and I leave it unlocked, so he comes and goes as he pleases. He might be there now, even, if you wanted to—"

"Ah, well, I think it can wait until tomorrow," I said. "Might scare him worse if I pop in out of nowhere."

Arthur tittered a high and nasal laugh, the sound not unlike an out-of-tune flute. "Perhaps it's for the best. If you'll please excuse me, I must be going."

I let him pass and watched him scurry down the street for a few seconds, trying to figure out what he reminded me of. A praying mantis, maybe? Strange and spindly with too-big eyes and hands always rubbing against each other. He turned and looked back at me in what I assumed he thought was a furtive manner. I shook my head as he doubled his pace to get away. Poor lovesick weirdo.

I went to Judith's door and knocked. A few seconds later, she opened it about an inch. "Is he gone?" she whispered.

I checked. Arthur had rounded the corner. "Yeah."

She relaxed slightly but remained hidden behind the door. "I hate doing that to him. He's persistent, and I'm not at all interested." She cocked her head. "How did you know I was here?"

"Well, I knew you wouldn't be at church. Plus, I could see you peeking out the parlor window."

She sighed. "At least Arthur didn't notice." She gave me a suspicious look. "And what are *your* intentions, Mr. Carrow?"

"Well, not to drag down your ego or anything, but I'm here on business. Can we talk?"

Her eyes darted around, and I realized she was terrified. Of me or Arthur or something else? She took a breath and stepped back, leaving the gap in the door open. I took that as an invitation and went in, only to almost walk smack into Maude Lamar.

"Oh, excuse me, Mr. Carrow," she said, keeping her head down. "I was just leaving."

Stunned, I looked to Judith.

"Maude is quite a dear friend of mine," she said. "She's been a great comfort these last few days. Haven't you, darling?"

"It's my pleasure. But I must be going now. Have a lovely Sunday." Maude took off like a shot through the door and down the stairs. I watched her go, fully aware of her bizarre and frazzled exit.

Judith shut the door and gestured at the parlor. "Please come in, Mr. Carrow."

She took a seat across from me in an armchair, neat and small and pretty, but there was a tenseness in the way she held herself that hadn't been the last time I'd come to see her.

"That's very kind of Miss Lamar to visit with you," I said.

"It is," Judith replied. She smoothed out her skirt, and I noticed the fabric was crinkled in unusual places. Her eyes skimmed over the covered mirror. "You learn who your true friends are in times of sorrow." She smiled politely at me. "It's good to know you aren't put off by such trifles."

There was something off about her face, and I studied it for a second. Her mouth? Yes, that was it—it wasn't a uniform color. Patches were redder than others, and in fact, some of the color extended past the line of her lips. She caught me looking, and daintily coughed, using the back of her hand in an attempt to discreetly wipe it away. It almost worked.

"Please excuse me. I've been a little overwhelmed, as you can imagine. To what do I owe the pleasure of your visit?" she asked.

Overwhelmed was one way of putting it. *Distracted* was usually how I ended up describing petting sessions. At least now I knew why she hadn't been too broken up by Trask's death.

"Mr. Carrow?"

In my startled confusion, I asked, "Is your dad home?"

Her eyes narrowed. "He's upstairs sleeping. He had a trying night last night. Is there something you need to talk to him about?"

"No, I thought I'd pop in." *Congratulations to you for managing to keep all that under wraps with him in the house.* "There's no reason to disturb him. I'm just asking people about Mr. Trask."

Judith continued to eye me. "What about him?"

"Why were you engaged to a man you didn't care for much?"

She blinked. "I loved Walter."

"It's pretty obvious you didn't. You were standing there with his rotted-out corpse, and you came over to comfort Sev and me. No one's that nice. And every time I talk to you about him, you have no reaction." I leaned in to whisper, "And you've still got Miss Lamar's lipstick all over your mouth."

Judith's fingers flew to her lips, her eyes widening. She turned her head away as she flushed. "I don't see what difference it makes to you," she snapped. "Why should you care about a man you've never met?"

"So, here's the thing. I don't care about him. I care about my family. Robert Kelly arrested Mrs. Ferri on trumped-up charges, and he's going to do everything in his power to have her executed, and I'm doing everything in *my* power to make sure that doesn't happen."

Judith shook her head. "I don't understand, why is she so important? Isn't she a...a..."

"Oh, Bella is a lot of things, and many of them are pretty terrible. But Sev cares about her, so I care about her." Judith still looked baffled and flustered, so I decided to say it. "He's not my brother-in-law; we're together."

It was the first time I'd said it out loud to someone, and there was an odd rush to it, less like I was telling a secret and more like being able to reveal a surprise. Dawning passed across Judith's face, and all at once, she relaxed and smiled.

"I wouldn't have guessed," she said.

Wouldn't have guessed? Well, we weren't smeared-lipstick levels of obvious. But better not to be noticeable, right?

"Yeah, so you see my problem here. If Bella gets hurt, Sev gets hurt, and I can't have that." I lowered my voice again. "I understand hiding, and I even understand you might feel you have to do what's expected of you, but there are plenty better men to attach yourself to than Walter Trask. So, why were you going to marry him?"

She sighed. "He has, no, *had* money, a lot of it. My mother's illness burned through our savings, and now my father is not well either." She cast a glance at the stairs.

"He can't work anymore, and I'm an only child." She sighed. "What else could I do besides marry rich and local?"

She looked tired, maybe scared, and who could blame her? People were descending on her like vultures, me and my nosy questions included.

"For what it's worth, I think Miss Lamar is very sweet," I said.

"She is." The last of Judith's tension eased. "I knew the first day I saw her that we would be something special." She glanced at the stair as if making sure her father wasn't going to come down them. "I'd tolerate a hundred Walters to see her every day."

I nodded. There wasn't anything else to say. Sure, Judith had been evasive, but she was also a scared young woman trying to blend what she wanted with what was needed. I stood. "Thank you for taking the time to speak with me."

"My pleasure." She started walking me out. "Perhaps you and Mr. Arrighi will do the same for me sometime."

"Sure." As long as Sev and I weren't still fighting by then. "Anytime."

Judith smiled softly and shut the door behind me.

BY THE TIME I got back to the house, the Oldsmobile was sitting in the driveway. Sev and Pearl were home. As I stepped onto the porch, I heard Crista's voice. I stood with my hand on the knob, waiting, listening. She was chittering in Italian, and when she stopped, Sev answered and laughed. My stomach clenched up, and my ears burned.

I stepped back. I didn't need this right now. But if I didn't go in, where would I go? The library was closed along with every store, and I had no desire to pop into whatever church services were happening. I could try hunting down Ed again. Something was happening with him, and I was going to need to find out at some point. The question was whether I was more scared of Ed and his weapons or of what I might find if I opened the door?

I started walking toward the woods.

The path to where Trask's body had been found was now familiar to me, and I got there without a problem, besides the usual one of sweating through my clothes. Once there, I headed in the direction Ed had indicated when we'd met. The track twisted, going one direction and then the other until I wasn't sure where I had come from. After what felt like forever, the path petered out—less of a track and more of a slight dent in the undergrowth. Still, I followed, stepping gingerly over the roots and branches and rocks in the way. I cursed aloud when I tripped for the fourth time. If I ever got out of this place, I was never going to set foot in the country again.

The smell hit me first: blood. I quickened my pace on the rough terrain. Between the trees, I saw some kind of structure made of slatted wood and stone. As I got closer, I realized it was supposed to be a house. Or, well, if not a house, at least something with an approximation of a window and a door. I stopped in my tracks. I was being astonishingly stupid running into the woods by myself.

I heard footsteps crunching through the undergrowth. I looked up the path, hoping my heart would get out of my throat and quit choking me. Sure enough, Ed was making his way through the woods, a rifle slung over one shoulder and a couple of rabbits over the other.

"Hello, Ed," I squeaked.

"Hello, yourself." He stopped. "I thought I told you not to come by."

"I wanted to ask you something about Walter Trask."

Ed snorted and turned in the direction of his house. I could have walked away, but I knew Bella was boiling to death back in town, and Sev was slipping away from me. The faster I got this done, the faster we could all get out of this godforsaken place.

Ed noticed me tailing him and grunted. "Stubborn."

"Driven."

Instead of going into the house, he went around the back. I followed. Then I regretted it. Not only was there a butchering block set on a tree stump, but several racks with hides stretched across them propped in a semicircle. And if that weren't enough, there were carcasses hanging from tree branches: a deer, a turkey, and something fat and furry with buck teeth that wasn't a beaver. A large number of tools—shovels, picks, axes, and spikes—lined the back wall of the house and squatted in rusty piles. This was where the smell of blood was coming from.

"Bears," said Ed.

"What?"

"You're looking at the meat strung up. To keep the bears from getting it."

Somehow that wasn't comforting at all. I managed to drag my attention away. He dropped the rabbits onto the butcher block and turned back to me. The rifle swung, catching my eye and making me jittery.

"Can you maybe put the rifle away?" I said.

He squinted at me. "You got a problem with guns, boy?"

Was I really going to be bullied by someone who probably didn't know what a shower was? "A-actually, yeah. I saw people murdered with a rifle in front of me, so I think I have a right to not like them."

He watched me in silence and slipped the rifle off his back. "Fair enough," he said as he laid it in the grass next to the block. My heart rate went down a few notches. Then he got out a knife as big as my forearm, and it shot right back up. I pretended I didn't see him slicing into the rabbit's body.

"Anyway," I said, "were you up here when Walter Trask was killed?"

"Always up here," he mumbled.

"And did you see anything?" *Did you maybe kill him?*

"Nah."

Right. This wasn't going to get me anywhere. It was all-in or none. "You and Mr. Trask were arguing about land."

I braced in case Ed decided to take a swing, but he kept concentrating on removing the pelt from the rabbit. "We did. I didn't kill him over it though. Besides"—he straightened—"if I was going to murder him, I could have done it any time. And I wouldn't've left him there." He held up a hand dripping with blood. "Think I don't know how to get rid of a body?"

If my stomach had been unruly before, it was nothing compared to now. But he did have a point. If my surroundings were any indication, Ed knew how to disassemble a corpse, and he probably knew very well how to hide his tracks. Plus, the man was armed to the teeth, so why bother using a tree branch?

"Did you see anyone else up here the day Trask was killed? Robert Kelly, maybe?"

"There was someone around, but I didn't see. Just the tracks later in the day." Ed looked at my shoes. "Not proper boots."

"Well, that could be anyone."

"No. Bobby Kelly's got boots. Mr. Wallace too."

Did they? It hadn't occurred to me to see what they wore on their feet as part of their police uniforms. And if they had boots, Oscar Gaines probably did, too, since he was out here all the time. Not to say any of them had been wearing their boots at the time. Using a tree branch as the weapon hinted that this had been a spur-of-the-moment choice, so whoever had done it probably hadn't intended to be hiking.

"You're giving me a weird look, boy."

"Women's shoes or men's?"

"Well it weren't no heels. Most of the women here are sensible. Wouldn't come out here wearing them anyway. I don't remember the size if that's your next question. Everybody came walking through later, so no point in trying to go back now and look."

Once again, it seemed the mass search party had scrambled up the evidence. I still needed to figure out who suggested it. "Anything else odd?"

He paused. "There was glass in the path. Wasn't there later though."

Glass, out here? "Like a bottle?"

"No. Clear. Like window glass, maybe."

Even stranger. But I wasn't going to go searching for a shard of glass in the middle of the woods. That could be a new phrase if *needle in a haystack* ever went out of style.

"Do you think Walter Trask's death has anything to do with Leo Manco's?" I asked.

Ed shrugged. "They say Leo got shot by the border police for smuggling."

"And you believe that?"

"It doesn't do no good to poke around in other people's business." He gave me a sidelong look as the knife in his hand slit through another piece of flesh.

I swallowed the bile creeping up my throat. "What do you know about James Smith? He'd been staying at the Reed house when Mr. Manco died. Supposedly, he was here to hunt."

"Well, I can tell you I saw him out here twice. And whoever he was, he was no hunter. Made an unholy racket stamping around. Wouldn't be surprised if he didn't catch one thing."

Finally, someone to confirm my suspicions Smith wasn't who he said he was. But why had he killed Manco, and would it have brought him forward to kill again?

"Right. Well, thank you for your time, Ed," I said. "I might come back if I have any more questions."

He nodded. "I'll be here."

Since I figured that was about as good of a goodbye as I was going to get out of him, I wandered out of the forest. It was well into the afternoon when I got back to the house. Still, I hesitated in front of the back door, unsure of what I was going to find. But I'd faced down the roughest-looking man I'd ever seen in my life. Surely Crista wasn't more frightening?

I walked in on Crista, Pearl, and Sev chatting around the table, a large bowl of pasta in the center. And, kind of strangely, Sev was sitting in his undershirt. He turned his head.

"There you are, Alex," he exclaimed. "We were wondering where you'd gone."

I stood in the doorway. I'd accidentally done the exact thing I'd wanted to do last night—disappear with no note or explanation to make him realize how panic-inducing it was—but it seemed like he'd barely noticed. That, combined with the sickeningly sweet domestic scene I was witnessing, tipped my temper.

"Can I see you in the living room for a minute?" I said.

Sev's face fell. "All right." He nodded at Crista and Pearl. "Excuse us."

He followed me into the parlor. Even as we stepped into the other room, he had a curious expression. Well, I'd cure him of that.

"What the *hell* are you doing half dressed?" I hissed.

He blinked, shocked at my sudden and admittedly confusing chastisement. "There's marinara sauce on the pasta, I don't want my shirt to get stained—"

"Did you even notice I was gone?"

"I did? I just asked you where you were?"

"I went up to see Ed."

That surprised him. "The man living up in the woods like some kind of wild animal? Alex, that was dangerous! You might have gotten hurt out there. You should have told me where you were going."

"I don't have to tell you everything."

He sighed and rolled his eyes. "No, you don't. But you can't be angry that I am not worried and angry when I am."

He edged around me to return to the kitchen, and I let him go since I didn't know how to stop him without raising my voice. I didn't want to let Crista know we were having another argument, and I didn't want to panic Pearl again.

"*Va bene?*" Crista called.

"*Alex non sta bene così va a letto presto,*" he answered with a brief look over his shoulder at me. "*Dovremmo salvargli del cibo.*"

I had no idea what he'd said, but I didn't like my name being batted around. Frustrated, I stormed up the stairs and slammed the door to my room. I leaned against it and groaned, already regretting what I'd done. Was I really going to spend another night like this? Jealous and scared and angry, not to mention starving because I'd walked off without supper again? Well, it was done now. Maybe I ought use the time to piece together what I'd learned about Trask. I dug my notebook out of the drawer of my bedside table and wrote everything down.

Trask had had money but not a lot of friends, not real ones anyway. His brother hated him, and his fiancée had been using him as a beard. Judith's dad hadn't liked him much either, mostly because Judith hadn't seemed to like him. The Gaineses couldn't have thought well of him since it was Louise's employment with him that had put their marriage on the final rocks. Apparently, Sheriff Kelly hadn't cared much for him, nor had Ed, though I was sure Ed didn't care for anyone. And of course, Crista hadn't liked him since he'd—either directly or indirectly—been responsible for her husband's death.

Of those, I was pretty sure neither Ed nor Judith had done it, though for different reasons. Despite the land dispute, Ed probably didn't care enough. And if he had, he would have been much better about covering the evidence. Judith had been using Trask for money, money she wouldn't get if he was dead. Still, that left a lot of people, Crista included. She'd have had all morning to off him before Sev and I showed up. Then again, she was awfully tiny.

And who were the Reeds and James Smith? Bella hadn't come clean, and no one else I'd spoken to had much in the way of interaction with them. *Meaningless*, Bella had said. But how could they be when they were the linchpin to at least Leo Manco's death?

I shut the notebook. The sun had shifted angles toward evening. I didn't hear any movement downstairs. Tentatively, I opened the door. Silence. Something caught my eye on the floor. It was a note in Sev's handwriting: *We left you a bowl.*

Now embarrassed, I crept downstairs. I saw Sev and Pearl in the parlor, sitting on the couch—Pearl was doing her best at reading one of the books Bella had given her, and Sev was doing his best to guide her along. He caught my eye as I moved past the doorway, but he didn't say anything before going back to what he was doing. God, in what universe was I anywhere close to being worthy of his patience?

On the kitchen counter was a bowl of pasta, as promised. I ate standing over the sink, alone, and it was only after I snuck back upstairs, I noticed a reddish-brown stain on my shirt.

Chapter Fourteen

IN THE MORNING, I bolted straight for the front door without even stopping in the kitchen. I was about to open it when Sev called my name. I froze, hand on the doorknob. I couldn't face him, not yet.

His arms slipped around my waist, his face pressed against my back. "What's wrong, Alex?" he asked quietly. "You're not yourself."

I stayed motionless. How could he know what I considered myself? He'd only known me for a month. And yet he wasn't wrong. I didn't feel like myself when I snapped at him. Or maybe I was just dredging up the nasty parts of me I kept hidden, that Donnie and Martin had kept down. If that was the case, which pieces were the real me?

"I'm fine," I answered, though the tone of my voice betrayed me.

He took a breath, and it whispered around the base of my neck. "Please don't lie to me, *caro*." When I didn't reply, he continued in a low tone, "I know I fell in love with a good man."

God, why did he have to say that? "You can get Pearl to school okay, right?" I asked, my voice hovering on the edge of cracking.

He let me go slowly. "Of course."

"Thanks." Without looking at him, I turned the knob and stepped outside.

He didn't follow me out. Good or bad, I couldn't decide. I couldn't do anything, not even tell the truth. Maybe if I tried to make it up to him somehow? Not sure what I could do, though, besides getting Bella out of jail. Or maybe I should start with something simpler, like getting his suit back from the cleaner's. When he got home from work, we would talk.

But it seemed even doing something as easy as picking up dry cleaning wasn't going to be so quick. Main Street buzzed, particularly around the post office. A telegram, no doubt, and probably important. I shouldered my way into the building.

It looked nothing like the big government post offices in the city, the ones with soaring ceilings and marble and glass kiosks. This was more of a wooden table with a pigeonhole cabinet behind. The place had been built to fit five people at the most, and I was number six. Luckily, I was taller than everyone else by some inches and got a view of the small crowd; Richard Trask and Mr. and Mrs. Gaines were making the most noise, yelling over each other, but Judith and her father were there too. The postmaster, a Black man—the only one I'd seen in town— was behind the counter trying to keep order. He held a piece of paper in his hand, keeping it back to prevent anyone from snatching it. So, I'd been right; there was a telegram, and apparently the news had come as a shock to some people.

"Please," he begged, "I'm just the messenger." He glanced at me. "Excuse me, sir. I'll be right with you."

Before I could say anything, Richard Trask took a leap for the letter. The postmaster jolted backward out of the way. Almost as soon as he did, Fran burst in with Crista.

"I brought her, Joe!" Fran exclaimed. Crista just looked bewildered.

Now there were eight people crammed into the space, and Judith got shoved into her father. She yelped and he grunted and the volume in the room increased to a grumbling roar. The counter tilted, and Joe the postmaster scrambled away, losing the telegram in the process. Oscar Gaines dove for it, but I moved faster.

Will be there Wed but for now: business to Mr. O Gaines to continue as he sees fit. House to Mr. R Trask. Remaining personal assets to Mrs. C Manco.

The parts about the business going to the partner and the house going to the brother I understood, but bank accounts and everything going to Crista? I glanced at her. She looked as confused as I felt.

Richard started shoving his way toward me. I held him off with one hand. Joe tugged the telegram, and I let him pull it away. He cleared his throat before reading aloud what I'd seen. Everyone paused for a moment, shocked as badly as I had been.

Then Louise shrieked, "You little slut!"

"What?" gasped Crista.

"Hey, hey!" I stepped between them, or rather I nudged Fran—whose mouth hung open at her mother's foul language—about a foot to the left. "Mrs. Gaines, that was uncalled for."

"I bet she's been fucking him behind everyone's back," she continued. "I bet they got together to get her husband out of the way."

She shouldered her way out the door. Her husband tromped after her. I caught a glimpse of him, but I couldn't read his face. Anger? Frustration? Fran bolted after them. Richard kept lunging at Joe, trying to read the telegram for himself. Judith and her father both looked somewhat lost. Behind me, Crista began to sniffle.

I sighed, hating myself for what I was about to do. I guided Crista to the door by her elbow. "Come on, let's get you out of here."

She nodded and let me move her outside. Once in the humid, sweet-smelling air, she slumped against the wall of the post office and pulled out her handkerchief. I scanned the area for Mr. and Mrs. Gaines—Louise wasn't anywhere in sight, but Oscar was stomping his way back toward his house, Fran trailing behind. Where could Louise have gone within a minute?

"She's a terrible woman," Crista wailed.

"Well, she's jealous you're going to get all that money," I said. I waited a beat. "You *weren't* sleeping with Walter Trask, right?"

"No," Crista whimpered. "We didn't even talk. I hated him for leaving Leo to die out there."

"Then why would Trask leave you money?"

"I don't know. And I wish to God he hadn't. It's hard enough here, and now that *punttana* is going to spread the rumor. She was the one having sex with him, not me."

"Wait, what?"

Crista's mouth shut tight, and she looked away. Well, if that was true, that explained why Oscar and Louise were getting a divorce. And if she was the one involved in adultery, she'd get very little, if anything, out of the proceedings. Maybe she'd been hoping once the paperwork had been signed, Trask would give up on disinterested Judith and marry her instead. At the very least, it seemed she'd been expecting he'd remember her in his will.

Maybe she'd even killed him on the anticipation. It wouldn't be too hard for her to take a pair of her husband's shoes. I glanced over my shoulder at Oscar's continuing retreat. *If I can hustle Crista along, I might be able to catch up.*

"Look, why don't you go back on home," I said to Crista. "Forget what Louise said. No one'll believe her anyway."

Crista sniffed and nodded.

The post office door swung open, and Judith and her father walked out, giving us polite nods as they did. I caught a glimpse of Richard Trask hurling abuse at the poor postmaster before the door shut all the way. I was almost sad I hadn't actually broken his nose. Then he would have had something to yell about.

I peeked in Oscar's direction, but he had booked it. No way I would be able to catch up without running, and that would look very odd. Worse, Robert Kelly was scurrying up the street. Just what I didn't need. I did, however, sneak a look at his shoes. Heavy boots, as expected.

"Mr. Carrow," he said, almost cheerfully. "I'm a little concerned about your amazing ability to be at locations where there's trouble."

"There's no trouble here," I protested.

He tilted his head at the door to the post office, which only partly muffled Richard's tirade. "Mrs. Gaines told me about someone disturbing the peace. Maybe in Boston that's not such a big thing, but we take it pretty seriously here." He noticed Crista wilting into the brickwork behind me. "Mrs. Manco."

She lowered her head. "Sheriff."

He returned his attention to me. "So, when is this lawyer for Mrs. Ferri supposed to show up?"

Oh right. I shrugged. "Maybe he got delayed. You know how traffic in Boston is."

"You know what's funny, I called up my uncle on the Boston police force last night, and they were *very* confused when I brought up your name, and they didn't find any record of you or Mr. Arrighi.

Shit. I'd have to think fast. "Are you sure you were spelling it right? Because there's an *h* in Arrighi—"

"Mr. Carrow—"

"And the church I was christened in burned down at some point and all the records—"

"Mr. Carrow!"

I shut my mouth, hoping the choking feeling creeping up my throat wouldn't kill me.

A nasty smile passed across Kelly's face. "You may think you're being clever"—he leaned in and lowered his voice—"but I *know* you and Mrs. Ferri are up to something. Probably Mr. Arrighi too. I haven't seen much of him though. Which makes me wonder even more. Oh, and don't think I don't know what happened in the library Saturday afternoon. I'm choosing to ignore it right now." With one motion, he pushed past me and opened the door. "Richard Trask!" he bellowed before the door slammed shut behind him.

"I should go," Crista whispered.

"Wait, before you do, is there anything else you want to tell me about your husband's death?"

She shook her head. "They went on a job. Only Mr. Trask came back. Mr. Kelly ignored it until Bella had her men bring Leo's body back. That is all I know, and that is all I will ever know."

"Right." I sighed. "Well, feel better."

"*Grazie*, Mr. Carrow."

She turned to go, but as she did, the post office door swung open, and Kelly dragged a flailing Richard outside. The scruffier man squirmed and yelled in Kelly's grip. In either a burst of luck or genius, Richard struck Kelly in the stomach. The cop gasped as he let him go. Instinctively, I grabbed for Richard, but he dodged more quickly than I'd expected from a drunk and I missed. He spun and took off onto one of the side streets.

"Well, what are you waiting for?" grunted Kelly, still hunched. "Catch him!"

I remained where I was. "If you let Bella out, I'll give it a shot."

Kelly grumbled and straightened, using the wall as support. His face contorted as he forced himself to take a deep breath. "You better hope he runs fast because as soon as I catch him, I'm coming after you for aiding and abetting."

I should have been unnerved by his threat, but I was already at the end of my rope and landing in jail didn't sound so bad in comparison. "Does he have good shoes?"

"What?"

"Are his shoes good? If they're bad, he can't run very far in them."

Kelly blinked at me. "The hell? I don't know what his shoes look like. What are you going on about?" He looked at Crista and gestured at me. "He's *your* friend."

She glanced at me, probably thinking the same thing I was: friend was a stretch. But she raised her chin. "Yes, sir. But this is not his town. He does not owe us anything."

Kelly rolled his eyes and muttered some curses and stumbled after Richard Trask. Crista released a breath.

"You should not press him like that," she said.

"I've seen worse than the likes of him."

"And what did they do when you tried to stop them?"

That seemed like an odd question, maybe a translation error, but as I watched her face, I realized I knew what she meant. What had happened the last time I tried to defy someone with power? I didn't even need to say—she already knew, or at least she had a vague inkling since Sev and I wouldn't have fled to the middle-of-fucking-nowhere Vermont if something terrible hadn't happened.

"Listen, Crista, let *me* worry about me, okay?" I said.

"And will you also worry about Pearl and Mr. Arrighi?" Her brow furrowed in a way I'd noticed some women had perfected—equal pieces defiant, disappointed, and concerned. "You are not by yourself."

She may have been tiny, but she knew how to take a man down a peg or five. "I won't do anything that will get them in trouble. I promise."

She stared at me for a moment, and without another word, she turned on her heel and left. Shame burned me from the inside out. She was right; I had been reckless and not just about Trask. I'd done some awful things to Sev in the last few days, things he didn't deserve for betrayals I couldn't prove.

I caught sight of Mrs. Gaines returning from her tattling on Richard, and I decided my own embarrassment would have to wait. She ducked into the front door of the factory. How inappropriate would it be for me to follow her in? Well, Sev wasn't there yet, so it wasn't like I'd embarrass him on his first day. I hurried after her.

Between my height and general frantic energy, I wasn't much one for stealth, and Mrs. Gaines whipped around to face me almost as soon as I stepped in.

"Can I help you, Mr. Carrow?" she snapped.

I opened my mouth to speak and gagged on the smell of maple. As bad as it was on the street, it was nothing compared to inside. The sweetness was choking, seeping, unavoidable, contained by thick wooden walls and a concrete floor. How did anyone work in here without losing their mind? Well, I'd have to make this quick.

"You had no right to shout lies about Mrs. Manco like that. Slurs either."

Louise's face bloomed scarlet, and her eyes darted around. I glanced around the room. It seemed it was too early for anyone else to have arrived. Still, workers might walk in at any second, Sev included. I turned back, and Louise had raised her chin in defiance.

"You can't prove she's not a little hussy."

"Maybe not, but you can't prove the reverse. I've heard her talk about Walter Trask, and she *despised* him. If they gave out prizes for that kind of thing, she'd have a trophy bigger than she is."

Louise rolled her eyes and started for a staircase against the nearest wall. Could I, should I, follow her into the offices? If I chased her, she might call the cops on me, and she would be well within her rights. But I *had* to make sure the rumors were true.

"Where are you going anyway?" I called after her. "Got another lover on the side? Did you pick him up before or after Mr. Trask got killed?"

She froze, foot on the first step. "How dare—"

"I hear you're in the process of getting a divorce, Mrs. Gaines. Care to comment?"

"Who told you that?" she hissed.

"Not important. Though I will say it was a different person than the one who told me you're divorcing because you were sleeping with Walter Trask."

Her mouth fell open and she sputtered into crying. I stood well back. Her over the top emotions reminded me too much of Emma and her crocodile tears over her husband's murder. And this lady? She was nasty for the sake of it, insulting Sev for no reason. No amount of crying was going to make me reconsider.

"Walter," she sniffled. "He always told me I was beautiful. And he never blamed me for things that aren't my fault. He knew what I do for this company. He knew I tried my best with Fran. Which is more than I can say of Oscar."

There was a lot of depth in there, to be sure, but I wasn't about to dive into someone's marital problems. That was for shrinks and spinsters. I just wanted to know who'd killed a guy.

"I'm assuming you'll deny killing him."

"Of course, I didn't kill him!" she snapped. She scrubbed at her nose with her handkerchief. "Why would anyone kill him?"

"Funny, I was about to ask you the same thing. Did you think it was strange how his will got parsed out, maybe?"

She shook her head. "The business to Oscar is understandable. They've been working together for almost twenty years. And Richard might as well have the house, but—"

"Crista."

"Yes! He loved *me*. Me!" Louise got fierce again. "So, she must have tempted him away. Said something, made promises, blackmailed him, I don't know. Just she got him to stuff her in there and forget me. The little whore—"

God, Sev was supposed to sit with this horrible woman three days a week? "Mrs. Gaines." I straightened up to my full height. "Language like that is not called for, so I advise you leave off before I get angry. Now, I want to know the answer to one question," I said. "Where were you Wednesday, oh, before two, say?"

Louise's eyes narrowed. "I was here in the factory. On the floor with the men, even, giving them their assignments for next week. And I stayed there when Walter didn't show up. Someone had to keep an eye on things. Wait around until they come and ask any of them."

"And your husband?"

A breath, a pause. "Presumably he was in his office, but I can't be sure."

Well, at least she hadn't thrown Oscar completely under the train. "Thanks, that's all I needed to know."

"I'd be careful about the waves you make here, Mr. Carrow," she called after me. "As I'm sure you've been told by now, Chickadee is not Boston."

"That might be frightening, Mrs. Gaines," I answered, "except this petty, incestuous squabbling you've got going in this town is *nothing* compared to the hell I just came out of, so I advise either keeping your mouth shut or thinking at least a little outside the box with your threats."

She gaped in silence, and I scuttled away before she found her voice. *Now you've done it. The pitchforks are going to come out any minute.* I hadn't thought I'd quite had that in me, but after weeks of an unending stream of shit being poured on me, it was only a matter of time before I lost it.

Chapter Fifteen

I STEPPED BACK into the less heavy air of Main Street. This place, these people—they were going to drive me insane. If I wasn't insane already, of course. Even if I ignored the nightmares and the nerves I couldn't seem to shake, I had made a lot of stupid choices: needling cops, chasing dangerous strangers, and—worst of all—shoving Sev away.

I glanced toward the house. If I ran back right now, I might be able to catch him before he left to take Pearl to school. I didn't have a good plan about what to say to him though. What if I rambled, made him late to his first day at work? I didn't doubt Mrs. Gaines would use anything as an excuse to fire him. And if she fired him, he wouldn't be able to discover anything, and Bella might roast to death in prison and Sev and me would get found out and—

Breathe.

Letting one thought leap to another wasn't helping anything. I could talk to Sev later, when I'd cooled down enough to be rational, and he wasn't in a rush. In the meantime, I'd get his suit back from Maude, maybe fix the coffee maker. Hey, and maybe I'd even manage to cook something so Crista wouldn't have to come by. It would probably be boiled eggs, but he'd appreciate it, surely. Oh, and I'd apologize too. For real this time.

No one was behind the counter at the dry cleaner's when I walked in. Maybe Maude was in the back? I rang the little service bell. Nothing. Leaving the building with the door unlocked would be very silly, wouldn't it? I rang the bell again, anxiety starting to creep up my shoulders. There had already been one murder in town. What if it had turned into two?

"Miss Lamar?" I called. "It's Alex Carrow."

Her voice came through muffled after a long pause. "I'm so sorry, I didn't finish the suit. Come back some other time."

Yeah, like that wasn't suspicious. "Are you okay?"

"Fine!"

Well, she had definitely been crying, but at least she wasn't dead. Maybe she was avoiding me after what had happened Sunday?

"You know," I said, "I think you and Judith make a nice couple."

After a few seconds of silence, Maude poked her head around the doorframe. "I heard. Judith came by a few minutes ago."

"Did she say something else? You don't look very happy."

"Oh, no, I'm a little disappointed in something, is all."

Maude tucked a loose strand of hair behind her ear, and I saw the red mark on the back of her hand again. That was not a burn, chemical or otherwise. The skin was too smooth. And I *knew* I'd seen a similar mark before, but not... Wait, yes, I did. It'd been pointed out to me, but I'd been too preoccupied with the pulpy mess of Walter Trask's skull: the birthmark on his hand.

Maude must have seen the change in my expression because she covered the one hand with the other. "Judith said you were clever. He was my father."

I was almost too astounded to answer. This town gossiped about everything else, and I hadn't heard that. "Who else knows?"

"You might have noticed most people here don't take foreigners very seriously"—she rubbed at the birthmark—"so no one thought to look; no one thought to ask. I only told Judith. I had to tell her when she agreed to marry him." Maude took a breath to steady herself. "She said she still had a responsibility, but she wouldn't leave me."

"Did Trask know?"

Maude nodded.

And he hadn't left her a cent according to the telegram. Well, I'd have been disappointed too. Even if he hadn't left her much, at least it would have been a declaration.

"When did he find out?" I asked, hoping it had been too little time to change a will.

"Almost as soon as I got here, so four, five years ago."

Bastard. "And he didn't—"

"No. He didn't want anything to do with me. I was a mistake made on a business trip. What was my mother but some exotic plaything for him?" Maude lowered her voice. "She was half-Indian, you know. Ojibwe. He probably didn't even think of her as a person."

"Why did you stay? Why did you even come?"

Maude took a few moments before answering. "I was eighteen, and my mother told me about him just before she died. I decided to look for him. And I found him. And he was awful. I'd never met a more selfish man. So, I wanted to go home. But by the time I got here, I'd run out of money. I started working here to earn." She waved at the shop. "Judith's mother owned it. That's how we met, though it was only because Mrs. Howe was doing so poorly. She'd come back from college to take care of her. Mrs. Howe left me the shop in the end. It was very kind of her. More than I can say of my father. But I do have to thank him for one thing. He knows how to keep a secret. Even after he's dead, he's still hiding me."

"Well, if it makes you feel any better," I said, "my father was an asshole too."

Maude sighed. "I think some men were not meant to have families." She rubbed the back of her hand again. "I did mean it about the suit. It's been quite a week. I'm not even through all the regular customers. Tomorrow? I'll bring it over to your house, even."

"Don't worry about it. I don't think he'll start missing it right away."

Maude watched me expectantly. Probably she wanted to know how someone with a bespoke silk suit had ended up with someone like me, and maybe she did deserve the story after telling me her own, but I wasn't ready. Oh, I'd talk about Sev until the sun went down, but the whole story? The one where I lost Donnie and Martin and what shreds of innocence I'd had left? That would require a hundred years and several bottles of alcohol.

"Tell Judith I said hello," I said as I hurried out.

If I was going to be frank, I felt a little humiliated it had taken me so long to figure out Maude was Trask's daughter. Did it make much of a difference? Sure, she might have killed him on the expectation of inheritance money, but apparently, he hadn't acknowledged her at all. It would have been very stupid of her to make such an assumption, and she didn't seem stupid. Maybe she had felt some kind of jealousy over Judith using Trask as a beard. Such an arrangement...well, unorthodox would be putting it nicely, and it couldn't have felt comfortable, no matter how in love they were. Empty-handed, I started the walk back to the house to think some more.

"Mr. Carrow."

Oh God, what now? I spun, trying to make my expression into one that might be interpreted as compliance. "Yes, Sheriff Kelly? What is it this time?"

He stood in front of me, his hands on his hips. "Richard Trask is missing."

"You mean you didn't catch him."

"Because *you* let him walk right past you. So, if you don't want to be arrested for obstruction of justice, you'll start looking for him."

I considered protesting since it wasn't my job to go chasing drunk lunatics, but Kelly had a look that said he would be all too happy to see me suffer. A word popped into my head, one that I'd heard Sev use: penance—one had to pay for one's sins.

"Fine," I grumbled. "I'll look, but no promises."

Kelly sneered. "They told me you were a smart man. Now I almost believe them."

I held my huff until he walked away. How could such a small town have such a high percentage of terrible people? They weren't even mean for good reason!

"The sooner you get Bella out," I muttered to myself.

Based on what I knew about Richard, I figured he hadn't gone far. For one thing, he couldn't be all that steady, and for another, he was probably aware of the dangers of the woods beyond town. He'd want to be somewhere safe and preferably quiet. And, well, Arthur *was* the only person I'd spoken to who seemed to hold any kind of pity for him.

I pushed open the door of the library. The smell of books overtook the smell of sticky maple, and I found incredible relief in it. How did anyone manage to stay outside in such a cloying scent for more than a few minutes? Arthur Parrish sat behind his little desk stamping books, his glasses balanced on the tip of his nose. He pushed them up with one finger.

"Devil take these," he muttered.

"Mr. Parrish?"

His head snapped up. "Oh, Mr. Carrow, I didn't know you were there. Apologies for the language. They're my spares, and they don't fit well. What can I do for you?"

"Well I don't know if you heard, but Richard Trask caused a bit of a commotion in the post office this morning. He broke away from Mr. Kelly when he went to arrest him."

"Oh dear." Arthur glanced at the shelves behind him. "Well he may be here. The fire door is unlocked, but I haven't seen him."

I pointed and mouthed, asking if I could look. Arthur nodded and shrank back. I crept between the shelves, ears tuned to any sounds of movement. Didn't mean he wasn't there. I edged closer to the back. Step, pause, listen. Step, pause, listen. The bench came into view. Nothing. I sighed my disappointment and went back to the front.

Arthur craned his neck as he saw me approach. "He's not there?"

"Nope."

"I would say I'm sorry, but I would rather not have another tussle in my library."

"Any idea where he might have gone instead?"

"I'm afraid not. I think I will go lock the door so he can't come sneaking in during the night. I'd hate for Mr. Kelly to have to drag him out."

I drummed my fingers on the desk. If I were Richard Trask, where would I go?

"Is there anything else I can help you with?" asked Arthur.

Was there? "Actually, yes. Do you happen to know who called the search party for Mr. Trask?"

"Hmm, I don't recall. Is that important?"

"Maybe. I went up to see Ed—"

Arthur flinched, and his glasses slid back down his nose. "Good Lord, you went up to see that beast of a man?" He shoved the glasses back up. They slipped again like they didn't seem to want to stay. "You're a far braver man than anyone here could boast."

"I mean he's weird, true. He didn't seem aggressive or anything though. Anyway, he said he saw someone's tracks before he learned Trask had been killed, but the search party muddled them. So maybe someone knew they'd left tracks and decided to wipe the evidence with the help of people wanting to be neighborly."

Arthur gaped. "How horrid." He stared into the middle distance for a moment, thinking. "Well, I'm sorry to say it, but Judith most likely suggested it. Walter *was* her fiancé."

True. Yet he'd left her nothing in his will, preferring to give his money to Crista. And his house to his brother. Technically, homeless Richard did have a real place to go now.

"One more thing, can you give me directions to Walter Trask's house?"

"Oh, sure." Arthur leaned over the desk and pointed out the leftmost window. "Down that street, west side. Beautiful brick building, built in the 1780s. In fact, if you're interested in the historical architecture of town, I have numerous archives—"

"No, that's unnecessary, thank you."

I nodded my farewell and made a beeline for Trask's home. Maybe I'd find a fight there, maybe I wouldn't, but there was only one way to find out.

Chapter Sixteen

I STARED UP at Trask's house. Yep, brick and imposing. Probably historical, too, but since I'd declined the archives, I couldn't be sure. I rattled the knob. Locked. After checking I was the only one on the street, I tried the nearest window. Also locked. Odd. These country folk tended to leave things open, didn't they? Trask wasn't one of them, though, not completely. At the very least, he'd been a bootlegger, and that was something worth hiding.

Maybe I should have thought about searching the house sooner. However, I took meager pride in knowing my gut instinct wasn't to do something illegal. I'd never picked a lock before—one of those things Donnie had never taught me in his effort to make me respectable. *Sev might be able to*. But I would have to drag him out of work, and possibly apologize and maybe even give an explanation of my behavior, and I wasn't quite sure I was ready to do that yet.

What if someone had a key? Judith? Or more likely Louise. Judith would hand it over if she had one, but Louise definitely would not, not after our little showdown. What if I got Fran to steal the key for me? A horrible thought, but I was desperate.

Well, I'd try Judith first. That way, I'd be able to smooth my conscience. I walked the two blocks to Judith's house within minutes. She opened the door with a confused expression.

"Mr. Carrow," she said, "you'll give my father ideas."

A series of coughs burst from somewhere inside. "Who's out there, Judy?"

"It's Joe," she answered. "He's got a package with bad handwriting and wanted to make sure we weren't expecting anything."

I was impressed with the plausibility and speed at which she'd lied. Then again, I'd spent a lot of my time lying about who I was seeing. It came with the territory. Maybe I did want to talk to her dad. He'd told me flat out he'd disliked Trask, which was more absolute than everyone else's vague objections, and had told me exactly why: he suspected criminality and infidelity, both of which had been true. How had he known, and had he done anything about it besides voice his objections? Trask's house could wait.

"Actually, it's your father I want to see," I said.

"Oh." Judith took a step back. "Well, he just got in." She glanced at the entrance to the living room. "But he does enjoy guests. He gets so few now. Please, come in."

She led the way to the living room with its draped mirror. George Howe sat in an armchair, a blanket draped around his shoulders even in the heat. He stood to shake my hand but lost his strength halfway through the action and flopped back into his seat.

"Mr. Carrow, you're here too?" he wheezed. "So sorry, I think I overdid it at the post office earlier."

Was I really going to interrogate a man who looked like he might keel over any second? He hadn't hiked into the forest and cracked Trask across the head. Or, he could have been faking. That was always what happened in the pulps—the person in the wheelchair could always walk; the person on their deathbed was perfectly healthy. But those were books, and books were fiction, as I well knew. How would George have known to fake for me anyway? He hadn't even known I was there until I walked in. And maybe catching him off guard would make him tell me more than he intended. If there was anything to tell, of course.

"Sorry to disturb you, sir," I said. "I wanted to ask you something about Walter Trask."

George shifted uncomfortably, but it was impossible to distinguish between emotional discomfort and physical pain. "I'll try to answer."

I glanced at Judith, who had come from behind me to take a seat. "The last time I spoke to you, you said Trask wasn't worth marrying, even though he was rich. Was it just the infidelity you were worried about?"

George glanced at Judith before answering. "Well there was all that business with Mr. Manco. Suspicious. Oh, I know Bobby said it wasn't his gun that killed the smuggler, but," he hesitated, "I'm not sure I trust Bobby much either."

Judith sighed. "Papa."

"Don't papa me. Bobby Kelly is as much of a weasel as Walter Trask ever was. Both of them selfish and bullying and—"

A coughing fit interrupted the rest of his rant. I cringed. If he was faking, he was doing an excellent job. At the end of it, he pulled his hand away from his mouth. There were flecks of bloody spittle on his palm. Not faking then.

"Anyway," George continued, "I told Mr. Trask if he wanted to marry my daughter, he was going to have to prove his worth to me. He would have to start being a better man."

"And what did that entail?" I asked.

"I didn't tell him what to do, just that he needed to do *something*. A few people told me he tried to reconnect with his brother, but rumors are rumors. I haven't seen them pleased to be near each other in years."

"When I spoke to Richard a few days ago, he said Walter tried to offer him money, but they ended up in a fight."

George shrugged. "Neither of them are very pleasant. Their parents tried, bless them, but those boys came out crooked and stayed crooked. Wouldn't be surprised if Richard snapped."

I nodded. So much for this side trip. I hadn't learned anything except George was too sick to do much, let alone chase a man into the woods and bludgeon him to death. There was nothing for it. Unless Mr. Howe knew something others didn't. "Did you ever speak to James Smith? He was here around the time Mr. Manco was killed. I know it was a few years ago—"

"No, I remember him. Kept to himself, mostly. I did have a conversation with him right when he came in though. Thought it odd at the time, so I remember. I saw him in the general store buying bullets, and I said, 'What're you planning to do with what you catch?' You know, because one person can't keep all that meat, so I was hoping to talk him into selling me some venison since it's been a time since I could go out myself. He said he was there to take some trophies. So, I asked him if he was hiring local, because the only person around here doing that sort of thing is Ed, and I thought he might need to be warned. And he mentioned he had a guy in St. Albans. So, I said, 'Oh I grew up in St. Albans, I probably know them. Who is it?' Then he looked at me funny and said he had to go. Rushed right out of there. Didn't even take the change for the ammunition."

Another burst of coughing ended the story, and this time he didn't seem to get his breath back. Judith jumped up from her chair, but he waved her back down. She wrung her hands. I stood there awkwardly until it subsided.

"Sorry," he rasped.

"No, it's fine," I said. "I should let you go. Thank you for speaking with me."

"I'll walk you out," Judith mumbled.

I followed her back to the front door. She paused there with tears in her eyes, taking a moment to dab at them.

"My apologies," she said. "It breaks my heart to see him like that." She stuffed her handkerchief into a pocket. "I almost wish Walter had left me some money. If he had, I might have been able to arrange for somewhere more comfortable for him."

"If you don't mind me asking, what—"

"Don't worry, it's not catching," she answered, almost bitterly. "Cancer, the doctor said. He was given a year about six months ago. I keep waiting for the day." She took a steadying breath. "No point in worrying. We all have our hourglasses."

I didn't know what to say, so I decided to drive back to my original purpose for coming over here. "Um, Judith, I have a bit of a confession," I said. "I didn't come here to visit your father." I lowered my voice. "Do you happen to have keys to Walter Trask's house?"

"Oh! No," she replied. "What do you need them for?"

Sev could read lies in my face, and I prayed Judith wouldn't be able see the one I was about to say. "Mr. Kelly wants to get in there for his investigation. He'd have come himself to ask, but I think he's trying to be respectful of your, uh, loss."

Her eyes narrowed. Considering what I'd seen of Kelly, he wasn't the respectful type, and she would know that even better. But Judith's good nature won out. "Perhaps try Mr. and Mrs. Gaines," she said. "I'm sure they did business on the weekends."

Yeah, business. I thanked her and left. *There, conscience, you happy?*

I hurried back toward Main and up toward the row of houses at the end, turning what George had said over in my mind. Whatever James Smith was, he wasn't a hunter interested in taxidermy. My money was on hired killer engaged to take out Leo Manco, but who had bought his services and why? Sev had said nobody would be bothered with bootleggers this small-time, but that wasn't necessarily true. While I loved Sev, he always seemed to have a too-rosy picture about the kinds of things happening in the underground. Maybe Bella had upset someone, and they decided to prune some of her traveling vines just because they could. I wouldn't have put it past Bella to do something like that, so why would her rivals have any qualms about it?

Fran's bike was propped against the house, which meant she was in. I sighed. Well, I'd come this far.

Fran opened the door, her smile beaming like the sun. "Mr. Carrow!" she exclaimed. "How can I help you?"

Oh boy. "Hey, Fran. Are your parents home?"

Disappointment passed across her face. "Oh, um, my mother isn't, but my father is out around back with the truck. Should I get him?"

"No. I wanted to see you. Can I come in for a second?"

"Yes! I mean, yes, please come in."

She edged out of the doorway and brought me back into their flashy living room. Instinctively, I started looking for places someone might stash a key. In the blue-patterned vase on the side table maybe. Or under the ottoman. Could one of the bricks in the fireplace be loose enough to pull in and out, one with a small pocket behind?

"So, how can I help?"

My attention snapped back to Fran. I willed my fake smile to look at least semi-genuine. Considering how smitten she was, she might not have cared, but it didn't hurt to sweeten the pot.

"I'm sure you saw Richard Trask causing a commotion at the post office earlier."

She nodded, her eyes wide. "He's a brute, isn't he? Nasty man."

"Yeah. So, anyway, Sheriff Kelly went to arrest him, but he made a break and—"

"Oh how thrilling! No one's ever escaped Sheriff Kelly's custody, not ever. I bet they'll put this on the front page of the town paper. Well, maybe the second page. The murder would go on the first. Do you think—"

I interrupted her before she got completely off-topic. "Kelly chased him, and he got away. Since I was there, he asked me to help him look for Richard. I think he might be hiding out in his brother's house since it's his own now. Do either of your parents have a key? I'd like to have a look and help the police out a little."

Instead of jumping to my aid like I expected, Fran got very shy. "Why do you want to help Sheriff Kelly?" she asked. "Didn't he arrest your sister-in-law or whoever?"

"Bella? Oh, she's Sev—Seb's cousin. Long story. But I was hoping he might take pity on her if I was helpful. She only slapped him, after all."

Fran nodded. "She did, I saw him. He was being mean to her. I heard what he called her. Good men don't use language like that to ladies."

"Right. So, keys?"

"Hmm." Fran tapped her lips with a finger. "I don't know if either of them had keys to Mr. Trask's house, but we can ask my father."

"Well I would, but here's the thing." How was I supposed to tell her I suspected her mother had a key because she'd been fooling around with her boss without saying it? "I know it's sort of strange I want to butter up Sheriff Kelly, and I don't want it getting around too much. More people I tell, the more likely it becomes an issue. So I thought, Fran will keep this quiet. She's so—" *Come on Alex, think of a word. You write for a living.* "—capable. She'd help you discreetly. And people are sometimes careful about things like keys. They put them in hidden places. I didn't want to go rooting through your house."

"Oh no, of course not!" Fran exclaimed, her eyes now wide again with the thrill of conspiracy and compliments. "I can have a look. I know where they put things they don't want other people to see. I used to find all my Christmas presents ages before they wrapped them, and they never knew."

"Well look at you, like a spy. I knew I made the right choice."

She giggled. I felt sick with myself.

"So, I'll meet you outside," I continued. "I'm going to go talk to your dad to make sure he doesn't bother you while you're looking."

"Good idea," she whispered, followed by another bout of giggling. She flitted to the staircase, apparently on her way to riffle through her parents' things.

Free from her, I slunk out the door and went around the back. As she said, her father hunched elbow-deep over the motor of his truck. He glanced up as I approached.

"Mr. Carrow," he said gruffly. "You looking for my wife or my daughter?"

"Neither, sir. I wanted to talk to you about Walter Trask."

The dead man's name got him to pause, at least. "What about him? He was a good enough boss and my best friend for twenty years. I know what you'll hear, but I have nothing bad to say about him."

"Huh, interesting. Because I'm fairly sure most men get jealous when their wives start having an affair with their best friend."

He fumbled the wrench in his hand, and the clang of it against the engine echoed into the otherwise quiet atmosphere. He stared at the block under his hands, frozen. I watched him very carefully. A wrench could be a pretty nasty weapon if he decided to attack me. But he didn't look angry, just very tired. His birdlike body slumped against the chassis of the truck.

"Who told you Louise was going around behind my back?" he muttered.

"It's pretty obvious, considering the fuss she made in the post office, and the fact she was torn up over Trask's death. More than his own fiancée. And I know you're getting a divorce. Fran told me."

He raised his head. "Damn that girl," he hissed. "Can't keep her mouth shut."

"Well, what were you planning to tell the neighbors when one of you moved out?"

"Business," he said. "We were going to say I went to Canada on business."

"Wouldn't they have noticed you weren't coming back?"

"Yeah, well, what do I care?"

"Are you still planning on going now that Walter is dead? You've got the whole factory now."

Oscar's eyes drifted back to the motor.

"Mr. Gaines."

His head snapped back up. "I know what it looks like, Mr. Carrow. I'm not an idiot. A man divorcing his wife over infidelity, and then the wife's lover turns up dead? And somehow he ends up inheriting the lover's business? I'm surprised Bobby Kelly isn't here with handcuffs to pull me in right now."

"So why isn't he?" I asked. "What benefit is it to him to leave you alone?"

Oscar didn't answer.

I sighed. "Listen, I don't give a shit about whatever squabbles are going on here. I don't care about your divorce or your wife's affair or Judith getting screwed over because of it. I just want to get Mrs. Ferri out of prison before she burns to death in there. So, tell me what you have on Robert Kelly, or I am going to call up some very powerful people in Boston to come here and have a sniff around. And I guarantee they'll be less nice about it than I will. I know you had to know Trask was smuggling with Leo Manco. You don't work with a man for twenty years without knowing at least some dirty secrets."

The air hung sticky and cloying between us. Would he believe my bluff? Apparently, he did because his shoulders sagged again.

"Yes, I knew Walter wasn't on the straight and narrow, and that he and Leo Manco were smuggling. I didn't care. They'd always drop a bottle off on my desk and that was it. But Kelly got wind of it and since it was before

Walter started sleeping with my wife, I thought I'd do him a favor and find some dirt on Kelly. Turns out the story we got told about his family was a pack of lies."

Oh good, one more reason to hate the bastard. "So, he doesn't have family in Boston?"

"Oh, he does. Even does have an uncle in the police force there. Dad's alive too, some Boston banker's youngest son who could charitably be called a troublemaker. Had a fling with a maid and nine months later, Grandpa has a screaming bundle of problems named Robert. There was some back and forth, but in the end, somehow they paid Momma enough for her silence and they trucked themselves out here. Understandably, he isn't keen on all that getting around, so when I told him I knew, he decided bootlegging was outside his paygrade." Oscar shrugged. "A little peace of mind for us."

I blinked at him. It was quite the story. Maybe it was even true. "How'd you find out?"

"Momma Kelly moved back to the city when Bobby turned eighteen, and at that point, she'd already been starting to lose her marbles a bit, so I thought, well, a couple years later maybe she'd tell me something that was supposed to stay secret. And I was right. She was being cared for in a home, a nice enough place though I don't know who's paying for it and she wouldn't have recognized her own mother if she walked in the door. Took a couple days, but I put it together. And the look on Bobby's face when I told him? I knew it was true."

My skin was crawling. Poor Fran had to live with these two horrible people? No wonder she was lunging after me. She probably thought I was her ticket out of town.

"Kind of awful to hold a man accountable for his father's sins, don't you think?" I asked.

Oscar shrugged. "I may not be a good man, Mr. Carrow, but I am wise enough to know when to use something to my advantage. Same as you."

The sick part was he wasn't wrong. I'd convinced his own daughter to snoop through his house for me. That was tolerable, though, right? It wasn't like I chased down a senile old lady to blackmail a cop. Still, I had to swallow my guilt. A smile quirked on Oscar's face. He could see my uneasiness, no doubt.

"You know what, Mr. Gaines?" I said, careful to keep my voice indifferent. "Fine. Let's say I almost believe you. What were you doing Thursday morning then? Because your wife says you weren't at work. She was there and has a dozen of your neighbors able to vouch her."

Oscar snarled, "Bitch."

"A bitch who would be very happy to see you carted off to prison, so maybe you tell me the truth about where you were before she starts spreading rumors about whatever she feels like."

He regarded me for a moment. "I was in Burlington overnight on business."

"Business?"

"I went to see the divorce lawyer, for your information. And I'll give you his number if you want. Walter was long dead before I got back in the evening."

He might have been lying. But if he was lying, why offer me anything? I could call the number provided and check his alibi. Hell, he hadn't even needed to do anything, just hop in the car and speed his way to the border. Within forty minutes, he would be scot-free, and that option had been there the whole time.

"I just want to know one more thing," I said.

Oscar rolled his eyes. "Yeah, what else?"

"What do you know about the Reeds?"

His eyebrows raised in surprise, and he glanced at the house. "Not much," he answered. "Why?"

"There's a possibility Leo Manco was killed by their boarder, and there's also a possibility the same person killed Walter."

Oscar chuckled. "Well, if that's the case, good luck. They're like ghosts. I think I've seen them maybe three times in the last ten years?"

I looked at the house myself. It was well taken care of despite being all but abandoned. "Who keeps it up?"

"Mrs. Manco, mostly. Some other people come by every now and then. Cleaning girls and gardeners and the like. Make it look lived in. But it seems like there's a different person living in there every summer."

Interesting, particularly the part about Crista being the main caretaker when she'd said she didn't have anything to do with the Reeds. If they weren't the ones paying her to clean and whatever else, who was? I wanted to know more, but it was clear I had worn out my welcome several questions ago. I tipped my hat to Oscar. "Thank you, Mr. Gaines. You've been very helpful."

He snorted and went back to tinkering with the car. Didn't even say goodbye.

I circled back to the front of the house, and Fran was waiting there. If she was trying to be discreet, she had failed miserably, practically bouncing on her feet. I groaned.

"There you are!" she exclaimed. I waved for her to take her voice down. She gasped and leaned in, only lowering her volume a little. "I think this might be it," she whispered as she pressed a key into my hand. "It was in

Mama's drawer."

I examined it. It looked like a house key, and the location made sense. "Thanks. Hey Fran, listen." God, I was going to hate myself for this. "I know your parents aren't always thinking about the best for you, so if they ever end up getting out of hand, you come to me, okay?"

Anybody walking by might have thought I asked her to marry me, she got so starry-eyed. "Thank you! You're so kind to say so."

I forced a smile onto my face. "You're welcome. Now, remember, I never asked for this key."

She nodded. "I won't tell a soul."

Unlikely, but there wasn't much of a choice at this point. I hoped she wouldn't embellish the story I'd fed her too much when she told the people in town. Then again, maybe she'd stall a little. People in love did all sorts of crazy things.

"Great. See you around," I said, and I bolted before she thought up another thing to say.

Chapter Seventeen

I HOVERED ON the threshold of Walter Trask's house, waiting for I didn't know what. At the rate I accumulated horrific coincidences, I almost expected to find Richard dead on the floor. But he wasn't. There was nothing; just an empty, quiet foyer. I stepped in and shut the door behind me.

The area around me had sunk into darkness, except from the beam of sunlight spearing its way into the gloom from an uncurtained window. Nothing there either. This already felt stupid. I'd put on a whole show for Oscar and Fran so I could look at dust on some rich guy's furniture?

"Richard?" I called. My voice fell flat against the plush chairs and Persian carpet.

I meandered, looking for any signs of forced entry, or anything at all to suggest I wasn't the only person in here. But my sweep of the first floor came up empty. No broken glass, no footprints, no sounds beyond my own breathing. The quiet sent a little shiver through me. I'd never get used to the silence and loneliness of this town. Maybe that was why they all swirled around one another so much, focusing on every cracked little rumor. If they didn't, they'd drown in their own isolation.

I was pretty convinced Richard wasn't here—either stymied by the locks or too wasted to think to squat in his new home—but Walter's presence was still fair game. I still didn't really know the man, only a faceless shadow on the cave of other peoples' lives. That was almost the saddest part. As soon as he died, it was like he hadn't been real. The only things left were the money and the lingering sense most people were better off without him.

The stairs were steep, and I got winded going up. At the top was an empty hall with four doors. Bedroom, bathroom, other bedroom. I opened the last door and froze; there was a figure in front of me. But another second, and I realized it was a painting: a life-sized painting of a man, hanging so the head was at eye level. It hung behind a desk in a garish frame. Trask's office. And presumably the painting was of himself. I dared to turn on a light to get a better look.

For someone approaching fifty, Walter Trask had been a good-looking man, if kind of angular. Deep-set eyes, high cheekbones, and a strong nose made him look almost like the blocky angels in the architecture of the Westwick newspaper offices, but maybe that was the artist getting carried away with art-deco trends. The painting had him in a thick coat against a background of snowy maples with his factory in the distance. Well, at least he hadn't had himself done up like some kind of urban bank manager.

I skimmed the desk. Sheets and sheets of copy paper. Organized, everything in triplicate. Odd that such a neat office keeper would find his way into rumrunning and the maple syrup business. Then again, how had I found myself in the detecting business? Sometimes life comes at us funny and we do what we can to not let it smack us around too badly. Hell, maybe the maple had been the cover and he'd always had ambition to be a criminal. I'd known a few boys back home who had aspired to be something like Sev was. Funny how Sev had wanted to be anything but.

I grabbed a stack of notebooks and began going through them. I'd nearly failed math several times as a child, and I remembered why when I looked at the columns of fluctuating numbers. I'd gotten Sev to go through cooked books back home, but I didn't want to bring him into this. Anyway, what would running the numbers prove? That Trask had been hiding whatever money Bella gave him in his factory finances? We knew that already. Still, I flipped them open one by one to make sure nothing jumped out. When I was satisfied, I dumped them back onto the desk.

Next, I went for the drawer. Office supplies. Aggravated, I shoved the drawer back into the slot. It made an odd thumping sound as I did. Strange. Nothing in there was big enough to make such a noise. I pulled the drawer out and inspected it again. Now that I was thinking, there were surprisingly few things in the drawer. I pulled it all the way out and flipped it. Pens, pencils, and paperclips fell out in a flutter, followed by another thump. I shook it, and after a pause, a false bottom fell out, followed by a notebook about the size of my hand. I chuckled to myself. No matter where I turned here, the past was right there waiting.

I picked up the notebook. This one had words, thank God. I almost kissed the damn thing—exactly what I'd been looking for. I picked a random page. It was dated at the top left and was covered in lines of even handwriting.

> *Dec. 5, 1933: So that's it for the rumrunning as of this morning. B promised she'd keep an ear to the ground about other opportunities, but I think I will have to focus on what my father left me instead.*

A journal. I flipped back some, skimming for details about Trask's life in his own words. It didn't look like he used full names, and why should he have? He knew these people, and he had probably never thought anyone else would see this, but it made for difficult reading on my part.

I got the rhythm after a while though. He'd been, as several people had already assured me, self-centered. Everything everyone did was in relation to how he felt. Bella kept him on the payroll because he was a genius at figuring ways past the border patrol. Oscar Gaines told him what to do too often, so he was a blowhard. While he respected what he called Judith's "shyness," he was preoccupied enough with the thought of bedding her that he used the closest available woman, which had apparently been Louise. And Louise he didn't mention besides her body. When he mentioned Richard, it was pure vitriol. Sometimes he would wax on about how their mother never liked when they fought, and how, since he was the older brother, it was his duty to fix things. And maybe if he did, Judith's father would get on board with the marriage. Maude was barely a footnote, his own daughter unnoticeable.

And then there was Crista. I expected more slobbery descriptors like he used with Judith, but he wrote about her like he'd write about his favorite schoolteacher—awe and respect and curiosity. And also, sad. I flipped around, trying to find mentions of her and puzzled it out. Trask had no doubt been infatuated with her, though whether he comprehended was difficult to tell. She mostly ignored him, as was fair since she was married.

I stumbled across the entries surrounding Leo's disappearance and death. To my surprise and slight disappointment, the blotted pages described everything the way Crista and Bella had told it: border run gone bad, separation, Leo likely killed by the border patrol. There was more detail, of course, some more interesting than the rest. Trask had refused to go looking for Leo or even insist on Kelly going to look for him on the grounds that it would seem suspicious, but between the lines, there was a greedy, hopeful tinge: if Leo never came back, maybe Crista would find comfort in someone else. He mentioned feeling bad about it several times, even going so far as to say he felt guilty once he realized Crista had been left in near-destitution and now hated him.

James Smith was brought up occasionally, but in about the same terms everyone else had: quiet, kept to himself, claimed he was on a hunting trip. Trask, however, had at least some suspicions about him. A mysterious man turning up with a gun just as someone else got killed? Trask never put the pieces together. He was too busy lusting after pretty much every woman who came into view.

I skipped forward to the last page, hoping something would be incriminating, but there was only more of the same, with an additional very dull twist about how next time he went into Burlington, he was going to buy more of the good kind of coffee. I flipped the pages back and forth. Something was missing. What had it been?

Then it occurred to me: the Reeds hadn't been mentioned, not once. Odd, considering Trask had supposedly known them and worked with them. Any of his thoughts about Smith should have been followed up with thoughts about them since it was their house he had rented. Who were the Reeds, really? I'd never gotten a straight answer about them. Did they even exist? And if they didn't, had Bella created fake people to blame if something went over badly, like Leo Manco dying? That would explain their continued absence and Crista's willingness to oversee an empty house. And *that* would mean Crista had been lying by omission, and that Bella knew *exactly* who came and went.

I shut the journal and looked up. The sunlight in the room had gotten more yellow, dimmer. Late afternoon. Damn, how long had I been up here? I chucked the book and all the other odds and ends back into the drawer, which I slipped back. Kelly probably wasn't going to start snooping, but better everything stay the way I found it just in case. A quick tour of the bedroom turned up nothing beyond Trask's apparent ability to wear holes into all of his socks. Random prodding at floorboards and molding on my way out showed an outstanding level of craftsmanship and zero secret compartments. I cursed my wasted time as I locked the door again.

I bounced the key in my pocket, wondering how I'd get it back into Mrs. Gaines's possession without her noticing or getting Fran involved again. Did I need to? It wasn't like she was going to use a copied key anymore, not unless she wanted to start a fling with Richard. The other option was to dump it somewhere. What would a random key in the middle of the woods matter?

Random like a piece of clear glass. Much stranger than footprints, come to think of it. Broken glass didn't spring out of the dirt on its own. Beverage bottle? Medication? Why would anyone bring those out there? There was a possibility the glass had been part of a distilling apparatus, but why would it have appeared months after bootlegging was no longer profitable?

I passed the sugaring mill and nearly gagged on the sweet smell. It stuck in my lungs like tar. If I ever got out of this town, I was never going to have maple syrup again.

As I approached the house, I noticed a small figure on the ground on one of the grass patches near the street. Richard, perhaps, collapsed? A chill curled around my shoulders. But no. By the time I'd taken a few steps, the figure had resolved itself into Pearl, surrounded by various toys having a tea party. I hurried to her.

"What're you doing out here?" I exclaimed. "Shouldn't you be in school?"

"School ended a while ago, and Mr. Sev said I could go out and play."

"By yourself?"

"He said if I stayed in the yard, it was okay. He said he'd be cooking if I needed anything."

I was going to kill him. Leaving Pearl alone outside with a murderer and God knew what else on the loose? "Well, time to come in." Ignoring her protest, I swept two of her toys up with one hand. "Pick up the teacups and come in now."

She scrambled to grab the small pieces of ceramic. I waited for her to finish before I marched her back toward the house. I shooed her in and shut the door behind us.

"Go up to your room, please," I said.

She hovered next to me in the hall. "Why?"

Because I'm about to rip the stuffing out of Sev, and I don't want you hearing it. "Because I said so."

"That's not fair!"

"I never said it was fair. Now go or I'll be—" I caught myself. What had I been going to say, that I'd belt her? My insides curled up at the very idea. Not my idea, my dad's.

Her dad's. The idea of angry men everywhere. Men I didn't want to be like. "Go or I'll tell Bella not to give you any more new toys."

Pearl's face twisted into an exaggerated visage of anger, and she huffed before stomping her way up the stairs. Just as she got to the top, Sev came hurrying out of the kitchen. Apparently, he'd heard the pocket-sized argument.

"What has she done?" he asked in confusion.

I grabbed his hand more forcefully than I'd meant to and dragged him back into the kitchen. Hopefully, Pearl wouldn't hear us at this distance. Daisy skittered out of the way, my stalking steps almost crushing her tail.

I spun to face Sev. "What were you thinking"—the words came out of my mouth as almost a growl—"letting her play all the way out there alone?"

His eyes widened in alarm. "Why, where was she? In the street?"

"Almost on Main."

The distress turned back to confusion. "But that's less than fifty feet away."

"Yeah, and that's forty-nine fucking feet too far."

"You can't be serious. There's nothing out there—"

"First of all, there are bears. Second, there's a *murderer* out there—"

"Bears would not be in our yard. And the murder has nothing to do with her. Why should whoever killed Mr. Trask want to hurt a little girl who wasn't even there when it happened?"

"I don't know. Maybe she'll see something. Or hear something. And then she talks." My voice cracked as I lowered it. "That's why Emma and Logan decided to off Martin. Pearl got to talking, and they figured he knew too much and would piece it together, so they killed him." I was almost in tears now. "What if someone doesn't like the questions I'm asking and decides to take it out on her? Or you?"

Sev didn't answer for a moment, just stared at me. God, why couldn't I see his thoughts on his face like he could apparently see mine? Slowly he said, "We brought her with us because you wanted her to have a more normal life, yes? So, you should not stop her from being a child because you're afraid."

Afraid? Oh, I was way beyond afraid. I was dancing somewhere between petrified and about to throw up. And not just afraid. Guilty, depressed, adrift. Missing Martin and Donnie more than words could say. Paranoid that my nosiness was going to get us all killed. I was falling through space, and there was nothing to hold on to. Nothing except a rag doll and a teddy bear apparently.

"Alex?"

My attention snapped back to Sev. This time I *could* read the concern and confusion in his expression. I swallowed.

"You're right," I murmured. "Sorry."

"You should tell Pearl, not me."

"Oh, right."

Almost absently, I turned to go upstairs, thinking of all the things I needed to apologize to Pearl for. Sorry I'd snapped, sorry I'd sent her to her room for no reason. Sorry for dragging her down with me...

"Alex." I turned back at Sev's voice. His gold eyes tracked across my face. "Did you want to talk about something else?"

Embarrassment flamed up the back of my neck. "No."

I hustled out of the kitchen before he called me out on my terrible lying skills. Fortunately, he didn't follow me. Unfortunately, that meant I had to sort everything out with Pearl on my own.

She sat on her bed cross-legged, hunched and pouting, with the occasional overdramatic sniffle as punctuation. Daisy had beat me up the stairs and was now curled in a ball next to Pearl's knee. She blinked at me but headbutted Pearl's hand until she relented and petted her.

I knocked on the doorframe. "Can I come in?"

Pearl glared. "No. You were mean."

"I know. And I wanted to say I'm sorry."

She unfolded herself. "Yeah?"

"Yeah. You didn't do anything wrong, but I was angry about something else, and I took it out on you, and I shouldn't have done that."

"You can come in."

Some of the guilt I held lifted off my shoulders as I crossed the threshold and sat next to Pearl. After a second of consideration, she burrowed her way under my arm to lean against me. I tucked the toys I'd accidentally stolen behind her.

"I like being outside," she said.

"I know. I'm glad Sev let you go out. I've been keeping you too cooped up here, and I'm sorry for that too. After everything, I just want you to be safe." I hugged her a little closer. "I promised Martin I'd take care of you."

She raised her face to me, and her green eyes seemed enormous. "Are you?"

"Absolutely. I won't let anything else bad happen to you, I promise."

She kept staring. God, those questioning eyes were going to kill me. "Mr. Martin said that, but then he died."

I sighed. "All right, I can't protect you from everything, but I'm going to try my best. And we're going to make Martin proud, okay? We're going to do our best all the time."

"Do you miss him?"

"Every day."

She nodded. That was enough proof for a six-year-old. After a beat of silence, she said, "Can I ask you something else?"

"Sure, what is it?"

"How did Mr. Sev get the scar down his face?"

"Well it's not an interesting story," I said, scraping through my brain for something innocuous to say since the truth—that he'd been cut up for being queer while in prison waiting for his murder trial—was not child—friendly. "Machining accident. A part broke off and *pfft*! Caught him right in the face."

"He said he got it from a fight."

Well, close. "Did you ask him to tell you? Because you can't ask people about their scars. It's rude."

"He said he didn't mind. I like Mr. Sev. He's nice."

This kid was *definitely* trying to kill me. "Yeah, he is."

"He's nice to Daisy too."

"Of course, he is. Daisy is great." I dared reach across and graze my fingers against the cat's body. She gave me an eye and made a sound that wasn't quite a growl and went back to laying quietly. Oh good, an improvement in one relationship.

As I got up to leave, Pearl tugged my hand. "Alex?"

"Yeah?"

"Can I go back outside?"

I nodded. "Go have fun."

She sprang up with an exclamation of joy and snatched her toys from where I'd placed them. Daisy spooked and bolted under the bed. Ignoring her, Pearl hugged me and started for the door.

"You're nice too!" she called over her shoulder.

My face burned. *Nice.* I'd bullied a woman into admitting her affair and tricked a sick man into talking to me. I'd leveraged a teenage girl's fascination with me into getting her to steal. I'd implied blackmail to a man, so he'd tell me secrets. I'd broken into a dead man's house. Plus, I was sniping at the two people I loved most in the world. None of those things were nice, and that was just what I'd done *today*. Amazing how the sins piled up. What would Donnie and Martin say if they could see me now?

Chapter Eighteen

I WENT DOWN the stairs cautiously, not sure what I'd find. Sev was sitting on the couch, reading. As I got closer, I realized the book was the damaged copy of the one novel I'd gotten published. He didn't look at me as I stepped into the living room.

"Back to that old thing?" I asked.

He continued to not look at me. "If you write something new, I will read it instead."

I glanced at my typewriter. I hadn't worked on a project in almost a month, and I couldn't see myself starting something new anytime soon. Stupid me, I should have gotten him something out of the library while I was over there. I should have—

No, stop. This isn't helping.

"I thought your aunt threw it out for being smut," I said.

The corner of his mouth twitched like he was trying not to smile, but he still didn't look. "She saw sense when I reminded her what the Romans sometimes painted on their walls." He raised his head. "Are you ready to talk now?"

"Yeah." He shifted over, and I slumped next to him. "I'm sorry about today. And yesterday. And Saturday. I don't even know what got into me. I—"

"Already forgiven." He slid an arm around me. "I want to make sure you're all right, *caro*." He stared me in the eye. "I know all of this is hard."

I almost couldn't look at him. Yes, it was hard—insanely hard—but it couldn't be any harder for me than it was for him. He'd left far more than me and, as he'd mentioned, had the burden of having actually killed Emma Carlisle instead of being the idiot who'd been too cowardly to do it.

I leaned against his shoulder. "I'll be better. I promise."

He didn't answer, and I realized he was waiting for me to continue. But what else was there to say? I couldn't very well start listing all my personal tragedies when I knew his tragedies had to be at least as bad as mine.

"As long as you're all right." He kissed my cheek. "So, should I tell you what I learned from that horrible Mrs. Gaines?"

"Is she was having an affair with Walter Trask?"

His eyebrows raised. "How did you find out?"

"Crista told me this morning."

"Oh. Though I expect everyone knows now. Mrs. Gaines screamed at her husband when he came in. She said quite a lot of things. That she wished her husband was dead instead of Mr. Trask and she'd have done it herself if she'd gotten the chance. Such a temper!"

"Temper enough to kill a man in a fit of rage?"

"Perhaps." Sev ran his fingers through my hair. "What would she kill him for?"

"Well, he *was* engaged to Judith Howe, and a couple people tell me he was at least trying to play it straight for her. Maybe he told Mrs. Gaines to get lost. Or maybe she found out he had a kid."

"He did?"

"Does. And she lives in town. Maude Lamar, the dry-cleaning woman. Who still has your suit. Sorry."

Sev waved a hand. "Never mind. What do you know about her?"

"Maude? Not a whole lot. She and her mom are Canadian. She came here to confront Trask, but he didn't care." I paused over how to say the rest. Her relationship with Judith wasn't my secret to tell. "She fell in love and stayed."

"Who told you?"

"She did."

Sev shifted away from me and gaped at me like I'd lost my mind. "And you believe her?"

"What, you think she hung around for five years to kill him? Why wait that long? And if you were going to wait, why do it so obviously?"

"People are not always predictable. Many little things add up. How long was Mrs. Carlisle married to the mayor? Ten years? More?"

Well, he had a point. What proof did I have Maude *hadn't* gone out to kill Trask? Just the men's shoes? Those were easy enough to buy or steal. "I guess I have to find out if she has an alibi," I said. "I have to get the suit tomorrow anyway. Maybe I can—"

Knocking interrupted me. I glanced out the window. Crista. This time she was expected. So much for me attempting dinner.

Sev stood, using my knee as leverage. "I assume you will be polite to her today?"

I ducked my head so he wouldn't see me flush. "Yeah."

"*Bene.*" He brushed past me to answer the door, a beaming smile on his face.

I MANAGED THROUGH dinner without making an ass of myself, though I could have *sworn* she made eyes at Sev half the time. But I'd promised I'd be better, and she was gone soon enough.

The night settled in, humid and dark, and—as had become normal for me—full of nightmares: *Blood and screaming. Gunshots. The flash of iron against Emma's throat. A shattered vase of white irises. Pearl weeping in my arms. Bells—*

Bells? I snapped awake, the noise having intruded on my recurring nightmare. I reached for my alarm clock instinctively, only to remember I still didn't have one. I peered into the darkness. Had I imagined it? "Oh, the phone!" I exclaimed to myself.

Phone calls in the middle of the night were never good. I scrambled down the stairs, only to stop short to avoid colliding with Sev, who was exiting his room. He glanced at me only for a second—not even long enough for me to read his expression—and hurried to the kitchen. I followed, skidding on the wooden floor.

He snatched the receiver midring. "*Pronto?*"

I waited, panting. The night sank into my skin, lying heavily against the sweat refusing to dry around my neck. Why should I be so panic-stricken when everyone I cared about was accounted for?

Still, I watched Sev's face. Bad news for him was bad news for me. His eyes, normally gold and full of easy pleasantness, darted around and narrowed. He chattered rapid Italian into the phone.

"What's going on?" I whispered.

He held up a hand to keep me quiet. Another burst of Italian; then he hung up. He shook his head in disbelief. "Someone broke into Crista's house," he said.

Oh. Not quite what I had been expecting. "Wait, how did she even call? She doesn't have a phone."

"She's with Miss Howe and her father. She screamed and they ran, and she ran for help."

"If she got help, what's she calling us for?"

"She thinks it has something to do with Mr. Trask's death." Sev grunted and slid past me into the hall. "I'm going to go get her."

I wandered after him, unsure what my role in this was supposed to be. "Should I come with you?"

"What's happening?" I looked up. Pearl clutched the rungs of the stair rail like a prisoner at the bars. "What's wrong?" she asked.

"Nothing's wrong. Go back to bed."

Sev ignored her and grabbed the car keys off the sideboard before ducking back into his room. He returned a few seconds later with his shoes and a dressing gown thrown over his shoulders. One of the pockets had something in it—his knife, no doubt. Pearl took in the scene and started creeping down the stairs. Daisy appeared on the landing and began her own descent. Great.

"Stay here with her," Sev whispered. "I'll be right back."

He smiled briefly and squeezed my arm. When he released me, he let his fingers linger before he swept out the door. As soon as he was gone, the only thing I heard was the thumping of my heartbeat.

Pearl stared up at me, shaking. "Alex?"

"It's fine. It's fine," I said as I took her hand. "Come here, we're going to watch him from the window, okay? He's going to get Crista. Something scared her, so she's going to stay here."

I scooted Pearl to the couch. Luckily for my blood pressure, I heard the Oldsmobile igniting and revving, and I had a clear view of most of the street from the window. Once the car pulled out of the drive, its lights beamed in the humid night. As they turned to pinpricks, I began thinking about how odd it was Crista's house had been broken into.

No, more than odd. This might be a trap. If she was with Judith and her father, she was safe already, so why bother calling? Just because she suspected someone burgling her house might have something to do with Trask's death? That couldn't wait until morning? All I had were rumors about what had happened to her husband, and I didn't have anything even half as vague when it came to Trask. What had I said when she was present? Had I accidentally implied I was getting too close?

"Alex," Pearl whispered, "are you scared too?"

What was the point in lying to her? "Yeah, I am."

"Mr. Martin said it's okay to be scared because that's when you can be brave."

Dammit, Martin. Even from beyond the grave, he was better than I was. "Tell you what, we're going to count to one thousand. And if Sev isn't back by the time you finish, we're going to…" Oh God, what were we going to do? I couldn't very well chase after him weaponless with Pearl in tow. "We will call the police to help us."

Pearl gave me a skeptical look. "They put Miss Bella in jail though."

"It was an honest mistake." Great, back to lying. "We're working on fixing it. Maybe we don't even need them. We have to get to one thousand first. You can count that high, right?"

She answered with an enthusiastic yes and proceeded to number the seconds. Fortunately, she only got somewhere in the seven hundred range before the car came rumbling back. I sprang off the couch to the porch, keeping an eye on Daisy to make sure she didn't make another break for it.

Sev guided Crista out of the car and she clung to him. I found some consolation in her disheveled appearance— an unflattering gingham housedress and ratty slippers, not to mention clumps of mussed hair. She took the stairs quietly, too small and light to make the boards creak, but sniffled the whole way.

"Pardon me, Mr. Carrow," she whimpered. "I look like a mess."

"Yeah, well, I always look like Clark Gable at two a.m. myself." I herded them in and shut the door. Sev nudged her toward the couch, where Pearl still sat wide-eyed. "What happened? Did they take anything?" I asked.

Crista shook her head as she sat. "I don't know. I heard the crash and went downstairs and saw someone breaking things, and I screamed, and they ran, and I ran for help. Miss Howe is so good to let me use their telephone."

Yeah, good. But not good enough to let her stay or offer to call the cops? "Why didn't you stay with them?" I asked.

"I am not stupid. Do you think I am not suspicious that my house is broken into right after I inherit money? Miss Howe is a nice girl, but he gave her nothing even though they are to be married and gives it to me instead. Very unfair of him." Crista glared. "But I don't even know why he left me money. I don't even want his money, the bastard." She made a spitting gesture. "Of course, he keeps ruining my life even after he's dead."

Pearl flinched at the sudden anger. It was very much time for her to go back to bed. Sev also noticed.

"*Gattina*," he called. "You are up so late past your bedtime. Let me take you back up, hmm?"

She hesitated a second before taking his offered hand, her eyes darting between the three of us. Eventually she gave in and let Sev lead her toward the stairs. Daisy prowled after them.

I waited until both cat and girl were out of sight before I said anything else. "Did you see anything about the person who broke in?" I asked. "Man, woman? Were they tall?"

Crista's face crinkled. "Do you see how short I am? Everyone is tall to me!"

"Okay, well, were they more Sev's height, or my height?"

She shrugged. "Not so short as Mr. Arrighi."

Right, taller than five seven. Not Judith Howe since she was considerably shorter. Not her father either, since he probably wouldn't be able to move fast or at all without hacking up a lung.

"So, you think this has to do with Trask?" I asked.

"What else would it be?"

Well, here went nothing. "Something to do with Leo's death, which seems to be getting dragged up a lot." I looked her in the eye. "What else has Bella done for you? Because, yeah, it's very nice you're friends, but I *know* you're not telling me something, and keeping your mouth shut is only keeping us from getting her out of jail."

Crista looked away for a moment. "She saved me," she whispered.

"From?"

"Did you ever hear of a man named Salvador Sarto? He ran a speakeasy on a side street off Beacon."

"Not up on my small-time Boston gangsters, sorry."

"It's just as well. He wasn't a pleasant man to know. An even worse man to be married to. And Bella knew. We'd all grown up in the same village in Italy as children. So when she figured out what was happening, she arranged for me to get away. She was sending Leo up here anyway, and it's quiet, and it used to be safe."

"Were you and Leo already a couple or?"

A faint smile crept up Crista's face. "No, I didn't meet him until he picked me up. But it was *ver'amore*, love at first sight. But we couldn't get married, not really, unless I called for an annulment, and if I did that, Sal would find out. But he disappeared. When I asked, Bella said she'd made sure he'd never hurt me again."

"And you didn't think that was important to tell me?"

"This was over eight years ago!"

Of course, Sev picked that moment to come back downstairs. "I just got Pearl to calm down," he hissed. "What are you arguing about?"

I took a breath before answering. "I'm trying to figure out if Leo's death has anything to do with Trask's. There was a man here a couple years ago when Leo died named James Smith, and that is a fake name if I ever heard one, and I am ninety percent sure he's responsible for Leo's murder."

Sev blinked at me. "Who— When did you decide this?"

Shit, had I forgotten to tell him about James Smith? Ugh, there were too many things running through my head. "It doesn't matter. What's important is Leo and Trask were working together, so it's possible that if Smith bumped Leo off, then maybe he did Trask too. So." I turned back to Crista. "Your first husband, Sal Sarto. He have family? Friends? And more importantly, did James Smith look like any of them?"

"Don't bully her," Sev muttered.

"I'm not bullying her. I just want her to answer a question."

"Well the answer is no," snapped Crista. "He had no one who would dare cross Bella. They were far more afraid of her than she was of them."

"And yet she's afraid to set foot out of her jail cell right now."

Crista sighed. "Mr. Carrow, I have told you everything now. If I knew the answers to your questions, I would give them. Do you think I like being scared? Not knowing what is happening?"

Sev laid a hand on my arm. "*Basta*. We are all tired and not in the right state to be discussing this." He nodded at Crista. "You will stay here overnight. You can stay in my room, and I will stay out here by the door in case of anything."

What was he doing, inviting this woman to sleep here? She was lying, or if not lying, at least holding something back. She had to know the Reeds were imaginary, and if she knew that, then she probably knew who James Smith was. And if she knew *that*, what else did she know? How could I prove her supposed break-in was even real?

"You can't be serious," I said.

Sev frowned. "Why am I not serious?"

It was too much to explain. And if Crista *was* hiding something, and I pulled the rug out from under her, who knew what she would do. "I mean, we're going to leave her house all trashed?"

"We can help her clean in the morning."

"And give whoever broke in a chance to come back?" I looked to Crista. "What if they're looking for something? Now there's no one in there, they can take whatever they want. Or maybe they left something! We have to go back. At least to check."

Sev shook his head. "I don't think we should leave Crista and Pearl alone—"

"I'll go. You can stay here with them if you want. I can do it by myself. Don't worry about me."

Sev sighed. "I would feel better if you waited until morning, but you know what, Alex? Do what you want."

I stood there awkwardly. Not quite what I had anticipated. Or wanted. But if I backed out now, I would look very silly indeed. So, I stumbled upstairs and threw on a set of clothes before coming back. Crista still sat on the couch, shaking.

Sev shoved a flashlight into my hands. I hadn't even known we had one in the house. "I assume you're walking?" he said.

Breathe. "I'll be back soon."

I went for the door, and Sev's brows came together like somehow what I was doing confused him. Well, if he hadn't wanted me to call his bluff, he shouldn't have presented the option. I stomped out the door.

My annoyance carried me all the way to the library before the logical part of my brain kicked in. What was I doing walking over a mile in a strange place with nothing but a flashlight and indignation? Ed's warning about bears came creeping back to me. And, honestly, who was to say the person who had broken into Crista's wasn't lying in wait somewhere, ready to pounce?

I paused, holding my breath, listening. Just cicadas and crickets. I shone the light against all the nearest

214 - | Thea McAlistair

houses. No movement, not even glowing eyes in the darkness. Somehow that made my uneasiness worse. The emptiness of this place choked me. I'd been an idiot, I needed to go back—be with Sev and Pearl and—

No, I was doing this. I was going to show Sev and Crista and anyone else who cared to think of me as incapable that I was worth something. And hey, the only time I could say I was brave was if I was scared first. I sped up. If anyone was stalking me, they would have a hard time keeping up. *See, the indignation is worth something.*

Crista's house loomed out of the darkness, a ramshackle shadow. I climbed the stairs, and they squeaked almost as loud as the cicadas. The weak beam of the flashlight fell on the shattered window next to the front door. So, she hadn't completely made it up. I squinted at the glass. There didn't seem to be any blood on the broken bits, which showed the trespasser had put at least enough thought into this to cover their hand.

I jiggled the door handle, but it was locked. I sighed. Silly thing to do when I could reach right in and undo it. However, unlocking the bolt proved easier said than done. It took some contorting on my part, and even then, I barely reached the knob. Judith hadn't done this—her arms were far too short. Of course, Crista still might have done it herself and not noticed such a little detail.

The place was trashed. The rocking chair had been tossed against the stone fireplace, where it had broken into several pieces. The rug was crumpled and displaced, and the couch was no longer flush against the wall. I took a step forward, window glass crunching beneath my feet, and shone the light into the corners. No one was there.

I let go of the breath I'd been holding and realized there was something off. The last time I'd been in here, it had smelled of bread. Now it smelled of whiskey. I'd know the stench anywhere. I followed the scent like a hound and discovered the source under the overturned chair. I picked up the flask from the puddle of its own contents. I doubted Crista had owned such a thing, which meant the burglar had brought it in. I turned the flask over in my hands. It was old and dented and dull. While a flask wasn't uncommon, one in such poor condition could only belong to someone as destitute as Richard Trask. I stuffed it into a pocket to be evidence in the morning.

Lights reflected in the remaining window glass. I froze. Who had a car? Mr. Gaines had a truck, but aside from him, I had no idea. I flattened myself against the wall and pushed the curtain aside. Blinded by headlights as the car curved, my heart beat faster. But as I blinked and the spots dissolved, I realized the car was the borrowed Oldsmobile. I sighed in relief and made my way to the porch as Sev stepped out of the car.

"I thought you didn't want to leave them?" I whispered.

He looked up at me, and I couldn't quite see his face in the dark, but his tone was enough to tell me I was in deep trouble. "I didn't want to, but I had to go running after you, didn't I?"

My cheeks burned up again. If I wasn't careful, they'd go permanently red. Without giving him the satisfaction of me speaking to him, I slank down the stairs to the car. He huffed as he got back in. The roar of the engine cut through the static silence humming in my ears. Well, at least he'd come after me. That had to count for something, right?

"So, where are they?" I asked.

He glanced at me from the corner of his eye as he slid the car back onto the road. "I told Crista to go into Pearl's room and lock the door."

I nodded. Was it possible to die of shame? Maybe I'd be the first, and doctors would exclaim over the medical oddity. Maybe Vern would be able to squeeze something about it into the *Westwick Journal*.

"And did you find anything useful?" Sev grunted after a few moments of silence.

"Maybe." I dug the empty flask out of my pocket. "I think this is Richard Trask's."

He peeked at it before turning his eyes back to the road. "That could be anyone's."

"Well it's not yours, and it's not mine, and I don't think it's Crista's." Already the house was in view, so I condensed my speech. "Look, you didn't meet him. He's not a pleasant guy. Kinda unstable." I touched the bruise he'd given me. Most of it was hidden by my hair, but it was still sore even if no one could see it. "I wouldn't put it past him."

"If you say so, *caro*." Sev pulled the car up next to the house. "But I still think you should have waited until daylight."

I wasn't about to admit I was wrong, not after that whole production, so I kept quiet. I hopped out of the car, the flask and the flashlight still clutched in my hands. Once we got in, I shoved the flask into the desk drawer while Sev coaxed Crista back downstairs. I saw her before he herded her into the bedroom: terrified and relieved all at once.

"Hey, Sev?" I called as he left her. He turned to me. He looked exhausted and, frankly, a little nervous. Had my reckless trip upset him that much? "Why don't you go upstairs?" I said. "I'll stay down here. I won't be able to sleep anyway."

He hesitated. "Are you sure?"

"Yeah. Consider it an apology for having to come after me."

"Alex."

"I'm serious. Go."

He raised a hand like he wanted to touch me and then thought better of it and let it drop. "Thank you," he whispered.

Heat rose in my cheeks again. "Don't mention it."

His typical half smile hovered on his lips as his gaze lingered on me for longer than it should have. What did that mean? I thought about asking, but he was already on the stairs, and I was left in the foyer. Alone.

Chapter Nineteen

AS EXPECTED, I didn't get much sleep after the mayhem. Even if I had wanted to, the sun poured in through the window by half-past six. The sun's appearance was followed by Crista's. She stood awkwardly in the doorway to Sev's bedroom.

"I am sorry about last night," she said. "I didn't mean to upset everyone."

"Not your fault," I mumbled as I tried to rub the exhaustion out of my eyes. "Do you want me to get Mr. Arrighi to drive you back?"

"I can cook breakfast first, if you'd like. In thanks."

My stomach was too knotted up to even think about food, and I wasn't keen on Crista staying in the house longer than necessary until I got to the bottom of whatever she was hiding, but Sev and Pearl were probably hungry.

"Well, lemme ask what he wants to do," I said. "Maybe we should all spring for something at the diner instead?"

I stumbled past her and up the stairs only to find Sev already awake. He smiled at me as he tied his robe. "Oh, I'm surprised you're up," he said.

I stifled a yawn. "Crista's up too. Asking if she should make breakfast."

He shrugged. "Why not? Maybe she will make something that isn't eggs."

"Do we even *have* anything that isn't eggs?"

"Well, there's oatmeal."

"Pearl won't eat oatmeal," I said.

"Maybe Crista can convince her to try it."

"Bella couldn't even get her to try it."

"Alex," he sighed. "You're arguing for the sake of it now. Just say what you're thinking and save us some trouble."

Just say? Just say? How could I? There were a hundred thousand things to say, I'd never get through them all. Crista was probably lying to us. Louise Gaines was a despicable woman, and her husband nearly as bad. Wallace and Kelly were a couple of jokes, if not downright obstructionist. Richard Trask was a drunk who had assaulted and now burglarized people. Not to mention Bella refusing to tell me anything.

And that was just about the murder. I felt more and more like I was going insane, like I was falling and couldn't catch myself. My only two friends were dead, and Martin's was all my fault. If I'd left well enough alone, kept my mouth shut, maybe he'd still be alive. And I'd, what, dragged Fran along on a hook earlier because it was convenient? What part of me had thought that was acceptable? Why was that part winning?

And here Sev was, expecting me to blurt out all. And the even more crazy part was I wanted to. I wanted to tell him I wasn't who he thought I was, and he should leave me and not look back. Because what had I brought him but pain? I'd made him leave his family, his job, his home because I had a big mouth and a nose for trouble. He couldn't love me that much; he couldn't.

"You're making faces, *caro*," he huffed. "What's wrong?"

The now-familiar heat flowed through me. He wanted to know what was wrong? I'd start with the simplest. "Fine," I snapped. "I want to know what the hell is going on with you and Crista."

"What?"

"You're always gossiping and flirting with her. Favoring her. Don't think I don't notice."

He gaped at me. "I'm not going to even dignify that with an answer."

"It's not crazy. I can see it happening. If you're saying it's not happening, then you're saying I'm crazy for seeing it."

He sighed. "That is not what I meant."

Why couldn't he get angry? If he would yell with me, maybe I could let it all go and everything could go back to how it was. But no, it couldn't go back. There was nothing to go back to.

"Get out of my room," I growled.

"Alex, you're being childish—"

"I said get out."

I pushed his arm. He apparently hadn't been expecting it and stumbled back a step, his head smacking into the low ceiling. He flinched. All at once, my anger sank away, leaving me staring in horror.

"Oh, Christ, I'm so sorry! I didn't mean it," I squeaked.

He didn't respond except to look at the floor with betrayal scrawled across his face. He raised his head and straightened his robe. "I will see you downstairs when you're ready," he said as calmly as he had ever said anything to me, but still not meeting my eyes.

He swept out of the room and down the stairs, too quickly to be natural. It was only as he reached the bottom

I noticed Pearl was peeking out of her room. If she hadn't seen me shove him, she had heard. Shit.

Instead of doing the smart thing and going after Sev or trying to talk to Pearl, I panicked and slammed the door, trapping myself in my room. Breathless with remorse, I leaned against the frame.

Now look what you've done. Sev hates you. Pearl hates you. Bella's going to die in prison. You're going to be stuck in this flea-bitten town. Broke. Homeless. Alone.

And I was really alone. Donnie and Martin couldn't bail me out anymore. They weren't even there to give me a stern look, to warn me off whatever terrible thing I'd come up with. Was this who I was without them?

I continued to wallow until I heard the door open and close and the car start up. A glance at my watch showed I'd been pouting for over two hours. Part of me was furious no one had bothered to check up on me before leaving, but why should they have? Clearly, I wasn't in any state to be talked to like a civil person.

If only we hadn't come here. No, actually, if only someone hadn't decided to off Walter Trask as we were driving up. Then Bella wouldn't have had any reason to come up or get arrested. I wouldn't have spent the last few days hunting down irritating neighbors instead of being with Sev and Pearl. Maybe I would have learned to cook so Crista wouldn't have had to come around every day. But no, someone had killed him and then someone had broken into Crista's house, making her cry and then she'd had to go and call and—

Wait, I knew who had broken into her house. It was Richard's flask hidden in my desk. I was sure of it. Why had he tried to burgle her? Just to cause trouble? Or was he trying to cover up something? There was only one way to know: I was going to have to find him.

Listening at the door, I didn't pick up any sounds from downstairs. A quick pace around the house revealed only Daisy's presence. Presumably Sev had taken Pearl to drop Crista off, but my brain started doing circles, convinced they had run off and left me. I shoved the thought away and cleaned up. I wanted to be out of sight by the time they got back, and more importantly, I wanted to punch Richard Trask in the face.

I STORMED INTO the library. "Arthur!" I called, letting my voice boom through the otherwise silent building. "Where is Richard?"

Arthur jumped in his seat, sending papers scattering. "Mr. Carrow, I would like to think you know better than to shout in here."

I stomped up to the desk. I was in no mood at all for being chastised by a human beanpole. "I want to know where Richard Trask is right now."

"Whatever do you—"

"Crista Manco's house got broken into last night, and I have reason to believe it was him. So, quit sheltering some good-for-nothing drunk, and tell me where he's hiding."

Arthur straightened and stilled his face into something more severe than I expected. "He is not here, Mr. Carrow, and you are welcome to check. I told you I would lock the door to him, and I am a man of my word. He has disturbed the peace of many of the ladies in town and has caused Mr. Kelly quite a bit of distress as well. I will not allow him in again."

Pretty speech for a man sitting behind a desk all day, but pretty speeches weren't always the truth. I swept into the stacks, scanning every person-sized hiding spot and even squinting into some smaller ones. No Richard. No one at all. Just the stacks of books going dusty. I stomped back to Arthur and his desk.

"Are you satisfied, Mr. Carrow?" he huffed.

"I'm only satisfied that he's not here. Any ideas where else he might be hiding?"

"No. I don't think anyone has seen him since yesterday. Though I heard a rumor" —he leaned in and lowered his voice, as if there were anyone else in the room to hear—"that he was the one who killed Walter and has hopped the border to escape the police."

"He what?"

He looked at me over the top of his glasses. "Just repeating what I heard. I can't say one way or the other."

"Who told you?"

Arthur shrugged. "A few people. I believe they heard it from Miss Gaines. You must know by now how that child loves to gossip."

Well, he wasn't wrong. I sighed. The last thing I wanted to do on a total of four hours of sleep was ask Fran where she'd heard about Richard's escape, or worse, have to talk her into admitting she'd made it up for attention. I muttered my thanks and left.

Someone almost ran into me as I stepped out the doorway. They mumbled an apology and kept going. I looked in the direction they were headed. A small parade of people was hurrying down one of the side streets. The one Walter Trask's house was on, in fact. Possibly coincidental, but considering my luck, probably not. I followed.

The parade turned into a crowd in front of the brick building I'd snuck into yesterday. That couldn't be good. I edged around people until I got to the front. The door was swung wide open and Officer Wallace stood on the threshold blocking the way.

"What happened?" I asked.

"Ain't your business," he answered.

"Huh, like it's not my business what you read on the weekends?"

His face went flame red.

"Great, so you're going to let me in before I turn around and tell everyone here, right?"

Still flushed, he edged just enough to the side so I could slip past him. There was some general mumbling behind me asking why I was being allowed in, but Wallace shut it down with some sharp words.

It took my eyes a few seconds to adjust from the bright sunlight outside to the dim foyer. The shapes of furniture loomed beyond. A person stood amongst them—Kelly, hands on his hips, looking up. Confused, I followed his line of sight.

Well, I'd found Richard Trask. Too bad he was hanging by his neck from the balustrade of the second-floor landing.

Kelly turned. On seeing me, he glared and said, "Should have known you'd show up."

"What happened?" I asked.

"I imagine he hanged himself. Note was on the table."

I glanced over—there was indeed a scrap of paper under a weight on one of the solid side tables. I hurried over before Kelly stopped me. In bold, almost elegant cursive the note said:

> *I killed Walter, and I am sorry. May God forgive me. —Richard*

Remarkably smooth handwriting for a fidgety drunk. If Richard had written this note, then I was the King of England.

"How'd he get in here?" I asked.

Kelly rolled his eyes "The back door was broken in if you must know, but that's the last you're hearing from me. Wallace! Get this man out of here!"

Wallace's gripped my shoulder and pulled me out. For a split second, I considered fighting him, but what good would it have done except get me in more trouble? He dumped me outside with the other spectators.

I WAITED AROUND for what felt like forever before an ambulance crew arrived and got the poor drunk bastard down. Richard's death wasn't suicide, that was clear. He finally had the house and no brother to share it with. And he hadn't seemed like the type of person who wore guilt like a mantle. But Kelly didn't see it like that. Richard, the troublemaker, was dead, and his note tied up Walter's murder nicely. Two birds with one stone, as far as he was concerned.

They brought the body out covered by a sheet, and I watched the sad procession from a few feet away while Wallace shooed off the townspeople who weren't blackmailing him. Should I let them go without voicing my suspicions? These deaths didn't concern me. In fact, they helped me. If Richard was decided to be the killer, Kelly would have to let Bella out of jail. I glanced at the sheriff. He frowned at me.

"There, are you happy?" I said. "Now let me post whatever the bail is for assault and let Bella go."

He watched me as the stretcher headed toward the

ambulance. "Richard might have killed Walter," he said, "but I still can't prove she didn't assist him."

"Oh, come on! Even you have to know that's bullshit. Let the lady out."

"She's not a lady, Mr. Carrow. She's a fire-breathing harpy with a gang of cronies stretching from Maine to Delaware. I know it, you know it, and the feds know it. The thing is no one's ever been able to tie her to anything until now. So, I will hold her for assault and keep holding her until something else settles into the pan or she decides to make it easy."

"So, you're torturing her because you can," I growled.

"I'm not doing anything she wouldn't do, given the chance." He began to step away. "Brother-in-law's cousin. Seems like an odd person to care about."

Of course, he was trying to pin me. I shrugged. "My family's all dead. Gotta stick with someone."

Kelly eyed me but didn't make a move. "I advise you to drop this, Mr. Carrow. Extended family or not, she will very soon be up a creek with no paddle, and I'm sure you'd rather not get splashed when she falls in. You or Mr. Arrighi."

Threatening Sev—even vaguely—was the final straw. "Richard didn't kill himself," I snapped, "and you're a fool if you think he did."

"Oh? Is there something you'd like to confess?"

I ignored him. "You saw the note. I only met Richard twice, but even I can tell that's not his handwriting. *I* couldn't write that nice if you gave me a new pen and twenty minutes, and you think Richard Trask—whiskey-soaked Richard Trask—dashed it off on his way to hang himself? He probably didn't even hang! Go look at his neck!"

Kelly froze. Oh my God, had I gotten through to him? He turned back to the ambulance and shouted at them to wait a moment. They obeyed, and he rushed to the body. I followed, not about to let my chance to gloat in Kelly's face escape me. In one sweep, the sheet slumped to the ground. As I suspected, Richard's head was on straight—no snapped vertebrae—and the bruising on his neck was in a distinct handprint pattern.

"See?" I said. "Someone strangled him and draped his already-dead body over the rail and planted the note. You've been had, Sheriff Kelly."

He flushed a brighter red than I'd ever seen anyone go and whipped around to face me. "And where were *you* last night?" he snarled.

"Well, at some point after midnight, Crista Manco's house got broken into, and she panicked and came to us. She stayed in our house the rest of the night. I think she's home right now if you want to ask her."

He squinted. "She went to you and not the police?"

"Funny thing, she doesn't seem to trust you. I told her that was ridiculous, of course, but you know how women are. Always getting ideas into their pretty little heads once someone ignores them for a week when they ask for help finding their husband's murderer. Who isn't Bella, by the way. I just want to put that out there plainly."

Kelly regarded me for a moment with an expression that said he wanted to hit me as much as I wanted to hit him. He ended up being, if nothing else, a man of restraint because he only rammed my shoulder a little as he stomped away.

One of the stretcher bearers tutted as he retrieved the fallen sheet. I stepped out of the way. Maybe Richard deserved a better send-off than me, a pissed—off cop, and two random strangers, but that wasn't what he was going to get. I got a twinge of memory from the smell of alcohol still radiating off him: I'd found my father dead of a stroke at the kitchen table, glass still in his hand. His body had been carted off in a similar way, except the cop had been more disinterested than angry. And Donnie had been there, leading me away from my near shack of a house that had held no joy for me.

Suddenly, I was very sad. Bits of the past like that got to me. Unexpected and small, they still brought all the pain back. Donnie hadn't deserved what he'd gotten.

The slam of the ambulance door broke me out of my musings. Murdered men, even dissolute ones, needed someone to pick up their pieces. Donnie had done it for my father, and as loathe as I was to do it, I would do it for Richard Trask. Donnie would have expected no less.

I walked away, running the facts through my head. There weren't many for Richard, or at least not any I'd have easy access to. Kelly wasn't going to let me get near the note or the body again. But that didn't matter. Clearly his death was related to his brother's.

So, what had it been? Had he known something? Possibly, but everyone was sure Richard avoided his brother whenever possible. He hadn't been a confidant for any secrets. He might have been a witness or been someone's alibi, but there was no way I could find out now.

The property? I glanced up at the brick facade again. Unimpressive. Besides, most people here had their own houses. What would be the point of having a second house in the same tiny town besides selling or renting it, and it wasn't like Chickadee was hot real estate, the Reed house notwithstanding. Then again, Crista's house had been broken into last night, and the only logical reason was someone had wanted to spook her after she inherited from Walter. But my main suspect for that was now very dead. Had he died before or after the house had been broken into? If it was before, how had his flask gotten there?

Because someone planted it, idiot.

Unfortunately, that didn't help much. Richard might have abandoned his flask pretty much anywhere, or someone could have stolen it off him when he was passed out. And how Richard had even ended up at the end of a rope. The back door being broken in didn't tell me whether he'd been killed inside, or outside and dragged in.

I paced around the back of the house to look for signs of a struggle. Nothing except the shut door. I got closer to it. It was less broken than merely loose. Someone had jimmied the lock. Would Richard have been able to manage such a thing? Just like the graceful handwriting, I found it unlikely. But why drag the corpse anywhere? If they'd dumped him in the yard with no explanation, probably everyone, including me, would have assumed he died of alcohol poisoning or some such. So, someone had brought his body in for the drama alone. What good would that do?

I'd have to go back to Walter's circumstances. Forest. Blunt force trauma. The only evidence seen before half the town traipsed through were the footprints and broken glass Ed had seen. Maybe there was some bit I was missing? Could Ed have—

My stomach pitched like a hawk in a dive. If Richard had been killed for almost nothing, then what had happened to Ed, who had been the only source of clues to who had killed Walter?

I started running for the woods.

Chapter Twenty

IN MY FRANTIC state, I made my way down the entirety of Main Street in about a minute, and before I knew it, I came up on the Reed house. I glimpsed Sev on the porch, a cigarette burning lazily between his fingers. My already-speeding heart skipped a bit, but there was no avoiding him.

He straightened when he saw me. "Alex, there you are!" he exclaimed. "Come here. I want to talk to you."

Oh God. This was it. This was going to be the conversation where he broke it off with me. But I didn't have time! I slowed just enough to pant out an answer. "Sorry, can it wait a little? I have to check on Ed's shack. He might be dead."

Sev blinked as I moved past him. "You have to what?"

"Ed. Shack. Woods. Dead." I'd have to stop moving if I said any more, so I shouted over my shoulder, "Back in less than an hour!"

I booked it across the backyard down the rutted little path, past the place where Walter Trask had met his end, all the way to the hut in the clearing. The smell of blood slithered into my nose, but I didn't think much of it. Ed had a butcher's shop hanging in the trees, after all. I skidded to a stop next to his butcher block and scanned the area. There was no sign of him.

I groaned. How was I supposed to find him out here? I should've thought this through. Should've gotten Sev to come along and help. Should've told someone what I suspected. Should've done a lot of things.

Exhausted and ashamed of myself, I found a patch of gore-free grass and sat. I couldn't go home, not yet. Not when I knew what was waiting for me there. Maybe I could convince Ed to let me live in the woods here, so I'd never have to go back.

Something flickered at the edge of my vision, and I turned. A fox was in the underbrush, tugging on something. A carcass, I figured. There were plenty of them around, and Ed probably didn't bother to pick up everything. The fox was actually kind of cute—like a small, sleek dog—and I'd never seen one that wasn't a pelt draped over a lady's shoulders. Whatever it was after ripped away, and the animal turned. I got a good look at what it had in its mouth. It was a human ear.

I yelped, and the fox bolted. Vomit threatened to crawl up my throat, but I managed to choke it down. After a few deep, hard breaths, I gathered enough courage to have a look. I crept forward, my heartbeat thudding out every noise.

Sure enough, there was a body. Ed's, to be specific. His skin was pale, and his blue eyes stared into the canopy. I bent down to touch him. Cold. Or at least as cold as he could be in the ever-present heat. I chanced moving his arm. Stiff. So, he'd been dead somewhere between half a day and two, probably closer to the half since he wasn't nearly as far gone as Trask. How had he died? The fox had gotten his ear, but the rest of him seemed intact, and considering everything else, I doubted Ed had keeled over from old age.

Ignoring my squeamishness, I flipped the body onto its front. A fair-sized hole near his shoulder had spilled quite a bit of blood onto the leaf litter. Murder. With something pointy and on the thin side. A pickax maybe? Maybe even his own.

I stood and walked back toward his shack, hoping to see something out of place, but I hadn't taken enough stock of Ed's organizational skills the first time I'd been up here to determine the usual order of things. Tools were lined up along the walls, some on hooks, some propped.

Something rustled. I whipped around. The fox again? No, it was a person. I could feel them—they were making the hairs on the back of my neck stand up. I swallowed and scanned the clearing edge. No one showed themselves. Not taking my eyes off the forest, I groped the wall for something to use as a weapon. My hand came back with a regular hammer. Not the best thing, but it would have to serve.

I took a breath and crept forward. If I bolted, I might be able to reach the track before anyone caught me and run home. Hopefully whoever was here wouldn't follow me.

I took a careful step. Nothing. Another step. Still nothing. *Running in three, two—*

Something metallic flew toward my head and searing pain exploded above my left ear. My eyes filled with water, and the world pitched to the side. The underbrush shattered beneath me, sending the distinct scent of crushed leaves into my nostrils.

"Alex?"

My name echoed in the trees. A shovel, bloodied along the curving edge of the scoop, dropped next to my face. I caught a glimpse of a man's shoe as its owner turned and fled, rustling plants as he ran off. I struggled to find the strength to stand amidst the pain. I heard my name again, closer this time, and more rustling. Running.

"Alex!"

I realized I knew the voice. Sev? His hands were on me, turning me, clutching me, pulling me in. I blinked, trying to focus on his face, but everything blurred to gray. Then it faded to black.

SEV WAS TALKING; that much I could tell. The words were muffled, like someone had jammed my ears full of cotton. I opened my eyes and got ready to tell him to let me sleep, but the world wheeled around me. In my disoriented state, I could just tell this wasn't my room— the ceiling here was flat. Where was I? I turned my head, and pain roared up along its side. I caught a glimpse of Sev's brass headboard before I squeezed my eyes shut again.

"Alex, can you hear me?"

I peeked again. Sev's face floated above me with a concerned expression. He said something else, but the words got lost before I could understand. I reached up to brush away whatever made everything so dulled, and my hand met nothing until I touched the side of my head. The feeling of cotton being packed against my ear was almost accurate; there were bandages wrapped around my head and piled into a pad in the space around my ear.

Everything came rushing back. Ed's fresh corpse hidden in the undergrowth. The shovel careening toward my head. The sound of someone making their escape. I lurched up and turned lightheaded. I flopped back down with a groan. My skull felt like it was going to break apart.

Sev grabbed my shoulder. "It's all right; you're safe."

"You don't understand," I wheezed. "Someone killed Ed."

"I know. I saw."

"Wait, how—"

"I don't know if you remember, but you told me you were going up there. I got worried and talked Mr. Gaines into coming with me to look for you." Sev made a face. "You enjoy taking years off my life, don't you?"

"It's not like I'm trying."

Sev ran fingers through my hair, but the action made the headache worse, so I batted him away. He drew his hand back. Unfortunately, I had gained just enough consciousness to realize I'd upset him, but not enough to figure out how to apologize.

I rubbed at my eyes. "How long was I out?"

"Forty-five minutes? We couldn't have been far behind you, and we brought you back here about a half hour ago." He glanced out the window. "Mr. Gaines has gone to fetch a doctor. They should be here soon."

Most of what he said scattered against the wall of pain engulfing me. I couldn't think straight. "Where's Pearl?" I asked.

"She's with Crista at Miss Howe's house. We didn't think it was safe for them to be alone while I went to get you."

Ugh, he was so much smarter about these things than me. "Good thinking."

He watched me for a few seconds. "I'm going to let you rest, all right? I'll be in the kitchen, so shout if you need me."

It was too hard to form more words, so I closed my eyes and grunted my acknowledgment. He patted my hand and then let me go. Something cool brushed against me, and I pried my eyes open to look. I caught a glimpse of something sky blue. After a moment, my vision focused enough for me to recognize Bella's rosary beads dangling from Sev's left hand. I looked at him, but he was already getting up. His lips were moving with silent words. The beads shifted.

"Are you praying?"

He paused. "Do you not want me to?"

I didn't know what to say to that, so I didn't answer.

He sighed. "I'll be back in a few minutes, *caro*." The beads pooled out of his hand onto the nightstand, a tangle of ceramic and brass chain. Without saying anything else or looking at me, he left the room.

I lay there, for I didn't know how long, piecing together what had happened. Ed had been murdered, most likely by the person who had killed Walter, since Ed was the only one who might have possibly witnessed it. And the killer had followed me as I went to see him. Were they the same person who had killed Richard? Quite possibly. What better distraction for a body than another body? And Crista's house could have been broken into as a distraction as well. If she *had* gone to the police, they would have been over there and nowhere near Walter Trask's house while the perpetrator rigged a suicide scene. But if Richard hadn't been the one to break in, who had?

I groaned against the pain making my brain slow. If I called for Sev, would he come listen to me ramble and tell me what I wasn't seeing? Would he come at all? He'd been trying to break up with me as I was running to Ed's place, and now I'd wrecked that too somehow. He was too nice to try to do it while I was laid up, so that made it, what, another two or three days before trying again? Could I make it three more days knowing what was coming? Maybe. Maybe I ought to use that time to apologize. Or would that make it harder for him? The last thing I wanted to do was hurt him more. I'd already done too much. No, in fact, I hadn't done enough. If I really wanted him happy and safe, I had to let him go. Or at least prompt him into letting *me* go. I didn't have the courage to do it myself.

It took me a few seconds to gather my strength and haul myself into sitting. I sat there, letting the world settle, listening to him bustle around the kitchen.

If you really love him, you'll do this.

With that thought burning in my mind, I stood and stumbled toward the door. *Maybe if I'm lucky, I'll die of this head injury before I make it to the kitchen.* But I had never been particularly fortunate, and I shuffled all the way there without keeling over. Sev had his back to me, facing the stove and muttering to himself in Italian as he glanced between a handwritten sheet of paper and whatever he was cooking. An apron was tied around him in neat bows. It might have been cute except I recognized it as the old floral one Crista had been wearing when we met her.

"Sev?" I called. My voice was weak with fear and pain, and he didn't hear me. Or maybe he'd chosen not to listen. "Sev!"

He turned. "What are you doing out of bed?"

I steadied myself on the counter, gripping the wood with my nails. "I need to talk to you."

"You *need* to go lie back down—"

"No!"

He blinked at me in consternation and annoyance. Good. It would be easier if he was angry with me. "What?"

"First of all, stop ordering me around. I'm your boyfriend, not your nephew or some kid you're babysitting." He opened his mouth, but I kept going. "Second of all, if you're planning on leaving, get on with it because I can't take the heartbreak of being yanked around."

My head throbbed as he stared at me. After a few seconds of silence, he asked quietly, "Why do you think I want to leave you?"

The tears I'd been holding back overflowed and I sniffled. "Because I ruined your life. Who am I but some punk kid you fell in with who fucked up and got you into trouble and we're fighting all the time now!" I lost whatever semblance of poise I had and dissolved.

Between the tears and my pounding head, I didn't see him approach, only felt his hands on my arms. *"Caro,"* he whispered, "I want you to sit please. Before you hurt yourself more."

I didn't have any energy left to fight, so I let him lead me a few steps forward and set me in a chair. The wobbly one, of course. I only looked up when he dragged the second chair around to face me and sat so we were at eye-level.

"I am going to tell you three things," he said, "and I don't want you to say anything until I am done, all right? The first thing—and do not be offended—is that you are very young. I know that this is maybe the most you have ever hurt, and you think it's the end of the world. Please believe me when I say it is not."

He paused, maybe waiting for me to interrupt, but I was too busy trying not to look him in the eye. He continued.

"The second thing is that even with everything you think you have done, I love you, and you make me very happy."

"But I can't!" I exclaimed. "We've been fighting on and off for days. And I *hit* you, for God's sake!"

"That was not hitting, I would know. That was an accident." He said it so kindly I almost believed him. "And yes, we fought. I would have been surprised if we had not fought. We are both anxious and concerned and have our own ideas. We will fight again sometime. This is what I mean when I say you are young. You believe an argument is the end, and it is not." He smiled at me. "Even fighting, you make me think. You make me want to be a better person than I am. And that is why I love you. All right?"

I nodded as I went to scrub the tears off my cheeks with my hands. He tutted and pulled out his handkerchief for me.

"The third thing," he said, "is maybe the most important thing." He tilted my chin up to look me in the eye again. "I would like it if you trusted me."

"I do though!"

"Yes, some." He smiled softly. "And where I come from, that is amazing. But I know there is a lot more going on in here"—he gestured at my head—"than you are saying. And I want you to know you can tell me." For the first time in the conversation, he looked hesitant, but he kept going. "I have known a lot of pain, and I survived, and if I can help you, I will. I don't want you to have to be alone."

I couldn't answer him right away; I was crying too hard. He was right, of course. All my angst could have been avoided if I'd just spoken up, acted like an adult. "Okay, okay." I looked up into his golden eyes. "Everything's a mess and I can't sleep." *Breathe.* "I miss the city. And I miss Donnie and Martin. I miss everything so much. And some of the people here are awful. And I'm so afraid I'm making everything worse. And—"

"Alex." He put his hand on my cheek. "I didn't mean you had to do it all now. No need to get overexcited when you should be resting." He brushed his thumb against the bandages and chuckled. "You're always in such a rush. There are many tomorrows."

I liked the sound of that: many tomorrows. There was time to figure it all out. My tears started drying up, or maybe I had run out. Either way, it gave me some semblance of calmness. Sev smiled at me, and I found myself drifting on his presence.

And then I noticed the smell of smoke.

Sev jolted up and swore as he turned back to the stove. The pan on the burner was indeed smoking and charred. He muttered to himself in Italian as he twisted the gas off. I jumped up and snatched a dish towel for him. He took it gratefully, using it to grip the pan's handle and tip the contents onto a plate on the table. Now that it was close to me, I could tell the blackened mass was supposed to have been meat.

"Pork chops?" I asked, waving the smoke away with my hand.

"Yes," he groaned. He tossed the towel onto the counter. "I told you, one of us has to learn how to cook." He nudged the plate with a disappointed expression. "And I know you don't eat right at the best of times. So, I asked Crista to help me. That whispering you think is us gossiping and flirting behind your back? She was trying to teach me. But I am a bad student."

Even burned, his attempt was more impressive than anything I would have been able to manage. "It's mostly fine. You just need to chip off the burned part. Perfectly good otherwise."

"I appreciate you trying to make me feel better."

He smiled, crow's feet crinkling at the corners of his eyes, and everything terrible I'd thought in the last few days melted away. I pulled him closer, partially to stay steady, but mostly because I wanted to hold him. Even just touching him softened my aching skull somewhat.

"Hey, Sev," I said, "I love you."

"*Ti amo, caro.*"

He brought my face down to close the distance between our lips.

Something clattered, breaking my reverie. I looked up. Fran stood on the threshold of the back door, openmouthed, an overturned pie at her feet. She'd seen everything.

I broke away from Sev. "Fran—"

She bolted.

Chapter Twenty-One

SEV RIPPED AWAY from me and chased Fran onto the porch. I might have done it myself except I didn't have the energy. If she was both scorned and shocked, there was no telling what she'd do.

"Miss Gaines," Sev snapped. I cringed. He didn't show the mobster part of him often, but when he did, it was terrifying. She froze with one foot on the stairs. Hell, I'd have stopped if he'd used such a commanding tone on me.

After a second, she crept back onto the porch and back inside, her eyes flicking between us. Sev let the screen door slam after her. Angry tears streamed down her face.

"I just wanted to bring you food!" she wailed. "Mama said you got hurt and I... You could have said!" she snapped. "You could have just said instead of being nice and letting me think I had a chance..." She trailed off and sniffled.

"Look, Fran, I didn't mean to lead you on." Well, I had, but I'd had the best of intentions. "I just wanted to make sure your parents weren't hurting you. And believe me, if I could get you out of here, I would, because they're both kind of shit."

She laughed bleakly through her tears. "They are pretty terrible, aren't they?"

"Please, Fran. You *can't* tell."

She set her jaw. "I don't tell everyone *everything*. I know to keep my mouth shut if people ask. I didn't say anything about the key."

"What key is this?" Sev asked.

"I'll explain later," I said. "But Fran—"

"No, I'm very good! I never told anyone that Joe keeps a squirrel as a pet or that Judith and Maude fancy each other." I sighed. Fran's eyes widened as she realized what she'd said. "But I wouldn't do that to *you!*"

Sev rubbed at the bridge of his nose and mumbled to himself, resigned to the fact we were going to be the talk of the town in about fifteen minutes. How were we going to be able to get out of this one without Bella doing all the hard, dirty work? And if we left or were chased out, who was going to spring Bella?

But Fran was right here. If she was in the mood for being honest maybe she could tell me something else.

"Well, Fran, here's the thing. I believe you when you say you aren't going to tell." I ignored Sev's incredulous expression. "I'm going to have to have you make up for barging in, okay?"

"Oh, yes! That was rude, wasn't it? And Mama always says, 'Fran, you're so rude!' And I say—"

"Great. So, I have a question. Did you know Richard Trask died last night?"

She nodded. "I heard! So, did you see him when you went into the house after you got the key?"

Wait. "Didn't you tell Mr. Parrish you'd heard he ran to Canada?"

She shook her head. "No. I only knew that he was hiding from Sheriff Kelly. I thought you might have found him hung in his brother's house and left him because it scared you. It would have scared me!"

So if she hadn't told Arthur that Richard fled, that meant Arthur had lied. And if he'd lied... "Who called the search party to look for Walter Trask when he went missing?" I asked.

Fran thought for a moment. "I think it was Mr. Parrish's idea. He said he was worried Judith would get worried, so we should all go help."

I stood there, stunned. Arthur had lied twice: he'd said Judith had tried to trash the crime scene and that he'd heard about Richard taking off for the border. He'd known Ed had found the footprints and the glass. I'd told him about those myself. And glass—he'd mentioned to me he was wearing his spares. He could have broken his regular ones in a struggle. Plus, he had lots and lots of access to Richard. He could have stolen the flask. He was tall enough to reach around to unlock Crista's door and probably just strong enough to lift Richard Trask over a balustrade. And he was head—over—heels in love with Judith and could very have been jealous of Walter. Did he have an alibi?

"Fran, this is very important, okay? Did you see Mr. Parrish between Wednesday night and Thursday afternoon? What about last night?"

"I don't think so?"

"Did anyone?"

"I don't know. I did see him going to the Howe's a minute ago though. You can go ask him."

Shit. I burst out the door and started running for Judith's house.

Sev called after me, "Alex, what's going on?"

"I think Pearl is in trouble!" I shouted back.

So many horrible thoughts ran through my head I barely processed them, but burning bright and constant was the fear I'd failed Pearl again. Me and my fucked-up, too slow brain. I should have kept my eye on everyone, regarded everything anyone said as a link. Stupid me, not figuring the quiet one as the culprit. Or had I been resistant? I was a quiet one, after all, and I still wasn't entirely sure what I was capable of in my worst moments.

I slammed into the door of Judith's house, turning the knob at the same time. Locked. I banged on the wood, hoping, praying I'd made a ridiculous leap in judgment.

"Judith!"

No answer.

Sev and his shorter legs couldn't be much further behind me, but I didn't dare waste the precious seconds. I squared my shoulder and rammed into the door, once, twice, and the lock gave. I stumbled in, off-balance and in pain, and almost tripped over George Howe. He was very, very dead. If the glassy eyes didn't announce it, the gaping neck wound would have. *Like Emma.* I choked on my own panic.

"Pearl!" I shouted.

"Alex!" she shrieked from somewhere deep in the house.

A male voice rumbled something, followed by her yelp. I leaped over George's body and careened into the parlor.

I heard Crista's pleading before I saw her. She stood in the doorway between the living room and some kind of den, hands out, begging. Over her shoulder, I saw Arthur Parrish's beanpole stature silhouetted against a large window. In one hand, he held Pearl's arm, stretched to reach his height, as she squirmed. In his other, he held a bowie knife, which he was using to keep Judith at bay.

Something clattered behind me, but I didn't turn my face away from Arthur and Pearl. Sev's voice followed. "Alex! What in God's name..."

He tripped into the room, shock and confusion on his face. Then he pulled his knife and charged forward. I only just managed to grab him and hold him back as Arthur brandished his own blade dangerously close to Pearl's arm.

"Alex!" Pearl cried again.

Arthur yanked her, sending her scrambling to keep her balance as he turned to me. "Mr. Carrow," he said. His proper, nasal voice clashed with the circumstances. "You've come at a bad time."

Judith whimpered. "I don't understand, Arthur. Why would you do this?"

"He wants you," I gasped. The wound he'd given me hurt so much it was almost blinding. "He was jealous, pure and simple. He didn't want you marrying Trask, so he followed him into the woods and killed him. And he killed Ed because he had seen evidence, and then he killed Richard so he would be the scapegoat."

Judith's mouth fell open.

Arthur almost looked impressed. "And how did you figure that out?"

"You don't give Fran enough credit. She told me you lied about who had called for the search party and that she didn't tell you Richard ran away."

"Ah, I should have known you weren't clever enough to figure it out on your own—"

"You should have let Richard run," I snapped. "He would have gone, and everyone would have believed your lie. You didn't have to kill him."

"He didn't run though. That would have been smart, and we all know—" Arthur paused and looked around the room as if expecting a flurry of agreement. "—Richard was not what they call a bright bulb. He came back to hide from Bob Kelly in the library. And that's when he told me he knew I had gotten in late Thursday morning. Little weasel tried to blackmail me. After everything I'd done for him! So, he had to go. Ed too. Good riddance to both of them anyway."

"And you followed me to kill me"—my vision was starting to go hazy again—"because I was putting it together."

He nodded. "I knew you were getting toward something. Otherwise, you wouldn't be poking around. Besides"—he glanced at Judith—"I understand you have been visiting this household uninvited."

Judith put out imploring hands. "He's just a friend, Arthur. Not even a friend, yet. He's been here, what, a few days?"

"It's only a matter of time." He looked to me. "She's the most cultured woman in this place. Writer from Boston? She's bright enough to know a ticket out of here when she sees one. Now"—he turned to Judith again—"I don't think you'll be coming willingly at this point, so I'm afraid I have to take some liberties."

He tugged Pearl again, and she screamed.

"Please!" I called. "Let Pearl go. You know she's not the one you want. She hasn't done anything."

He squinted at her for what felt like the longest second in my life and then tossed her at me. She whimpered as she tripped into my arms. Arthur's now-free hand clamped onto Judith's arm, and he moved the knife to her throat. "You're right, I don't need her. Now, you, on the other hand." He sniffed her hair, and she whimpered. "If you will excuse us. Please don't try to follow."

He dragged her backward toward the kitchen. I held onto Pearl, who cried into my shirt until they were out of sight. "You all right?" I asked.

She nodded.

"Good. Stay here." I shoved her against Sev. "I'm going after them."

He gaped at me. "Are you insane?"

I might have answered him, except I was too busy running through the house. A door to the outside was swinging open, offering me a glimpse of Arthur shoving and pulling Judith toward a truck I'd never seen. Did Arthur own a truck? I'd never bothered to ask, but a car would explain how he got in and out of the woods so quickly.

Within mere steps, I felt my heartbeat in my head, sending fresh blood gushing against the bandages and making me dizzy and slow. He would outrun me, even dragging Judith with him.

They were only a few yards from the truck when something flashed by the corner of my eye. Fran, on her bike, sped past me. She got closer and closer to Arthur. What the hell? She was going to hit him if she... Oh, that was the idea. But that was crazy! I shouted after her. She ignored me, ramming into the back of his legs.

Fran, Judith, and Arthur all went sprawling. I'd only have a few seconds to catch up before Arthur got to his feet. But a few seconds was all I needed. I pounced on him, pinning his arms into the dirt. He shouted and struggled, but by some miracle, I was too strong for him.

Judith pried the knife out of his hand and chucked it some yards away before clambering to her feet and screaming for help. Within a few moments, dozens of people appeared. Maude hurtled from wherever she'd been to Judith's side, hands and eyes skimming her for injuries.

Kelly and Wallace jogged up, late to the party, as usual. "Can someone tell me what in the world is going on here?" Kelly demanded.

Fran, back on her feet and dirt across her dress, started in right away. "You should have seen it, Mr. Kelly! I was telling Mr. Carrow I never saw Mr. Parrish on Thursday morning and—"

"Someone who's not *you*, Miss Gaines."

Kelly pulled me by the back of my collar while Wallace grabbed Arthur. The librarian twisted against his grip but gave in. His glasses were cracked and bent, and the whole left side of his face was scraped. I glanced at Judith. She too was dusty and bruised, with rents in the knees of her stockings, and she shook. Otherwise, she seemed all right. Maude pulled her closer.

"Arthur k-killed my father," she stammered, "and tried to kidnap me. And he murdered Walter and Ed too."

"And Richard!" I panted.

Kelly blinked and let go of me. I tried to straighten and look smug, but that last jump had taken everything out of me. I swayed, but as I was about to fall over, familiar arms wrapped around me.

"Hey, Sev," I said weakly.

"You really need to stop running into trouble," he answered.

"But then you get to come rescue me."

"Shush, someone will hear you."

Despite his admonition, no one was listening to us. They were all chattering over one another—arguing, accusing—as Wallace tried to wrestle handcuffs onto Arthur.

"Hey!" I shouted.

Everyone paused and looked at me.

"Sheriff Kelly," I panted as I leaned against Sev's arm, "I think you owe Mrs. Ferri an apology."

He opened his mouth to answer, but I missed what he actually said because I blacked out again.

Chapter Twenty-Two

I CAME TO only a few seconds later to Sev tapping my face. From the ground, I caught a glimpse of Arthur being hustled off. Somehow, I was dragged to my feet and helped into the back seat of a car, where I slumped against Sev's shoulder. He murmured things at me I either didn't quite hear or didn't understand.

When we got back to the house, the doctor Mr. Gaines had brought around was sitting on our porch, confused and frustrated. I got hauled inside and poked at. He declared me lucky to be alive between the hit, the blood loss, and the shock of overexertion. I could almost hear Martin in his indignant tone, though unlike Martin, he laid off the hour-long speech about how I was a self-destructive idiot.

I tried explaining to Sev everything that had happened with the murders while the doctor ran stitches into my scalp, but I got jumbled, and in the end, I was fairly sure he hadn't gotten any of it. He simply said it all sounded very fascinating, and that I should tell it again after I'd had some rest. When the doctor left, I was put back in the brass-post bed, and Sev stayed in the chair next to me until I fell asleep.

I woke up sometime later to the sound of a door opening and closing. It was night, and the lamp on the nightstand was on. It gave a soft, yellowish glow to the room. Both windows were open, letting in a cross breeze and the sound of cicadas. I felt less dazed, though my head was still very sore. I reached for Sev where I had last seen him, but he wasn't there. Only the rosary beads remained on the chair. Despite our earlier conversation, I still sat up in a panic, sure he had snuck away, and unsure of what exactly had happened after Arthur Parrish bolted.

But as I listened, I heard a hushed, excited conversation, though I didn't understand. I shook my head to clear it and realized the reason I couldn't figure out what they were saying was because they were speaking in Italian. The door opened a crack, and Sev poked his head in. His expression softened when he saw me sitting up.

"Good, you are awake. Are—"

"Is Pearl okay?" I asked. "I can't remember."

"She's fine," he assured me. "A little shaken and worried about you, but otherwise, she is fine. I just got her to bed, though, so—"

"Enough." Bella swept past him. "I do not have all night," she said as her heels clacked on the wood, sending little spikes into my aching head. She stopped next to the bed and peered down at me. Her hair was in disarray, and she had sweated through her clothes. Kind of smelled too. That was something special, the Queen of Sin not drowning everything in the heavy notes of ambergris and roses. Sev shut the door behind them as I leaned against the headboard.

"You look as bad as I feel," I mumbled.

She frowned. "I will forgive you for your smart mouth since I know you've taken some hits in the head." She sighed, and her icy energy thawed. "I have come to thank you for finding the true killer. The librarian, I understand."

I waved a hand or tried to. "He would've snapped anyway, and they would have had to let you go."

"Perhaps. Or perhaps they would have kept me because they could. Sheriff Kelly is a nasty man. But now he will get what is coming to him." She leaned closer. "You should learn to accept gratitude."

"I might, except I know you're trouble." I looked her square in the eye. "Why'd you have Leo Manco killed?"

Sev looked startled, Bella less so.

"Did Crista tell you that?" she asked.

"No, I figured it out between all the back and forth. After years with no problems, suddenly the feds show up and administer a little rough justice to an employee? Meanwhile, no one's actually living in this house. Then there's a man here who no one has seen before or since who happens to have been on a 'hunting trip' during that whole time. One who the police conveniently couldn't find afterward." I blinked back my increasing headache. "I assume Wallace was in on it rather than Kelly? He hopped to it pretty quickly when you started bossing him around."

"Bella, did you really?" Sev asked with a tone more appropriate to asking a child if they had put a frog in their sibling's sock drawer.

Bella's gaze bored into me. "Will you tell her?"

"No. I don't think that will help anyone. I just want to know why."

She sighed. "Very well. I found out Mr. Manco was going to turn on us, not just go to the police, but to the federal men. I would not have worried so much except he was very close. He knew everything about Crista's first husband and knew where the body is buried. I could not trust him, so he could not stay alive."

Sev frowned like hearing the story hurt. "Why would he betray us?"

"Their baby. He had the idea he wouldn't be a good father unless he got away from us." Bella gave me a side-eye. "He found no peace with himself."

"Couldn't just have scared him straight?" I asked.

"No. I have someone break his legs and then what? He adds that to the list of things I've done. He was very driven; nothing I could have done would have stopped him."

"And Crista never needed to know."

Bella looked away. "I did what had to be done to protect everyone. It was one friend's happiness or everything I ever built, everything my father built, and all the people who fit into it. I made the clear choice."

Clear enough if the things she had built weren't criminal all the way through, but I was in no position to fight, both literally and figuratively. And if Leo Manco had torn down Bella's empire two years ago, where would I be now? Not in fucking Chickadee, Vermont, but also not with Sev. Maybe I wouldn't even be alive. "Why did you come up here when you knew very well who had killed her husband?"

"She is still my friend, Mr. Dawson, and when my friends call, I come. As you well know."

"I think you need to rethink what it means to be a good friend."

Sev mumbled something under his breath in Italian that was probably something along the lines of begging for forgiveness, maybe even tossing in something about my brains being scrambled. Bella held up a hand, and he stopped trying to apologize for me.

"He is a clever man and brave. I'm beginning to see why you like him." Bella's mouth twisted into a nasty smile. "Have I told you I like that you're not afraid of me? I can find work for a man like you."

It took me a few seconds to figure out what she was saying. "No, thanks. I'll take my chances with the publishers."

She shrugged. "Your choice. But you only need ask." She put a small notebook on the side table before turning to go.

"Wait."

She turned back and rolled her eyes. "You are testing my patience now."

"Why did you let Kelly keep you in a cell for days? Even with your gang all mixed up, I'm sure you could have gotten someone besides me to get you out."

Silence.

"Yes, Bella, why?" Sev asked.

"He's making you bold, darling cousin," she said. "My business is my own."

He stared at her and asked her something in Italian. She seemed taken aback for a moment, but she answered. As soon as she finished speaking, she spun on her heel and clicked her way out. He trotted after her, and they disappeared into the foyer. I caught a few muffled sentences. The front door open. More conversation—Italian, of course—through the window, followed by Bella's heels on the stairs, the slam of a car door. A flash of headlights beamed through the window before moving away. A moment later, the front door opened and shut again. Sev reappeared and let out a long-suffering sigh.

"I wish you wouldn't pull tiger tails," he said as he returned to his chair. "One day, she won't be so forgiving."

I shrugged. "She seems to like you, so I figure we got a couple more months at least. What'd you say to her, anyway?"

He remained thoughtful and quiet for a few seconds, fiddling with the rosary. "I asked her when she last received at church. And she said she had at Dario's funeral, but she shouldn't have."

"I don't know what that means."

He waved a hand. "It doesn't matter." He went quiet again. "I think she stayed in the jail to punish herself."

"You're kidding! She made us run in circles and almost got me killed because she was *sulking*?"

"I wouldn't say sulking. She knows what she's done. And with Dario gone, I think she is thinking about what could happen to her."

"I mean, great, she's sorry, but she should have warned us she was going to be all depressed and religious."

He sighed. "She is family."

"Family isn't everything! My dad was shit, all right? Horrible. Worse than Taggart ten times over. And I have no problem leaving his memory in the gutter. Mom too. She walked off without me. I don't owe her anything. You don't owe Bella anything. You don't owe anything to people who bring you down, make you be something you don't want to be."

Sev watched me in silence for a moment and then said, "Imagine someone breaks in here and threatens us. Wouldn't you rather have a big, vicious dog between them and us than nothing at all?" He picked up the notebook Bella had left and handed it to me. "And there are other benefits."

Curious, I opened it. It contained a list of names, addresses, and numbers of people in the writing business, people everywhere from small-time magazines to the *New York Times*. Connections, presumably. Some had been underlined, circled, or starred, some all three. I shuddered to think what the coding meant—some of it couldn't be good. But the gift was sweet of her if kind of twisted. Maybe that was how she kept the wolves at bay: providing a woman's touch in a game otherwise filled with dead bodies and ruin.

It took all my willpower to shove the notebook back into his hands. "I don't want it. I don't even want to be tempted by it." After all the terrible things I'd done in the last week, I wasn't going to make anyone else suffer for my benefit. "Donnie taught me to be better."

Sev looked at the notebook before tucking it behind the lamp. "All right, I'll destroy it tomorrow." He gave a half-hearted laugh. "You are a better man than me, *mi amore*."

Ha, better? "No, no, no, don't say that." I reached for his hand and kissed his knuckles. "I was *awful* this week. Picking fights and ignoring you and not thinking about how you were dealing with everything. Do whatever you need to do to feel okay, okay? Go to church, talk to a priest, see—"

"I was going to do it with or without your permission," he said, almost sharply. "You think I do not know how to hold my ground against people I love, but I do."

I blushed. Of course, dumb, self-centered me would give him a lecture only for him to spit it right back in my face. "You're right," I said. "I was an ass. I *am* an ass. And I'm really, really sorry. I don't want to make excuses, but I'm new at this whole *in love* thing, and I'm so scared I'm going to lose you and Pearl like I lost Martin and Donnie. Only it'll be worse because I'll know I ran you off."

His expression softened. "Oh, Alex." Very gently, he ran his fingers along the side of my face. "If you are so new, then I will have to tell you: loving is not perfect. It can feel like it when things are good, but nothing ever is. You must work and learn and fix. Apologize. Maybe change, hopefully for the better." He smiled, and the crow's feet appeared. "I think you are doing all right in such a small amount of time." He patted my hand. "So now that I have reassured you, back to sleep, *caro*. Before you get too worked up."

I was already worked up, but I'd never be able to top that speech. "Can you stay here? Please?"

"Of course, *caro*." He slid next to me on the bed, clothes and all. I curled against him, and I felt relaxed, sure in his embrace.

"And can you do me one more favor?"

"Mmm?"

"Please never try to cook by yourself again."

He chuckled and pulled me closer, rubbing his hand along my arm. Something thumped onto the mattress and nearly gave me a heart attack. Daisy.

"I think this cat wants to kill me," I mumbled as she paced her way into the narrow space between us and onto his legs.

"Oh, I don't know. I think she's sweet," said Sev as he scratched her ear.

She leaned into his hand and purred. I expected him to start singing at her again, but instead, he hummed a song I'd never heard before, quite possibly because he got the notes wrong. But it was soft and light and very sweet, and for a whole five minutes, I found something that might have been peace.

Chapter Twenty-Three

IN THE MORNING, I stumbled out of the bedroom to find a small crowd in the parlor. Not only Sev and Pearl, but Crista and Judith as well. The adults were speaking in quiet tones while Pearl listlessly placed pieces into her puzzle.

She looked up. "Alex!" She jumped up and ran to hug me around the middle. "I was scared you weren't going to wake up."

"I know. I'm sorry," I said, stroking her hair. "How you doing, kiddo?"

"I'm good. I was scared when Mr. Parrish grabbed me, but it's okay because he's in jail now. Are you all right?"

I took a moment to assess whether I really was. My head hurt, and I was groggy and kind of weak, but overall—especially considering the circumstances—I was feeling decent. Finally. "A little tired."

"There you are, see," said Crista. "Didn't we say all would be well? Now will you eat your breakfast, *gattina*?"

"I hate oatmeal!"

"Will you try again for me?" I said.

She stared up at me with her enormous eyes. "*Fine.*" She released me and let Crista lead her into the kitchen.

Once they were gone, Judith came up to me. She looked like I had expected her to look when Walter Trask had died—red-eyed and vacant. More proof she hadn't cared for him at all. Still, she held herself with grace and smiled politely at me.

Sev caught my eye and cleared his throat. "Please excuse me, I believe I have got the coffeepot to work again."

He edged past me on his way to the kitchen, letting his hand brush against my arm. It was just me and Judith now.

"Shouldn't you be at home?" I asked.

"Why should I? There's no one there." She tried to smile, but it faded before it got very far. "I wanted to thank you for everything. If you hadn't come when you did..."

"Well, you're welcome, of course, but you'll need to thank Fran for timing herself right. I wouldn't have figured it out if she hadn't mentioned Arthur had lied."

"I already saw her." The smile spread. "She's quite proud now. Saying how she wants to race bikes when she grows up. Even so, you were the only one who looked into Walter's death." She shook her head. "I heard Bobby and Mr. Wallace got called in by their supervisors. I don't think it's going to end well for them."

I managed to keep my smug glee internal. "Maybe it's for the best."

"Maybe." Judith looked away. "I don't want to think this was all my fault, but—"

"It's not your fault," I said. "You're not obligated to be anyone's plaything. And you're *not* responsible for other people's actions."

"No, I suppose I'm not. Still, I wish it ended better."

"It can always be better. It can always be worse too."

"Also true."

An awkward silence sprung up. There was no clean way to do this, so I jumped right in.

"I'm, um, sorry I wasn't fast enough to save your father," I mumbled.

Judith looked up. "He was in a lot of pain, and I know he was worried about being a burden to me." She sighed. "He always protected me."

I nodded. "It was pretty clear he loved you a lot. And I don't think he would have cared about Maude."

"You know, I don't think he would have either."

More silence, but it wasn't as severe this time. Amazing the things honesty could do.

"So, what are you thinking of doing now?" I asked.

"Well, once everything is settled with the funeral, perhaps I will go back to school. It's been a few years, but maybe they will remember me. And I think there might be enough saved now that Maude can come with me. There are many students living together. I don't think anyone will notice."

"Sounds like a great idea. What were you studying?"

"Literature."

"Ah. Sorry."

"Don't be sorry." She looked away for a moment. "If I let Mr. Parrish ruin another thing I love, it's almost like letting him get his way, isn't it?" She raised her head again. "Unless you're apologizing for your writing for the pulps, in which case, I forgive you. Reading should be enjoyable for everyone."

"Thanks, I think."

She stood on her toes and kissed my cheek. "Thank you again for everything. I wish you and Mr. Arrighi all the luck in the world."

She stepped toward the door, and I let her out. I wasn't sure how I was supposed to feel. Yeah, I'd found the killer and gotten Bella out of jail, but it'd practically been an accident. Richard, Ed, and Mr. Howe might have not been murdered if I hadn't shown up, but Judith might not have been lucky enough to get away. But like I'd said, I couldn't be responsible for the actions of someone else.

I heard Sev's footsteps behind me in the hall, so I turned.

He caught me around the waist and pulled me close to him. "Is everything all right?" he asked as he moved a strand of my hair sticking up among the bandages. "You are making faces."

Time for more honesty. "I'm sorry I wasn't able to save more people." Christ, this was hard. "Maybe we can talk about it later? When Crista's gone and it's calmer."

"I will hold you to it, *caro*; don't think I won't. But right now," he said, "tell me what's this between you and Miss Howe?"

"Seriously?"

He smirked and let me go. "Just checking. Come, I have made coffee and you must try it."

"Why me?"

"Because if you accidentally get poisoned because of my incompetence, I can blame Mr. Parrish."

I snorted. "You think you're funny, don't you?"

He shrugged, still with his wicked little smile. "Only if you say so."

He herded me into the kitchen, where Crista was cajoling Pearl into eating a bowl of oatmeal with the consistency of cement. It slopped off the spoon when Pearl tipped it instead of putting it in her mouth. Crista sighed in exasperation. *Ha, so parenting can be hard for you too.*

"I thought you were going to eat?" I said as Sev handed me a cup. At least the contents smelled like coffee.

"You wanted me to *try* it," Pearl answered, "and I did, and it's still yucky."

I rolled my eyes but decided it wasn't worth the fight. Not when I was barely on my feet. "Fine, we'll make you some eggs. We'll call you when they're ready."

Pearl sniffed and pushed the bowl away before scampering back toward the parlor. Sev sighed and reached for a pot to boil water. I knew it was spoiling her to let her get her way all the time, but she *had* recently been taken hostage by a homicidal madman. And oatmeal *was* pretty disgusting now that I was thinking about it.

"So," said Crista as she moved the bowl from the table to the sink, "have you two finished your lover's spat?"

I nearly dropped my coffee. "What?"

"That is the right phrase, yes?"

"Did Fran tell you?"

"No, but if Fran knows, I think it will be through the town by the end of the week." Crista looked at Sev and then back at me. "I am not stupid. Sometimes people think I am because my English isn't always good, but I can see. You turn so red when I talk to him. Like you are jealous." She nodded at Sev. "And you look at Mr. Carrow like he is made of gold." Sev flushed, and Crista turned back to me. "And if I did not know, Bella stopped by and told me last night."

I groaned.

Crista ignored me and pulled something out of her pocket. Slips of paper? No, train tickets. Three of them. She handed them to Sev. He squinted at them.

"Boston?" he said.

She nodded. "The day after tomorrow. She says she will regroup."

"Well, thanks. I guess," I said. Why hadn't Bella given them directly to us? Or told us last night when she popped around?

"It is my pleasure." Crista lowered her head and started moving toward the back door. "Have a safe trip, Mr. Dawson. Mr. Argenti."

I opened my mouth to say my goodbyes only to realize she'd said our real names. She saw my confusion and smiled. Then she walked out the back door, the picture of delicate elegance.

Sev looked to me and shrugged. "I didn't tell her," he said. "Perhaps Pearl?"

"Pearl doesn't even know your real last name."

"It must have been Bella."

That didn't make any sense. Bella didn't tell anyone *anything*, even when it might be helpful. So, Crista had to have found out from someone else. Who then? Maybe Robert Kelly had told her when he had his Boston relatives sniff around our story. Except as far as I knew, he and Crista hadn't been on speaking terms.

Could it have been the same person who had set the Boston police on us in the first place? Had Crista known where we were, what we had done? She claimed she hadn't known how her husband had died, but how could she not? She was the caretaker of this house, she had to know the hitman had been here. And if she knew he was here, then she could have easily put everything together. What better revenge than to bring down everything Bella cared about, me and Sev included?

"Sev, can you do me a favor?" I asked. "Can you call Bella and tell her how grateful I am for those? I wanna see what she says."

His brow furrowed as he looked between the tickets and me. He could undoubtedly hear the suspicion in my voice. "What are you thinking?"

"I think Crista didn't tell us something. And I think we don't want to go to Boston. Where are those tickets out of, by the way?" I asked.

Sev glanced at them. "Montpelier."

"Long drive. We should start today. Spend the overnight somewhere else. Just in case."

He watched me, and I thought he might question what I'd said, but instead, he tucked the tickets into his pocket and went for the phone. I slipped into the living room. Pearl was there, finishing her puzzle. I scanned the room, searching for anything Crista might have left or taken. Nothing, or at least nothing obvious.

I sighed and went for my typewriter. It was the biggest thing and by far the heaviest, and I probably wasn't going to write anything new anytime soon. Might as well pack it away. As I went to pull the paper out of the rollers, I noticed someone had typed something on the sheet:

Love makes you do crazy things.

Acknowledgements

This book would not have been possible without the tremendous support of:

My parents, Eleanor and Bob, my uncle Louis, and my sister Diana, who have always been there for me, especially as I worked toward my publishing goals.

My friends Andrea and Tiffany and the rest of my D&D team Mike, Lindsey, Sam, and Nicole, who have listened to me complain, brought me joy, and kept me sane.

My writing partners Allie and Jonny, who have given me their time, energy, and suggestions to make this and all my books the best they can be.

My coworkers, who have been nothing but supportive of these very nichy books.

My partner Alex, who has boosted my confidence and has brought me brightness and peace.

About the Author

Thea McAlistair is the pseudonym of an otherwise terribly boring office worker from New Jersey. She studied archaeology, anthropology, history, architecture, and public policy, but none of those panned out, so she decided to go back to an early love—writing. She can often be found playing D&D, cross-stitching, cooking with her partner, or muttering to herself about her latest draft.

Email: vsheridanwrites@gmail.com

Facebook: www.facebook.com/vsheridanwrites

Twitter: @vsheridanwrites

Other books by this author

No Good Men

Also Available from NineStar Press

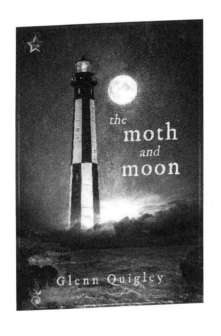

Connect with NineStar Press

www.ninestarpress.com

www.facebook.com/ninestarpress

www.facebook.com/groups/NineStarNiche

www.twitter.com/ninestarpress

www.tumblr.com/blog/ninestarpress

Made in the USA
Las Vegas, NV
16 March 2021

19632374R00162